THE BIG SKY COUNTRY SERIES #2

# THE DAWN OF AN
## *Adventure*

THE BIG SKY COUNTRY SERIES #2

# THE DAWN OF AN
# *Adventure*

## RACHEL MCBRIDE

**Pleasant Word**

Pleasant Word (a division of WinePress Publishing, PO Box 428, Enumclaw, WA 98022) functions only as book publisher. As such, the ultimate design, content, editorial accuracy, and views expressed or implied in this work are those of the author.

Unless otherwise noted, all Scriptures are taken from the King James Version (also known as Authorized King James) of the Bible.

ISBN 1-4141-0683-1
Library of Congress Catalog Card Number: 2006901022

Grateful acknowledgement is
given to the following:

First, I would like to thank the Lord for His
mercy, wisdom, and direction.

Second, I thank my parents for all of their
help, support, and encouragement.

Next, I thank my sister who is always willing to listen to my excited chatter about this
book.

A big "thank you" to Brother Stauffer who
took interest in my writing and helped make
this book a reality.

I also want to thank Mrs. Mercadante and
Brother Wagner for their proofreading.

Thank you, Brother and Sister Shirey, for
your support.

Thank you, Brother Ron Gearis and Rock of
Ages, for printing my first book.

This book would not have been printed if it
were not for all of you, thanks!

The "Big Sky Country Series" is dedicated to the people of Fellowship Baptist Church, in Cumming, Georgia, and is in memory of their pastor, Brother Randy Paul Holt.

Because of the kindness of Brother Holt and the generosity of the people of Fellowship, I was able to purchase a better computer on which to do my writing. Your sacrifice and love will never be forgotten.

Thank you!

We miss you Preacher Holt!

This book is dedicated to every parent who has a wayward child. Remember that God's power can reach wayward children, no matter where they are. Never give up on them.

Best friends Samuel Goodton and Thomas Sampson are starting their lives with their lovely brides. Sam and Esther and Tom and Carol are happy living on a farm in Indiana. Still, there is longing in Sam's heart for the wild and untamed West. If it be God's will, he wants to raise his family there.

Tyler Goodton has run away from his home and found all that his heart desired, or so he thought. To his surprise, he is not satisfied. There remains an emptiness in his soul that only ONE can fill.

# TABLE OF CONTENTS

# CHARACTERS=MAIN AND SPECIAL

Samuel Joshua Goodton=He is a strong Christian who longs to serve the Lord with all of his heart.

Esther Faith (Maker) Goodton=The godly, loving, and caring wife of Samuel Goodton.

Matthew Joshua Goodton=The oldest son of Samuel and Esther, Matthew is a leader.

Michael Thomas and MacShane (pronounced McShane) Tyler Goodton=Though twins, they are quite different in personalities. Mike loves books while Mac loves adventure.

Montana Laramie Goodton=The fourth son, born prematurely, he must be watched carefully to ensure his health.

Martin Samuel Goodton=The last son of Sam and Esther is a bouncy and energetic boy.

Tyler Andrew Goodton=Wild and unruly, he is the wayward younger brother of Samuel Goodton.

Thomas Joel Sampson=Eccentric yet trust-worthy, Tommy is Sam's best friend. He too is a Christian, and together they strive to serve God in all that they do.

Carol Joy (Grey) Sampson=Tom's sweet Christian wife and Esther's best friend.

Archibald Dunningham=Riverboat owner.

Clarissa Dunningham=His wife.

Cecilia Dunningham=Their tenderhearted daughter, who simply longs for a real family.

The names Jim and Marie Brownly are taken from my pastor and his wife, James and Mary Brown.

Jim Pryce is dedicated to my preacher buddy, Brother Jim Price.

The name Ricky Daniels is taken from my cousin, Rick Daniel Thompson.

The names, Scott McBride, Cheryl, Ann, and Kay are taken from my father, Brian Scott McBride; my mother, Cheryl; my sister, Bethany Kay; and myself, Rachel Ann.

The name Greg James is taken from my cousin, Gregory James McBride.

The names Nan and Max Pabis are taken from my mom's oldest sister and her husband, Nancy and Dave Pabis.

## Special Animals:

Bill is taken from my preacher's donkey, Bill.

Bear is taken from one of my preacher's Walker coon dogs, Bear.

Charlie is taken from my Aunt Robin's horse, Chuck-a-luck.

# Chapter 1

# MAINE

The sun had just come up and was casting its warm radiance over the land and sea.

"Isn't it beautiful, Tommy?" Carol asked as the early morning salt breeze teased at her golden hair. She knelt down, picked up an ornate seashell, and placed it in a sack nearly full of colorful shells and stones.

"Yes, it is," Tom answered. Her husband, Thomas Sampson, looked out across the sea and thought about the past couple years. He remembered the day when he and his best friend Sam Goodton had received their first piece of farmland. Their fathers owned a big farm together in Indiana and had given their sons part of their land. Tom smiled as he remembered how excited he and Sam had been. Then, a few years later, he had asked Carol Grey to marry him, and Sam had asked Carol's best friend, Esther Maker, to marry him. They had had a double wedding and the two couples were on their honeymoons in Maine.

Tom stopped his reminiscing as a sailboat floated by. "The sea is beautiful," he agreed again. "I can see now why Todd loves it. I imagine that the storms are something to see." With that, he spoke a rhyme that he made up.

> "With gentle calm the sea holds beauty,
> And in it's storm a frightening fury.
> Our friend Todd was right,
> The sea is a beautiful sight."

Sam grinned, knowing his friend loved poetry, though sometimes his rhymes were a little different. "Speaking of Todd, here he comes now," Sam said. They all turned to watch Todd as he ran toward them.

As Sam watched, his mind went back fourteen years to the day Todd Leonard and his family left Indiana because of Mrs. Leonard's health. Todd had been very close to Sam and Tom; but the Lord, knowing best, had sent Todd's family to Maine. The boys had remained in contact by letters, but the Lord worked it out that Todd and his family could go to

Indiana for the double wedding. Todd had invited them to spend their honeymoons with his family in Maine.

Sam's thoughts were interrupted when his wife said, "I wonder what it is Todd wants to show us. He told us not to plan anything at all today."

Todd caught up to them and took a moment to catch his breath. "Whew, that was a long run from the house to here. It is a beautiful day, is it not? I want to show you all something," he said in his clear and faintly British accented voice. Once again his friends were reminded that, because of a slight speech impediment, Todd did not use any contractions. "I waited all week until I had a whole day to show you," he continued, "and we needed to wait until there was a full moon. It is my favorite place in all of Maine. Mother packed us a picnic basket, because we will need to stay there until sunset. Are you all ready?"

"Yeah, but where are we going?" Tom wanted to know.

Todd just laughed. "You will have to wait and see. I have got a buggy waiting. Come on!"

Chuckling at his exuberance, the others trooped off after him.

Twenty minutes later, reaching their destination, the two couples saw what all the fuss was about. Most of the ocean beach they had seen was nothing but sand, but here it was strewn with boulders and rocks. In some places the waves beat against the rocks, sending the salt-spray ten to fifteen feet in the air. The air was rich with the smell of the sea, and the sound of the waves seemed reverberated off the rocks.

"Here it is, folks." Todd's voice spoke of his admiration far more than any words could.

"Oh, it's breathtaking! It's absolutely beautiful!" Esther exclaimed. "Todd, thank you for showing it to us."

They unhitched the horses, and tied them to a stake that Todd had driven into the ground for this very purpose.

"Now, I will show you around my castle of rocks," Todd informed them.

With Todd acting as tour guide, they began to explore. They walked down the beach in silence as Todd pointed out the loveliest spots.

Finally, after a thirty-minute walk, Todd spoke. "The prettiest spot is up there," he said, pointing to a tall peak. "I call it 'Zephath.' Ze'-fath," he repeated, pronouncing it slowly for them. "It is a Bible word that means 'watch-tower.' There is a great view up there, but it is kind of hard to get to."

"Oh, don't worry about us girls," Carol said. "We've done a good bit of climbing in our lifetime, and we wore our older skirts today. Let's try it, please."

"Could we try it, Sam?" Esther asked.

"Sure, we'll try. Will you bring the picnic basket, Todd?" Sam asked.

"Yes, I will," he answered.

They started up the incline. It was rough in some places and Sam and Tom were quick to lend the girls a hand. When they paused to let Esther and Carol rest, Sam watched as Todd scouted up ahead.

"He doesn't look like the captain of a ship, does he?" Sam asked. Recently Todd had bought his uncle's shipping business. He had wanted to be a sailor from the first time he saw the ocean. His uncle took him under his wing and taught him all about the sea. Todd learned fast and had become one of the best seamen in the business.

Tom turned to watch their friend scramble over wet, slippery rocks with the agility of a mountain goat. He looked like a young boy exploring new territory. Todd was neither tall nor short, neither fat nor skinny. His features were naturally dark, and his sailing had darkened them even more.

One thing about Todd stood out. He had an air of authority. He walked and spoke with confidence, but he did not gloat over his position. His actions reminded Tom of what a preacher had once said: "To execute authority rightly, you must first submit to authority." Todd was quick to submit to the Lord, and to those of higher rank. He was the perfect example of proper authority.

"No, he doesn't look like a captain right now," Tom agreed. "We're seeing the relaxed side of Captain Todd Leonard, but I'd really like to see him aboard one of his ships. I'll bet he handles his men well." Tom took a deep breath of the rich salt air.

"We're ready now," Carol said, and once again they started climbing. When they reached the top, the view was even more inspiring than the one from below. They could see for miles. Great ships were like toy boats sailing on a borderless lake.

They had lunch there on the cliff. Todd backed away and let the newlyweds enjoy the scene in privacy. There they sat, talking about their future together. It was not long until the sun began to go down. The foursome had seen a sunset on the ocean, but never one like this. The sun, whose light danced across the water, making it a million different colors, seemed so close that they were tempted to try to touch it.

"It's getting late, and Todd's family will be worried about us. Maybe we'd better go back down," Carol said reluctantly. Esther nodded, slowly stood up, and brushed the sand off her dress.

"Uh-oh. How are we going to get down? It's so dark I can hardly see the trail." Sam peered cautiously over the edge.

"I came prepared." Todd dove into the picnic basket and withdrew two large lanterns. "Between these, the moon, and the stars, we should be alright; but there is no rush. Mom and Dad know that when I come here it will be a while before I come back. Take your time and enjoy it. Besides," he said, leaning against a boulder, "this is my last night to spend here at Zephath. In three days I set sail again on my new ship, *The Pontius*. I always spend the last evening alone with my immediate family and the evening before that with my grandparents, aunts, uncles, and cousins. I am glad you are going to come to the party. It will be huge, with all three thousand members of my family there."

The others laughed at his exaggeration and decided to stay for another hour. The rocks echoed with their happy voices as they told each other story after story.

"Todd, how do you name your ships?" Tom asked. "I would have never thought of the name *The Pontius*."

"I like to use names from the Bible for some of them. I had to do a report on Bible names for school my senior year. Discovering what the names meant was quite interesting. 'Pontius' means, 'belonging to the sea.'"

When the hour was over, they started down the incline. Todd had been right; they had no trouble seeing the path. Soon they had harnessed the buggy and were on their way home.

The party the next night was amazing. There truly did seem to be three thousand family members. They finally met Todd's Uncle Jason Burns, a sailor who captivated them with his stories of battling pirates and storms. He was so interesting and descriptive in his narration that the two newlyweds would have stayed up all night and listened to him.

"Did you see the young man with a scar on his face?" Todd asked, after the party was over. "He is my cousin's husband, and he works with a detective named Mark Philips. Mr. Philips is quite possibly the best detective there is. His son Mark Jr. works with him, and from what I understand, he is turning out to be pretty good, too."

"Interesting," Sam said. If he could have looked forward into time and seen the wonderful role Mark Philips Jr. would play in their lives, he would have been more than just interested.

The young couples had to leave the next day after lunch.

"We had such a good time," Esther said, hugging Mrs. Leonard.

"Yes, thank you for putting up with us," Sam said. The others voiced their thanks.

"You know that you all are welcome any time," Mr. Leonard said.

"Yes," Mrs. Leonard agreed. The move to Maine had truly been what Mrs. Leonard needed. The

Goodtons and Sampsons remembered how ill she used to look and marveled at the health she now enjoyed.

They were soon on the train saying their goodbyes. "I sure am going to miss all of you," Todd said after they had prayed. "Thank you for coming, and do not forget," he added, stepping off the train, "I want to take you on a voyage one day."

"We won't forget!" they shouted as the train chugged away.

"It'll be good to be home, but I sure will miss everybody here. It all went by so fast." Tom gazed out the window and watched the scenery flying by. "Look at how rich this land is. A man could raise a good crop here, but our soil at home suits me fine, right now."

*Right now*, Sam repeated in his mind. He knew what Tom was thinking. They both wanted to go west one day. Where and when were, at this moment, uncertain, but Sam felt that the time was near when they would leave their farm and journey to the great wild West.

"Thank you, Sam, for my new dress," Esther said.

Sam turned to look at her and grinned. The deep green satin dress looked lovely on Esther. She had seen it in a store a few days before and had admired it. The day before they left, Sam had surprised her with it.

"You're welcome, Esther honey."

Early the next evening, the train pulled into the little station at Clear Water.

"Welcome home!" A crowd of family members was there to greet them, welcoming them as though they had been gone for years. Everyone seemed to have a question to ask.

"How's your health?"

"Is everything alright with the house?"

"How was your trip?"

"Was the ocean as beautiful as Todd said?"

"How are the crops coming along?"

Sam and Esther's dog Duke, in his excitement, knocked Sam down. Duke had been left with the elder Goodtons, and though he loved them, he had missed Sam and Esther. His big black body trembled with joy as he pounced on Sam, gave his face a good licking, and then more gently welcomed his mistress.

Seeing their families was wonderful, but the couples were glad to retreat to the quietness of their own homes. Esther set about cleaning as Sam checked the crops. He met Tom on the way and they inspected their fields together. They were pleased with what they saw.

"Well, looks like it's back to work again tomorrow, but I was ready to start back up anyway." Sam stood up from inspecting the soil. He swung into the saddle resting on the back of his faithful horse Dusty. He sat in the saddle for a minute, running his hand down the brown pony's neck. He had missed his horse. Dusty, glad to have Sam back, turned his head and nibbled on Sam's boot.

"Hey, none of that you rascal," Sam said, pulling the horse's head back. Dusty snorted and Sam laughed.

Tom, his inspections of the field complete, rode up beside Sam. Tom was astride Midnight, a black horse that towered above Dusty. Dusty, not impressed with Midnight's size, nipped playfully at his shoulder. The two stallions had grown up together and were, like their masters, best friends.

"How about a race, Sam?" Tom asked. "For old time's sake. We'll race to the point where the path to our houses splits."

"Sure," Sam replied, turning his horse toward home.

"On your mark, get set, go!" Tom shouted. They flew down the path. The two horses raced with a will, and yet they still ran side-by-side. The race ended, as usual, with a tie.

Sam jumped off and stroked the pony's neck. "Well done, Dusty," he praised. "It was a tie again, Tommy."

Tom, petting his horse and loving the feel of his silky mane, answered, "Yes, a tie between the two best horses in the world." They headed home.

Esther was waiting for her husband, with Duke at her heels. Sam wondered if there was anything Duke would not do for Esther. She loved him, and he rewarded her with loyal devotion.

"All is well," he reported, as she followed him to the barn. As he put away his horse, he told her how good the crops looked. When he was finished, they walked back together. Hand in hand, they stepped onto the porch and watched the sun set.

"It's good to be home," she whispered, "but I'll never forget this week. Thank you, Sam. It was one of the most wonderful weeks of my life."

"Just to know that you're happy makes me happy. Did I ever tell you that I love you very, very much?" he asked, putting an arm around her shoulders.

"Once or twice," she said with a chuckle.

"Only once or twice! Come on now, I think it was more than that," he teased. She laughed and leaned against him.

"Yes, it was."

"Well, I'll tell you again. I love you, Esther."

"I love you, Sammy."

*Chapter 2*

# RELATIVES

---

The rest of the year seemed to fly by for the newlyweds. The crops yielded a large increase and they were pleased. Winter was coming, but even the snow and wind could not dampen their spirits.

It was the week of Christmas and Esther woke up sick again. She had been sick the whole month.

"What's wrong with me?" she asked aloud as she tried to make breakfast.

"Are you still not feeling well?" Sam asked as he came into the kitchen.

"No, Sam, and I can't figure out what's wrong."

"Come on then, let's go see the doctor."

Esther felt bad that they had to go, especially since today was to be Esther and Sam's first Christmas together, but she knew seeing the doctor was the best thing to do.

Sam waited for the doctor's report impatiently. "Dear Lord, please don't let anything be wrong," he prayed.

Finally, Esther and the doctor came into the waiting room. Sam was relieved to see a smile on Esther's face.

"Well, Doctor?" Sam asked.

The old doctor said, "Oh, it's nothing that time won't cure." He turned around and walked back to his office. Sam cast a questioning glance at Esther.

"He said that it's not uncommon and that it'll go away," Esther explained.

"Praise the Lord," Sam said as they left the building.

Sam and Esther went home and had their special Christmas party. The next day would be Christmas with the rest of the family.

"I have one more present for you, Sam," Esther told him after the presents under the tree were gone. "I can't give it to you yet, but I *will* tell you about it." She smiled warmly, her eyes lighting up. "I'm going to have a baby!"

Sam nearly fell off his chair. He had to hold on to the seat to steady himself, and then looked at his wife. He tried to speak, but nothing came out. He finally managed to whisper, "Would you say that again, please?"

She laughed. "I'm going to have a baby. The doctor told me today. That's why I've been ill."

Sam was smiling. "I should have known." He knelt beside her, and kissed her hand. "Oh, Esther, I've been so anxious for us to have a child."

She grasped his hands tightly. "Let's pray, Sam. Let's pray for our child." She knelt down beside him and he began to pray.

When the others found out, congratulations and advice were given out right and left.

"Do you have any names picked out?" Carol asked.

"My, we were so overjoyed when we found out that we forgot to even think about it," Esther admitted. "We'll let you know when we decide."

At home that night Sam sat down on the couch and motioned Esther to sit by him. "Let's pick out a name right now."

First, they prayed and asked God to guide them in every aspect of caring for and raising their precious child. Then Sam said, "Why don't you decide on a name for a girl, and I'll pick one for a boy? How does that sound?"

"Fine, you go first."

"It's our first baby, so why not Matthew, since Matthew is the first book of the New Testament? I'd like Joshua for the middle name, after my father. What do you think?"

"Matthew Joshua… I like it; it sounds like a strong man. Now for my turn. I've always liked the name Mary. How about Mary Lisa, after both our mothers?"

"Beautiful. Matthew Joshua or Mary Lisa. They're both perfect. Now, you must be dead tired. I'll clean up the kitchen for you, and you can go on to bed."

"Why, thank you, Sammy." Stifling a yawn, she rose from the couch.

For Samuel and Esther the weeks dragged along. Every day they prayed for the little life Esther was carrying. Their families prayed as well.

One day, Tom came thundering into the yard. Enthusiasm was written all over his face and he clutched some old papers as if they were made of pure gold. Sam stepped out on the porch to greet him.

"You're not going to believe this, but we're re-lated!" Tom shouted, as he jumped off his horse and onto the porch.

"What!" Sam asked.

"We're related."

"What in the world are you saying, Tom?" He took hold of his friend's arms and led him to a chair on the porch. "Now," he directed, "sit down right there and get hold of yourself. I think you've been out in the sun too long." He felt Tom's forehead to see if he had a fever.

Tom laughed and pushed Sam's hand away. "I'm serious, Sammy.

> Though friends we are,
> We find we're more than that.
> For we find way back where at one man,
> Our family tree starts at."

Sam shook his head, bewildered at his friend's riddle.

"Here, listen to these letters," Tom began. "Oh, that'll take too long. I'll just give it to you in a nutshell." He took a deep breath and began to explain, glancing frequently at the papers to find and pronounce the right name. "More than a century ago, in the country of England, a man by the name of Uziah Gudten had two children, Miranda and Lance. Miranda married a man named Daren Samsen. Daren and Miranda had a son named Jeremiah. Lance and his wife Lydia had a son named Jeremy. Jeremy and Jeremiah, who of course were cousins, became best friends, but the Samsens moved to Germany and the Gudtens went to France. They lost contact with each other.

"Jeremy's son Jacob moved to America when he was twenty. Here he married a Tiffany Bowden. He changed the spelling of his last name from Gudten to Goodton, the way the Americans pronounced it. They had a son named Randal who had a son named Nathaniel Harry Goodton. Does that name sound familiar?"

"That's my Grandfather," Sam answered in disbelief. "What happened to the Samsen family?"

"I was coming to that. Jeremiah had a son named Malchum who had a son named Levi. Malchum came to America when Levi was two. Here their last name was changed to Sampson. Malchum died when he was only thirty years old, and his wife remarried. Levi was the only one of her three children that bore Malchum's last name. He had a son named George Oliver Sampson and..."

"Your grandfather's name is George Oliver Sampson," Sam said.

"Yes. I have a letter here from Jacob Goodton to Malchum Sampson. It seems that they came over to the States on the same boat. They began to talk and Jacob mentioned Uziah Gudten. Realizing they both had a man by that name in their ancestry, they began to compare facts. Both Jacob and Malchum decided they must be related. Upon reaching America, they separated but each managed to secure an address that the other could send information to. The letter

I found asks some questions and gives a few details from Jacob's past.

"Malchum kept this all a secret, hoping to surprise his family by finding the long lost relatives. After he died, his wife was so broken she didn't go through any of his personal papers. Therefore, she didn't know about the Goodtons, and Jacob was never informed of Malchum's death. When he didn't hear from him, he must have figured that they had been wrong and never mentioned it to anyone. Then one day, many years later, a Mr. George Sampson helped a Mr. Nathaniel Goodton who was trapped in a mineshaft. My grandfather and his wife were invited over to your grandfather's house, and from that night on the Sampsons and the Goodtons have been best friends."

By this time it was Sam who needed to sit down and get hold of himself. "So," he began slowly, quickly figuring the generations in his head, "you and I are sixth cousins?"

"Yeah, what do you think of that?"

"How did you find all this out?"

"Well, Grandpa had a trunk in his attic that was filled with Malchum Sampson's things. This letter, the one he got from Jacob Goodton, was in it, hidden inside a box. I was looking through the trunk, just seeing what was in there, and found the letter. *Then* I found a book filled with the history of the

Goodtons and Sampsons. Apparently, Malchum had written down what he knew about his family and what Jacob Goodton knew about his family. It all traced back to Miranda Samsen and Lance Gudten. I praise the Lord that I found it!"

"Have you told anyone else?"

"Not yet, but Carol and I are planning a party to-night, and everyone is invited. I'll tell them then."

Tom polished his history lesson and told it to the two families. It was quite a surprise, but a pleasant one.

No one could know that one day the Sampsons and Goodtons would once again become a family.

*Chapter 3*

# THE LONG-AWAITED DAY

It was the last day of August, and Esther was more than two weeks overdue. Concerned, she and Sam were staying with the elder Goodtons so that Mary could watch over her. Esther's parents had gone to Michigan to help take care of Mrs. Maker's elderly mother who had broken her arm.

Sam was reading the newspaper when Esther began to feel labor pains.

"Sam, I think it's almost time," she said.

He dropped his bundle of papers and helped her into bed. By the time he had called his mother, the pains were coming more quickly.

"Samuel," Esther cried softly. "I'm so scared. Pray with me, please, before you leave."

He grasped her hand and began to pray. "Lord, thank You for Esther and the baby. Please be with them and help them. Thank You, Lord. In Jesus name we pray. Amen." He kissed her before Mary ushered him out of the room.

Josh was sitting in the living room and he chuckled as Sam began to pace. "Sit down, son. You just leave your wife and child in the hands of God and your mother."

"I can't sit down," Sam moaned. "I've never been this nervous. I thought the wedding was scary, but that doesn't even come close to this." He ran his fingers through his red hair and sighed. Then he sat down and prayed with his father.

Finally, Mary came out of the room, and Sam rushed to her.

"Is everything alright?" he asked

She smiled and hugged her son. "Oh yes, Sammy. Esther is fine and your child is beautiful and healthy. Go on in. I want Esther to tell you what it is." She pushed open the bedroom door for him.

"Thank you for your help, Mother." He kissed her before stepping inside.

"Oh, Samuel," Esther said as Sam walked in. Her voice was weak but filled with joy. "Look, it's Matthew Joshua. A handsome and healthy Matthew Joshua." Tears streamed down her cheeks as she looked at the baby wrapped in a blanket.

"Thank You, Lord." Sam looked down at his firstborn son. "He's wonderful," he said, sitting down on the edge of the bed.

"Here, hold him, Sammy. See how strong he feels." She placed him in her husband's arms.

The tears fell as Sam held his son for the first time. It was then that he remembered a similar scene and his tears of joy turned to tears of sorrow.

"Why, Sam, what's wrong?" Esther asked, concern filling her voice.

"Honey, some years ago, I sat in this same place and held another baby boy, a boy named Tyler." He choked a little and had to pause. Sam was six years old when his brother Tyler Andrew was born. As Tyler grew, he became rebellious. His family witnessed to him, but he would not heed to their pleas. Five years ago, shortly after Tyler's sixteenth birthday, he had run away. Except for one note, the Goodton family had not heard from him. However, they were still praying for him, and trusting that the Lord would bring their boy home.

"I pray that our son will get saved at an early age," Sam said. "That way he'll not go through the heartache that I'm sure Ty has gone through." He cuddled the little bundle and whispered, "Matthew, there is *nothing* better than serving the Lord. I'll do my best to teach you that. I promise, son."

Esther wiped her tears away. "Yes, we both promise."

He handed the baby back to her and then reached up to touch her face. "I'll go spread the news," he said. "Will you be okay?"

"Yes, your mother will take excellent care of me. Go ahead, Sam, and don't worry about me."

After a kiss, Sam strode outside, and took a deep breath. *What a wonderful day,* he thought to himself.

Duke walked up to him, whined, and nuzzled his hand. Sam began to stroke the dog's thick fur. "Don't worry boy, everything's fine. Esther's doing good, and you'll soon have a new playmate. Now, let's go tell everybody."

He jogged over to the barn and bridled his prancing horse. Grabbing a handful of mane, he swung onto the horse's bare back. He touched his heels to Dusty's flanks and the horse responded with a lunge toward the gate.

His first stop was Tom and Carol's. They were sitting on the porch when he rode up.

"It's a boy!" Sam shouted, sliding to the ground. "We've got a healthy baby boy!"

Tom whooped, leapt off the porch, and nearly knocked Sam over with a big bear hug.

"A boy! That's wonderful!" Tom exulted. "Maybe if Carol and I have a boy they'll be best friends like we are. Oh, a boy!"

Carol, though just as excited, was much more reserved. "That's wonderful, Sam, and how's Esther?"

"She's fine and, as you can imagine, quite pleased with Matthew Joshua. Well, I'd best be on my way. I've got more people to tell." In an effortless motion he was back on Dusty and they were off.

He told his grandparents, Uncle Joel and Aunt Virginia, and Carol's family, and then made his way home. After caring for his horse, he walked into the house to find Esther sitting up in bed with Matthew. Sam sat down on a chair beside her.

"God is very good to us, Sammy. We have salvation, loving families, a good place to live, and now a fine son." She smiled. "For so long, I've dreamed of the day I would hold a child of my own. It's more wonderful than I ever imagined. I wish this day would never end."

He chuckled. "I'm afraid it will, so enjoy every moment." He saw that his mother had left a pot of tea in the room. Sam stood and poured some of the warm liquid into a cup for Esther. "I'll hold him while you drink this." He sat back down and reached for his son. After settling the baby in his left arm,

Sam held Matthew's tiny hand in his big one. "Thank You, Lord," he praised.

The next afternoon the younger Goodtons decided to make the short trip home. Sam and Josh fixed a comfortable bed in the back of the wagon for Esther and the baby.

"Now be careful on the way home," Mary said as Sam helped Esther into the wagon. "Take your time and remember there is no hurry."

"I will, Mom," Sam promised. "How can I ever thank you for all your help?" he asked, hugging her.

"Simple. Make sure you bring my grandson over to see me regularly," she said.

Joshua, holding his grandson, nodded in agreement. Sam noticed the glow in his parents' faces and he knew they were proud of the baby.

"Don't worry," Esther said from the back of the wagon. "We'll bring him over."

The ride home went by quickly. Once there, Sam helped his wife into the house and into bed. He then placed Matthew in the hand-carved cradle that had once been Sam's.

"You know, I've always had a hard time believing that I used to sleep in that tiny thing," Sam said, scratching his head. "It's so small."

Esther could not help but laugh.

"It's true, Esther," he said matter-of-factly. "Can you imagine a guy who's now six-foot-four sleeping in something that small?" That just made her laugh harder. She sat up in bed, her soft, bell-like laughter so contagious that Sam, as usual, could not refrain from joining in with her.

Sam looked down at the cradle again and remembered that Tyler had slept in it, too. The day had brought back many memories of his little brother.

Esther saw the far-away look in his eye. "Did Tyler sleep in it too?"

"Yes, he did. I sure do miss him."

"I wonder where he is," Esther mused.

"The only note he sent said he was enjoying his new job and was making a good bit of money. I really can't think of any job that he liked, so I'm at loss as to what it could be. I try to remember that even though I don't know where he is, the Lord does. Let me get my Bible and I'll show you a verse that has helped me." He lifted his Bible off the nightstand and sat down beside her. There was a fluttering noise as he flipped the worn pages to John chapter three. He pointed to verse eight. Esther cuddled close to him and read the verse silently to herself as he read it aloud.

"'The wind bloweth where it listeth, and thou hearest the sound thereof, but canst not tell whence it cometh, and whither it goeth: so is every one that is born of the Spirit.'

"The wind in this verse," Sam explained, "represents the Holy Spirit. The verse divides itself into five different truths about the Spirit.

"The first is that 'The wind bloweth…' This means that the Holy Spirit is always at work. He was at work in the first chapter of the Bible where it says '…And the Spirit of God moved upon the face of the waters' in Genesis 1:2, and in the last chapter of the Bible where it says 'And the Spirit and the bride say, Come…' in Revelation 22:17. This is the truth that helped me the most. It's calm and quiet outside, but in Maine, where Todd is, it could be storming. Just because I can't see the Spirit working doesn't mean He's not working. He may have Tyler in a spiritual storm right now. The Lord knows what Ty needs, and I have to trust Him to take care of my brother.

"The second truth is that the wind blows '… where it listeth…' Sometimes we tend to demand things of God, but God works in His own time, and it's always the best time.

"Number three, '…and thou hearest the sound thereof…' You can always see or feel the effect of the wind. There are all kinds of wind, from a cool breeze to a wild storm. What was it that Todd called that terrible storm he encountered at sea?"

"The 'Euroclydon.' It's a Bible word. He said it means, 'Wind from every direction.'"

"Yes, thank you. I can't pronounce it. You can always see what the wind has done. It always leaves a mark.

"Next we are told that we '…canst not tell whence it cometh…' Sometimes the Holy Spirit shows up even when you don't expect Him. I know He's always with us, but sometimes He manifests His presence in a more obvious way. I believe He will show Himself only where He is invited.

"Lastly, we don't know '…whither it goeth.' This part is simply stating that you need to be willing to follow the Holy Ghost in whatever He would have you to do."

Esther smiled up at him. "Thank you, Sam. I enjoyed that."

# Chapter 4

# TYLER'S JOB

Tyler started contemplating running away when he turned thirteen. He was sick of plowing, planting, hoeing, and harvesting. Yearning for adventure, he wanted to live life with the "high class," and he knew how he wanted to go about it. Every dime was carefully hoarded. He secretly sold a few of his belongings and his small pile of money began to grow. One year when Tom had been hurt and could not help Sam with the land, Tyler helped instead. Sam and Tom shared that year's profit with him. Tyler was elated. He had the money he needed and all he had to do was wait for the right opportunity, which had come not too long after he turned sixteen. The three other members of his family left one day and took Duke with them, leaving

Tyler to watch the house. Instead he saddled his horse and rode for Indianapolis, where he bought a train ticket to Kentucky. If he had left from the station at Clear Water, someone would have seen him and tried to stop him, but in the distant city he boarded the train without a problem. Once in Kentucky, he made his way to Georgia then to Louisiana. After a few days he finally reached his original destination, New Orleans. It was even more exciting than he had imagined. He found himself a cheap hotel and tossed his few belongings on the bed. He quickly cleaned up, donned his best attire, and went out to find a job aboard a riverboat. He tried five different boats and received the same answer each time: "No." Finally, on the sixth try he struck pay dirt. He was turned down, but as he stepped off the gambling ship a very fastidiously dressed man confronted him.

"Lad, did my ears deceive me, or are you inquiring about a job aboard a riverboat?"

"Yes sir, I, I am," Tyler stammered, somewhat taken aback by the man's formal manner.

"Well, your search can come to an end if you'll just follow me. I believe I can set you up as an errand boy for now, and if you prove yourself worthy, you can work your way up."

"Do you own a boat, sir?" Ty asked eagerly.

"Yes, yes I do, lad. The finest one that ever navigated these rivers, if you don't mind my saying so. My name is Dunningham, Archibald J. Dunningham, and yours is?"

"Tyler Andrew Goodton."

"That's a fine name, a fine name indeed. Tell me, Tyler Andrew, have you had any experience with riverboats?"

"Um, no, sir."

"Ah, an honest soul, that's what I like. I promise you that a man willing to try can make a life for himself aboard the ships."

"I *am* willing to try. I really want to work aboard one."

"Splendid! Splendid! I do believe that we shall get along famously. Step right this way, Tyler, and prepare to feast your eyes on the most beautiful sight you've ever seen."

Tyler liked the gentleman and his carefree attitude. The young man began to relax. *I think I'm going to enjoy working for Mr. Dunningham*, he thought to himself.

"There she is, Tyler, *The Mademoiselle Jewel*."

Tyler stopped dead in his tracks. She was beautiful. Anchored in port, she rocked slowly on the gentle waves. Even in daylight, Ty could see the lights that adorned her rails and cabins.

"I bet she is pretty at night when all the lights are blazing," Tyler commented.

"That she is, son, that she is. Now, come on aboard and I'll show you around." He stopped a moment and gazed at the boy. "You know, you look like you could use a square meal."

Ty's stomach growled at the very thought of food. His funds were low and he had not had a good meal for three days. "Yes, sir, I sure could."

"Then let's get to it. I never could discuss business on an empty stomach. By the way, all my employees call me Captain Dunningham, or just Captain."

"Yes sir, Captain Dunningham."

Together they walked up the gangplank, around the deck, down a stairway, and into the most lavish quarters Tyler had ever seen.

"Clarissa, I've brought us a guest, and he's in need of a nice warm supper." As he spoke, a tall woman with brown hair down to her shoulders stepped into the room. Her bright yellow dress and matching hat gave her a certain elegance, but they did not alter her obviously irritable attitude. She eyed Tyler in dissatisfaction.

"Who is he?" she asked coldly.

"Why, this is Mr. Tyler Andrew Goodton, a possible employee, Clara dear. Come, he is my guest."

After a delicious meal, the Captain gave Tyler a tour of his boat.

"Most of us who live and work aboard her decks call her *The Jewel*," he said, showing Tyler the living quarters. "Now, here's the part I think will most interest you." He pushed open a door. A large mirror reflecting a long bar stretched across the far end. Scattered around the room were card tables where dealers sat shuffling cards. To the left, a man stood wiping the dust off the wooden edges of a dice table that sat against the wall.

"This is our gambling room. Your job will be to make sure our guests want for nothing. Keep their glasses full and things like that. It's a seemingly small job, I know, but if you keep your eyes and ears open, you'll learn the ropes in no time. So, is it a deal?"

A young girl the same age as Tyler entered the room. She was a miniature of Clarissa Dunningham, but with sparkling eyes and a childish smile. She stopped short when she saw Ty. "Who is this, Father?"

"Tyler Goodton. Tyler, this is my daughter, Cecilia. Cecilia, this young man may start working for us. Isn't that right, Tyler?"

If there had been any doubts in Ty's mind about taking the job, they vanished. One look at Cecilia had answered the question for him. He nodded.

"Good." Mr. Dunningham turned to face his daughter. "Run along now, child, and let us discuss our business."

She gave Tyler another friendly smile, and then left the room. Tyler looked up at the Captain and asked, "When do I start?"

If Tyler could have heard the conversation between Mr. and Mrs. Dunningham that night, he would have realized that the man's friendliness was nothing but a front.

"Why did you hire that little runt?" Clarissa asked, disgust in her voice. She was sitting at the table in their room with a half-empty bottle of wine and a glass in front of her. She was so practiced that she did not have to look as she poured the wine into the glass and lifted it to her lips.

"I felt sorry for the poor lad," he said mockingly, pouring a glass for himself. "No, I'll tell you why. There are a couple of reasons. First, we *need* a helper at the bar. Second, he wants to learn. When someone wants to learn as badly as he does, you can bet your money he'll work hard. Third, it's obvious he's a runaway. If his parents locate him, we can tell them that we found him and have been looking for his family. There just might be a profit in that." Taking a sip of his wine, he said, "No matter how you look at it, we come out ahead."

His wife's eyes glistened greedily. "Maybe it wasn't such a bad idea after all," she conceded.

Tyler did his best at his new job, partly because he enjoyed it and partly because he desperately wanted to gain Cecilia's favor. When gambling was slow, she would sing to entertain the customers. Sometimes a large group would pay to have the entire ship to themselves, and again she would be called upon to sing. Ty had a hard time working when she sang. He often found himself perched on one of the barstools listening to her. Still, his attention was not totally devoted to Cecilia. He watched his fellow employees as they did their jobs. His favorite pastime was watching and listening to Clark Mason, the man at the dice table. Tyler would often question him about how he did his work, and Mason was quick to give out tips.

They were anchored again at New Orleans one night when Ty walked into the gambling room. The ship had been closed for two days for a few repairs. They planned to reopen the next day. Tyler reached the table and picked up the dice. He pretended that the room was full of people who were itching to gamble. He rattled the dice loudly and began talking to an imaginary crowd.

"Step right up folks and test your luck with the dice. You sir," he said, pointing his finger to the chair closest to him, "you look like the lucky type.

Step up to the table, that's right, and we'll see if my prediction comes true. Old Tag here knows a lucky man when he sees one." Tyler had noticed that many of the people aboard *The Jewel* had nicknames. Dunningham was Captain and Clarissa was Clara. Cecilia went by the letter C, and Clark Mason by the fitting name of Dice. Among the card dealers were Ace, Duce, Duke, Spade, and one they called Jack, who was only a couple years older than Tyler. The bartender was Shotglass. The name fit him well for two reasons. He was constantly filling the little glasses, and he looked just like one. He was short, quite round, and his bald head glistened. Tyler had spent many hours trying to come up with a name for himself. He thought about Tiger, the nickname his father had given him, but that brought back too many memories and a feeling of guilt. He had finally chosen the name "Tag," his initials, and he rather liked it.

"Ha ha, see what I mean? A very lucky man indeed. Shall we try her again? What, giving up so soon? Come now, not when you're just getting started. One more time? That's the way."

Unbeknownst to Tyler, Dunningham was watching him. A smile played about his lips. "You'll do," he whispered. Stepping out of the shadows, he asked, "What do we have here?"

"Oh, Captain Dunningham, I uh, I was just messing around," Tyler stammered, embarrassed that he had been seen.

"That's quite alright, Tyler, I mean Tag. I've got a proposition for you." Dunningham pulled up a chair, sat down, and motioned Ty to do the same. "It may surprise you to know that Dice started out as a card dealer."

"He did! Then how come his nickname is Dice?"

"He was called Dealer but Mason switched to Dice when he switched jobs. He took over the dice table when my man left three years ago." Dunningham did not mention the fact that, by means of fine print in a contract, he had drained the man's life savings and when he could get no more out of him had fired him. "I think Mason would like to get back to his cards, although the name Dice will forever stick with him. Why don't you take his place?"

Tyler's jaw dropped. "You mean it?" he asked.

"That I do. I take that question to mean, 'yes.'"

"Yes, yes I would."

"Fine," the Captain said, rising and heading for the door. "You'll start Sunday."

# Chapter 5

# CECILIA

---

Tyler, now known to the crew as Tag, launched into his new job with gusto. His boyish features and eager voice caught the attention of the customers. They could not resist his smiling face and carefree attitude. When *The Jewel's* profits began to increase because of Tyler, the crew warmed up to him. Captain Dunningham frequently invited him to supper with his family and Tyler was always willing to oblige.

As the year past, Tyler began to feel pretty good about himself. He was, in his own eyes, rather rich, and Cecilia seemed to take more notice of him. She even spoke to him occasionally, making his heart race.

One day, as he was leaning against the deck railing taking a well-deserved break, she approached him. "May I join you?" she asked. He stood up straight and nodded. "Thank you," she said. C stepped up beside him and let her eyes sweep over the scenery they were passing.

"It's beautiful, isn't it?" Tyler asked.

"I guess," she said rather dully. In answer to his questioning look, she explained. "I mean, I see it all the time. It gets boring after awhile, but yes, some of it is kind of pretty." She paused, and turning to look at him, asked, "Where are you from, Tag?"

"I was born in Indiana, but I've been to Kentucky, Georgia and a few places in-between." He had only passed through them on his flight to Louisiana, but he was trying to impress her.

"Really? What business was your father in?"

He winced inwardly. He did not want her to know that he had been a farmer, which to him was an insignificant profession. "Well, he was a, a farmer," he finally said.

"Oh, I've always wanted to live on a farm!" At first he thought she was making fun of him, but as she went on he realized that she was serious. "Did you have any animals, any cats or dogs, and horses, did you have any horses?"

Enjoying the opportunity to talk with her, he told her all about the farm, excluding only its exact location. She listened intently, a dreamy look on her face.

"Wasn't it fun to live there?" It was more of a statement than a question.

"It's really not all that great," he disagreed.

"You don't think so? I've always thought it would be wonderful to settle down in one place and raise animals, especially horses. I love horses. When I was little I used to put a quilt over my bed and straddle it, pretending I was riding my horse, Thunder." She laughed softly. "I grew out of *that,* but I still love horses. Tell me, did you ride a lot?"

"Sometimes, but enough about my past. Would you tell me about yours?"

She shrugged. "There really isn't much to tell. I was born on a riverboat, and I learned to walk on a riverboat's shifting deck. When I was nine, I sang my first solo on my father's gambling ship, *The Sailing Star.* My life has been centered around riverboats. That's all there is to it."

A bell rang and Tyler knew it was time for him to go back to work. "It's been nice talking to you Miss C, but I need to get back to work."

"Of course. Oh, I almost forgot. When we dock in three weeks, my father will be taking me to the opera. He said I could invite you to come along, if you like."

"It would be my pleasure," he assured her. She smiled and headed back to her quarters. Whistling, Tyler went back to work. "Life is good," he exulted, though there was no one around to hear him. "Things couldn't be better." Suddenly, a sense of loneliness swept through him. He could see his mother's face and hear her voice saying, "Things never make people happy, Ty. Only God can make people really and truly happy."

"I'm happy," he said to himself, but a question from deep within shot back, *Are you really?* He pondered that thought as he slowed his pace. He realized that C had what he had always wanted, yet she was not happy. Tyler had lived on a farm, which was Cecilia's dream, yet he had not been happy either. Maybe things did not make people happy. Or did they? He had to admit he was not sure.

By now he had made it back to his table. After a few minutes of rattling dice, he felt better. Soon he had pushed the thoughts of home out of his mind and was dwelling on the future "date" with Cecilia. He felt confident that he could make a favorable impression on her. Shotglass had taught him a lot about how the upper class lived. The last time they had docked, Shotglass picked out a new wardrobe for Tyler. It was a little extravagant for the country boy, but if that was the way people of his profession dressed, he would do the same.

Despite his earlier confidence, he still had butter-flies in his stomach as he mounted the steps into the hired carriage that would take them to the opera.

To him the opera was nonsense, but it was obvious that Cecilia enjoyed it. Tyler decided that he would put up with it if it meant that much to her.

Afterwards, on the ride home, she asked him what he thought of it.

"Well," Tyler began, "personally, I think she wasn't that great a singer. You see, I know this girl who can sing twice as good as she can."

"Oh, who's that?" she asked.

"She sings on this riverboat, oh what is that name?" He appeared to be concentrating very hard. "Oh, yes, *The Mademoiselle Jewel*, and her name is Cecilia Dunningham."

She chuckled but looked pleased. "Do you think I could meet her?"

"I might be able to arrange it, Miss C. At dinner tomorrow night, at that French café by the dock?"

"Yes, of course, and since I believe we're going to become good friends, you can call me C."

The carriage rounded a curve then came to a halt. Dunningham, who had fallen asleep, awoke with a start. "My, my, home already," he said stifling a yawn. "I do hope you both enjoyed yourselves tonight."

Ty and C said that they had.

"Splendid, splendid! Now I believe we ought to bid each other goodnight and get some rest. I'm hoping for a rewarding day tomorrow."

Tyler made it a practice to take Cecilia wherever she wanted to go when they were docked. They went to more operas, a circus, and several plays. One Friday, after making their way west to Galveston, Texas, they found a sign announcing a rodeo.

"Oh, Tag, a real rodeo. It starts tomorrow and ends Sunday night. After the competition, they're having a shindig and a costume contest," she said, reading the poster. "Have you ever been to a rodeo?"

"Yeah, we had a few in Indiana, but they were never this big."

"Well, then let's go. I've never been to a rodeo."

"Alright, if you wish, but you're going to want some western clothes." He withdrew his wallet and handed her some money. "Here, you go down to that store and pick you out some clothes. Go ahead and spend all of it if you like. I'll go find me a hat and cowboy boots."

Cecilia had a great time. She especially liked the barrel racing. The way those horses swung around the barrels was astounding. Late in the competition, she jumped out of her seat and cheered wildly as a beautiful Paint Horse came charging toward the barrels with the cowgirl urging him to go faster. Even Ty caught his breath at the sight of the horse. It was as though someone had carelessly thrown a can of brown paint on a white horse. The animal thundered down the arena, circled the barrels with style, and flew back toward the gate. The crowd applauded as his time was announced. He and his rider had won.

For Tyler the whole two days were quite depressing. The hat he bought reminded him of one his father used to wear. As they were watching the bronco busting, the last horse out of the chute looked like Dusty and the rider resembled Sam. Tyler shook his head. No, it was not them, but he still could not calm his frightened heart.

At the shindig he had another fright. They had just signed up for the costume contest when the cowgirl who had ridden the Paint Horse walked by. Up close, he saw that she looked a little like his mother. Memories of his family tore at him, making him feel sick. "Okay," he growled under his breath. "I'll admit that I do miss them, some." He tried to push the thought of them away, and for a while the effort worked. He enjoyed the evening. Though most of the people there were businessmen and women dressed in western garb, a few were honest-to-goodness cowboys and cowgirls. He pointed them out to C, who would gasp in delight.

At the end of the festivities, the man sponsoring the contest came to the front and said, "Our costume winners tonight are Tyler Goodton and Cecilia Dunningham!"

They made their way to the front and stood on the stage for a picture with the entire group of winning contestants. C was ecstatic. Tyler was excited, too, until he noticed who was around him. The barrel racer who resembled his mother stood by C. The man at his left elbow was the broncobuster who reminded Tyler of Sam. He talked like him and had the same long-legged stride. He offered his hand to Tyler and Ty felt the strong, calloused hand that reminded him of both his father and Sam. Tyler was quick to leave. He promised the photographer that he would come back the next morning to pick up two copies. All he wanted right now was to head for the small room he called home.

Cecilia jabbered the whole way back, and burst into her parents' room flashing the prize money and ribbons. Weary, Tyler bade them goodnight and was soon lowering himself onto his bed. Despite being desperately tired, he could not sleep. His thoughts kept drifting back to his farm and to that day he left it. In five days it would be two years since he had run away. Two years. How were his parents doing? How was the farm? Were Sam and Tom still working that piece of land? How were his grandparents?

How was his horse, Ace? Did he miss him? The thoughts whirled around in his mind long into the night. Finally, from sheer exhaustion, he fell into a fitful sleep.

As time progressed, Tyler kept bringing in money, and his and *The Jewel's* safes were getting fuller. He had moved to a nicer room, one almost the size of the Dunninghams'.

Dunningham all but doted on him and was quick to bestow praise and rewards on the lad. Despite the Captain's attention, Tyler never really found out much about him and his bitter wife.

One day, as Tyler was getting ready for work, there was a knock at his door. "Come in," he called, continuing to comb his dark hair. In walked Agatha, an old Negro maid. She and her husband Abel took care of all the maintenance on the ship. Every week she thoroughly cleaned all the rooms on the riverboat while her husband cared for the decks and the gambling room. Tyler often wondered if *The Jewel* could get along without Abel and Agatha.

"I's jest a comin' to git yo' clo'es dat need a washin'," she said in her thick accent.

"That's fine. Uh, Aggy, how long have you been here?" he asked, laying down his comb and turning to face her.

"Oh, I's been heah wif my Abe on *De Jewel's* first trip, an' I reckon we's still be heah on 'er last."

"What can you tell me about Captain Dunning-ham and his wife?"

"What does you wanna be a knowin'?"

"Things like where they're from and why they chose this life."

"Le' me see heah." She set down her basket and brushed back a stray wisp of her hair. "I believes dey come fum Miz'sippi. I really don't knows a lot 'bout 'em, 'cept when de Cap'n an' his wife first bought dis heah boat, dey wus purty nice folk. Dey wus almos' happy den. Missy C wus only 'leven year old. Sech a purty little girl she wus, an' is yet. Like I says, dey wus almos' happy heah at first, but den after 'bout a year or two dey began to drift apart. All dat money didn' make der family stronger. It done sep'rated 'em. Now, deys not happy at all, even wid all dat fancy stuff. Den, Missy C, the po' little girl. She's so very lonesome. Deys don't pay her much mind. Sometimes I's spec she give up all her money if'n dey could jest be a family again." Shaking her head in sorrow, she picked up her basket and left.

Tyler turned back to the mirror and considered the things he had learned. Looking at his reflection, he was surprised to see how much he still looked like his mother. Though he had grown taller, his facial features had not changed at all. To his disgust, that familiar pang of loneliness stabbed his heart. Once again he thought about what his mother had said about things not making people happy. In his mind he could see his father leading them in family devotions and could almost hear him pleading with his youngest son to heed the teachings from the Word of God.

Tyler noticed that his hands were beginning to tremble. "Snap out of it," he murmured. Trying not to think about his family, he grabbed his fancy jacket and hurried upstairs. As usual, once he started working all thoughts of home vanished.

# Chapter 6

# THE DESTRUCTIVE NIGHT

It was the beginning of Tyler's fifth year aboard *The Mademoiselle Jewel*. Since he was not like his fellow employees who spent or gambled away their paychecks, his account was second only to Dunningham's. He was saving to buy a boat of his own, and he was getting close. Even better than that, he was planning to ask for Cecilia's hand in marriage.

While they were docked in Mississippi, he spent three hours searching for the ring that he thought best suited his girl. Finally satisfied, and to the relief of the exhausted salesman, he made his purchase and hurried back to *The Jewel*.

"Agatha, have you seen C?" he asked.

"Last I saw her, she wus a headin' fer her room."

"Thank you, Aggy." He took the steps that led down to the living quarters two at a time, whistling all the way. His first stop was at his room. There he dressed in his best clothes and, after a final inspection, went to seek out the girl he hoped would be his bride.

Squaring his shoulders, he knocked lightly on her door.

"Come in," she called. The minute he heard her voice, he broke into a cold sweat. Taking a deep breath, he opened the door. She was sitting on her bed brushing her hair.

"Tag, did you need something?" she asked.

"No, yes, I mean I…" Tyler shrugged helplessly. He walked across the room so that he was facing her. "C, I've been saving my money ever since I got here, and I almost have enough to get started on my own riverboat. I'd like you to share my future with me." He handed her the ring. "Will you marry me?"

She dropped her brush and accepted the ring. "I was wondering if you would ever ask me. Yes, Tag, I will."

"Really?" he asked, raising his eyebrows. "I was afraid that you would say no. Come on, let's go tell everybody!"

"No, not yet," she pleaded. "If we try to tell them all now, we'll surely miss someone. Let's wait until tomorrow morning, when the crew is gathered in the gambling room for instructions. That way they'll all find out at once."

Tyler would do anything to make her happy, and if that was the way she wanted it, then that was the way it would be. "Tomorrow morning, sweetheart."

He floated out of the room and up the stairs. He wanted to shout to the world, but instead he worked out his enthusiasm by vigorously attacking his job. He began to sing out, "Step right up, Gents. That's it, step right up. Try your luck with the dice. There you go, sir. What's your first bet? Well, that's kind of low, but we've got time to increase." On and on he went. Later on in the day, Duce walked over to him.

"That's the way, Tag. This here's the richest crowd we've had in months. Keep it up."

Tyler did just that. His biggest haul was from a cowboy who seemed to have no control over his gambling. What little money he did not gamble away he spent on one beer after another. Tyler was amazed that the man could even walk after all the liquor he had drunk, but he managed to stumble out and make his way down the gangplank. Tyler shrugged then went back to work, but he could not forget the sight of the cowboy, dizzy, stumbling, falling, and broke. *He*, Tyler, was the reason for that man's misery. What if he had a wife and children who would go hungry that night when Daddy came home with no money? What if he struck one of them in a drunken rage? What if he had to sell his home to pay for his losses? Thousands of "what ifs" kept nagging at Ty. He tried to tell himself that anyone who started gambling took the risk of losing his money, but every time he convinced himself, the picture of the drunken cowboy came back to haunt him.

After all the "customers" had gone, Tyler was still having trouble. Leaning against the bar, he ordered a glass of whiskey. Shotglass filled one of the little cups and slid it toward Tag.

"What's eating at you?" Jack asked him, seeing the gloomy expression on his face.

"Nothing," Ty answered lamely.

"Nothing? Come on now. I've never seen you so down. Enjoy yourself, Tag, for today *The Jewel* doubled her money!" The man slapped Tyler on the back.

"You mean the money that she got from the hands of foolish and ignorant people," Tyler snapped.

Jack straightened his lean form. "What's the matter? You going soft or something? You know that every person who walks in here," he emphasized his lecture by pointing to the rooms' ornate doors, "takes the risk of losing every cent he has on him. I know that, you know that, and everybody knows that. It's the name of the game, Tag!"

"Yeah, yeah, Jack, I know, and no, I'm not going soft. I'm tired from the long day, that's all."

"Well then, you'd better get some rest. The Captain says to expect another big crowd tomorrow." Jack downed his liquor and walked away, and Tyler went to his room. There he emptied his pockets on his table, intending to get ready for bed, but the objects that tumbled out of his hands caught his eyes. He sat down on a chair and looked at them. One was the leather wallet that his mom and dad had bought him on his sixteenth birthday. Inside one of the pockets his parents had placed a note with two Bible verses on it. It was still there. He unfolded it, and for the first time in a long time he read it.

"Lay not up for yourselves treasures upon earth, where moth and rust doth corrupt, and where thieves break through and steal:

"But lay up for yourselves treasures in heaven, where neither moth nor rust doth corrupt, and where thieves do not break through nor steal:" Matthew 6:19-20

We love you, Tyler. Happy Birthday.

Mom and Dad.

The other item was the old pocket watch that Sam had given him for Christmas. It was still keeping time. As he fingered the watch and wallet, a question popped into his mind. *Why do you keep these? You have so much money you could easily buy newer and better ones.* As usual, he tried to rationalize away the true answer.

"They're in good condition," he told himself aloud. "There's no need to buy newer ones. It would be a waste of money, and I'm too thrifty to waste money on things that I really don't need." In his heart he knew the real reason. These insignificant items were all he had kept from his life at home, and all he had left from his parents and his brother. He brushed a tear from his eye and tossed the items and the note in a drawer. As he did, his eyes fell on the picture from the rodeo. Both he and Cecilia had one. He picked it up and looked at the young broncobuster and the barrel racer. Somewhere, from deep within, a cry for him to return surged through his body. He laid the picture facedown and tried to calm himself by reaching for a glass and pouring some wine. Dunningham had given him four bottles of the best French wine in New Orleans. Tyler liked it, but this time it did not satisfy his cravings. He tried another glass, but found that he needed something stronger. He put on a jacket and headed for the bar.

"Whiskey, Shotglass," he ordered.

"Now, Tag, you know I'm closed."

"To the public, yes. To the employees, no. Pour!" he demanded.

The bartender shrugged and poured. Tyler downed it and slid the glass back for a refill. He downed the second glass just as quickly.

"Tag, aren't you laying on this stuff a little heavy?" Shotglass asked, waddling over to him. As usual, Tyler could not help noticing how much Shotglass looked like his nickname.

"Not near as bad as you do," Tyler said studying his glass.

"Yeah, but you don't normally drink like this. You sure you're okay? Jack thinks you might be sick. You do look kind of peaked."

"Like I told Jack," Tyler said, feeling woozy from his liquor, "I am tired."

"Then get some sleep instead of getting drunk." The bartender grabbed Ty's glass and finished cleaning up.

Tyler was about to argue with him when they heard a commotion out on the deck.

"That sounds like the makings of a fight," Shotglass said. "Probably Duce and Duke again," he added. "Them two are going to kill each other one day I'm afraid."

"Yeah, I better see what's up," Tyler agreed. He looked toward the door and thought he was going to fall over. He held on to the bar and waited for the room to stop spinning. Then he walked out, bumping into a few chairs along the way. Stepping on the deck, he paused to determine from where the noise was coming from. It sounded as though it was from the other side of the deck. The cold wind whipping at his face helped to somewhat clear his groggy head, and he hurried toward the sound. He had to pass the stairway that led down to the living quarters. C and her mother, curious as to what was going on, were coming up it.

The argument was getting more intense. Tyler, recognizing the voices, thought to himself, *It's not Duce and Duke. It's the Captain and that cowboy who was here today.* Tyler winced as he heard the cowboy demand to see the kid who "stole" his money.

"You two stay here," Ty said to C and her mother. "I'll go see if I can straighten this thing out."

"No, Tag, please," C begged, clutching his jacket. "He's angry and he might kill you. Let father handle it."

Tyler's pride flared up. "I'm not going to stand here and let your father cover for me," he told her. "Now, stay here. I'll be fine."

"Tag, please don't go out there!" she cried, but Tyler had already turned the corner. She would have followed him, but her mother pulled her back down the steps.

Tyler, oblivious to the light rain that was falling, advanced toward the voices.

"I told you, we're closed for the evening," he could hear Dunningham say. "If you want to talk to Tag, you'll have to come back here tomorrow. Now go, before I throw you off!"

"I'll not leave until I see this Tag fellow!" the cowboy roared.

Tyler saw Jack, Duce, Ace, and Dice, holding tightly to the man's arms. At Dunningham's instruction, they began to pull him down the gangplank.

"I'm right here," Tyler said, walking up beside Dunningham. "Let him go fellows." The four gamblers looked up at the Captain, who nodded his head. Simultaneously they let go, but stood close by, ready to jump him again.

"Now," said Tyler, "speak your piece, then get out of here."

"I want the money that you stole from me!"

"I'm sorry, but you gambled that money away. You no longer have a claim on it," Tyler said coldly.

"You lied to me! You said I was lucky! You lied; you stole my money, and you're going to pay!" Before anyone realized what was happening, the man pulled out a pistol and fired! Tyler cried out in pain and slumped to the ground!

# Chapter 7

# DOUBLE-CROSSED

Spade came running to the boat with the sheriff and a couple of deputies at his heels.

"Drop the gun!" the sheriff barked. His deputies pounced on the cowboy and snapped a pair of handcuffs on his wrists. After making sure the prisoner was secure, the sheriff knelt down beside Dunningham and Ace as they surveyed Tyler's wounded left shoulder. "Is it bad?" he asked.

Ace, who was also *The Jewel's* unlicensed doctor, shook his head in bewilderment. "Yes, and no. It's not the bullet wound I'm worried about. It's the bump on his head he got when he fell. I think he'll be okay after some rest, though."

Just then, Cecilia came running down the deck. Seeing Tyler on the ground, her hand went to her mouth and she started to weep. She fell down beside him and grasped his hand. "Oh Tag, Tag, please speak to me Tag, please! Tell me you're all right! Tag, please!" she cried.

"There, there now, C darling," Dunningham said, pulling her to her feet. "He'll be fine." He looked at two of his men and said, "Ace, Duce, you two take Tag to the doctor." As they carried Tyler away, Mr. Dunningham turned back to his daughter. "Ace said he'll be fine with a little rest, and Ace has never been wrong yet. Dry your eyes, my dear. I'm going over to the doctor's office right now and see that he's cared for. Agatha, take Miss C to her room and fix her a glass of milk." Agatha put her arm around the trembling girl and led her to her room, all the while assuring her that Tag would be fine.

As soon as Agatha and Cecilia were out of earshot, the Captain motioned for Jack and Clara. Jack had told Dunningham that he thought Tyler was getting soft and might leave *The Jewel*. Dunningham knew that if one gambler began to wonder about the profession others might do the same. He considered Tyler to be a danger to his business and wanted to get rid of him.

"Listen," the Captain began, "I racked my brain trying to find a sensible way of disposing of our friend Tag. Now, thanks to the drunken cowboy, we have a splendid chance to get rid of him. Jack, you were a forger before you were a gambler. I want you to forge Tag's signature on a bunch of IOU's. Go through his room and find any account books he may have and get rid of them. In my office you'll find a blank account book. Make it look like Tag started gambling away his money about two years ago. Make him, let's see here, three thousand dollars in debt to me. I'll tell that to the sheriff and say that, out of the kindness of my heart, I'll forgive him the debt, but I must fire him."

"Oh how sad," Clara said with a sneer.

"Clara, you pack all of Tag's things and have them sent to the doctor's office. We'll leave here when I get back. Got it?"

"Yeah, but what about C? She and Tag were getting very friendly." Jack had always had a grudge against Tag for winning the heart of the girl he wanted.

"Thank you for reminding me about her. I'll tell her he decided that this was too rough for him, and he's decided to quit. He sends his love and regrets that he wasn't able to see her again. Now for another matter. We better make sure she doesn't try to sneak out to go see him. Jack, tell Shotglass to wait by her room and make sure she doesn't leave. Tell him if she gets out, it'll mean his job."

"Right." Jack ran toward the bar to set the Captain's plan in motion.

Meanwhile, Dunningham hurried to the doctor's office.

Tyler was still unconscious. The doctor's assistant, a Dutch/Swedish nurse named Matilda Bird, was carefully tending to him.

"Alright Dunningham, what happened?" the sheriff demanded. He did not like riverboat gamblers, especially Archibald J. Dunningham. The man was wicked and evil, but managed to stay just inside the bounds of the law, preventing his arrest.

"Why, Sheriff, surely you don't think that I am at fault here." To this the sheriff snorted.

Dunningham, ignoring the sheriff's disbelief, gave him the account and Ace and Duce backed him up.

"Poor lad," Dunningham moaned after he had finished. He stepped up to where Tyler was lying and shook his head sadly. "Such a nice young fellow, too. Tell me, Mrs. Bird, will he recover?"

"Aye t'at 'e 'vill. If'n t'e Good Lord sees fit to continue to 'elp 'im."

"Splendid! Splendid!" He once again faked a sad face. "Poor, poor lad," he repeated. "In so much trouble already, and now this."

"What do you mean by 'trouble already'?" the sheriff asked.

"Well, Sheriff, I hesitate to bring it up, but Tag is in debt. Terribly in debt."

"To whom?" asked the sheriff.

"To me. He owes me at least three thousand dollars, and I'll wager he doesn't have ten dollars to his name." At the sheriff's skeptical look, he quickly added, "I have the papers to prove it. If you wish, Sheriff, you could come over and see them." The sheriff shook his head.

Dunningham went on. "He did good for a while, but then he became obsessed with gambling and lost all his self-control. We tried to stop him, but he refused to slow down. It's such a shame. I had high hopes for him and my daughter, but now, I'm afraid I'm going to have to fire him. I got a letter from a friend of mine who lives a good ways from here, and he says there's a chance for me to make a good profit at a riverside fair he is hosting. We'll be leaving as soon as I get back to my boat, so we'll not be able to wait for Tag to recover. I've arranged for his personal belongings to be sent here. As inconvenient as it is, I'll forgive him the debt, and," he added, reaching for his wallet, "I'll leave him with fifty dollars. That should take care of his doctor bill, right, Doctor?"

"Yes, it will," the doctor said accepting the money. "Whatever is left over I'll give to him."

"Fine. Well boys," Dunningham said, addressing Ace and Duce, "we ought to be heading back to *The Jewel*."

Ace and Duce looked at each other questioningly. They knew Dunningham was lying. Tag had more money than everyone on *The Jewel* put together, except the Captain. Still, the men knew that if Dunningham said he had papers to prove his accusations, then he surely did. They would not put it past him to forge documents and alter account books. They wanted to speak out in Tag's defense, for they liked the kid. He had brought a lot of business to their boat, giving them a greater income. However, it would be Dunningham's word against theirs and they would undoubtedly lose their job. They kept quiet.

Abel showed up with Tyler's belongings and the Captain and his three employees started back to the boat.

"I wonder why he turned on Tag," Ace whispered to Duce.

"I don't know but the Captain better not see us talking about it," Duce warned. "Or we might be next and we might not get off the Captain's discard pile as easy as Tag did."

"Agreed."

The two gamblers said nothing more. When they reached *The Jewel,* Dunningham told the others that Tag was awake and had decided to stay in Mississippi. Ace and Duce backed his story and soon the boat was leaving the dock.

# Chapter 8

# THE BIRDS
# TO THE RESCUE

---

Tyler was unconscious for three days. All the while Mrs. Bird cared for him tenderly. Having had twelve children of her own, she was no stranger to illnesses. Due to her watchful care, he quickly began to mend.

"Wh, where am I?" he asked on the morning of the fourth day. He tried to sit up but was hindered by shooting pains in his head and left arm.

"Take it easy, Tag," Mrs. Bird whispered. "You are at t'e doctor's office," she explained, her pleasant accent calming him. "I am Mrs. Bird. I've been takin' care of you since you vere 'urt. You've been 'ere for t'ree long days. You yust vaking up. You vahs vounded and 'urt your 'ead ven you fell."

"Oh, yes, now I remember. That cowboy shot me."

"Ya, t'at is right."

"Whew, have I ever got a headache," he said, lifting his good arm to feel the lump on his head. He winced and let his arm fall. "Thank you kindly for taking care of me all this time. I'll be sure to make it up to you. Now, I think I need to get back to my boat." He attempted to sit up again, but sunk back down on the bed.

"No, no, Tag. You not vell yet. Lie back down." She helped him get comfortable and tucked the blankets around him.

"Thank you. Mrs. Bird, could you do something for me?"

"Ya, I vill try."

"Would you send for Cecilia Dunningham? She is probably worried sick about me. Her father owns the riverboat *The Mademoiselle Jewel*."

She looked at him sadly. "Tag, t'ey 'ave already left." She proceeded to tell him all that Dunningham had said.

"Why that no good, double-crossing swindler!" Tyler cried weakly, trying to get out of bed for the third time, but again he slumped back down. "This, this can't be true," he said softly. "I, I never gambled that money away. I had almost as much money as Dunningham did. Cecilia and I were going to get married." Feeling at ease with the caring nurse, he told her his story, starting from the minute he arrived in New Orleans several years ago.

"I see," she said. "Son, vere is your family?"

"I, I ran away from them five years ago," he answered.

"I see," she said again.

"I, I should have listened to them. They told me that money would never truly satisfy. They said that the friends of this world would turn their back on you without a second thought. I should have listened to them."

"Ya, t'ey sound like a vonderful family. Tell me, vere t'ey Christians?"

He looked up at her and nodded.

"T'at is good," she said, her face lighting up. "Me and my family, ve are Christians. I've been saved for fifty-five years. Vaht about you, Tag?"

"No, I'm not. I thought that Christianity was something to prop up weak people. Now, I don't know." Every message, every sermon, and every Bible verse he had ever heard was flooding his mind. "I don't know."

"Tell you vaht. I'll leave you my Bible, and you read it. If'n you 'ave any questions you yust yell. I'll be right outside t'e door. Start in First Yohn chapter five and verse t'irteen. T'en go to t'e next verse t'at is marked on t'e bottom of t'e page." She handed him a Bible and then walked out.

It had been over five years since Tyler had held a Bible in his hands. His fingers trembled as he turned its yellowed pages. Much to his surprise, he remembered where I John 5:13 was, and he found it rather quickly.

"These things have I written unto you that believe on the name of the Son of God; that ye may know that ye have eternal life, and that ye may believe on the name of the Son of God."

Tyler pondered the verse. How wonderful eternal life would be. When the cowboy had pulled the pistol out, Ty thought his life was over. What came after death? He looked at the reference marked in the margin of the Bible. It was Romans 3:23 and he turned there.

"For all have sinned, and come short of the glory of God;"

*All have sinned.* He knew that sin was disobeying God, and he knew he had been disobedient. He had run away from his parents and the Bible said to obey your parents. He had lied, cheated, drunk, and lived a life of rebellion toward God. Yes, he knew that he was a sinner and that all men were born sinners. He remembered his pastor saying, "We are sinners by birth and sinners by choice." Ashamed of his wickedness, Tyler checked the margin again. When he turned to Romans 6:23, the words paralyzed him with fear.

"For the wages of sin is death; but the gift of God is eternal life through Jesus Christ our Lord."

Death! The very word scared him. Again he wondered what would happen after death. He remembered Pastor Carson preaching that after death a man either went to Heaven or to hell. Tyler wanted to go to Heaven. Finding hope in the words "...but the gift of God is eternal life...", he continued to the next reference, Romans 5:8.

"But God commendeth his love toward us, in that, while we were yet sinners, Christ died for us."

"Why would Christ die for me?" Tyler asked himself. "I'm not worthy of that." Then he realized that the same verse answered his question. "'But God commendeth his love toward us...' Pastor Carson said that the word commendeth means to show or to give. That's why Jesus died," Tyler exulted. "He loves me. Oh, I never realized that God truly loves *me*."

The margin directed him to Romans 10:9 & 13.

"That if thou shalt confess with thy mouth the Lord Jesus, and shalt believe in thine heart that God hath raised him from the dead, thou shalt be saved."

"For whosoever shall call upon the name of the Lord shall be saved."

All Tyler needed to do was call upon the name of the Lord. He closed the Bible and began to pray.

"Lord," he began, "I've never done any praying, so this may be a little rough for me. You didn't say that I needed to feel some kind of emotion or that I needed to say all the right words. You just said call, so I'm calling. Lord, I know I've done wrong, and I don't deserve Your forgiveness, but You said You loved me, and I believe You. Please save me Lord, please." Here he paused and felt peace flood his soul. He had never realized that being saved could bring such peace. "Thank You, God, thank You."

"Mrs. Bird! Mrs. Bird!" he cried out.

She came running in. "Ya, ya, vaht is it?" she asked.

"I asked Jesus to save me!"

She smiled gently. "T'at is good. T'at is very good. I'm 'appy for you, Tag." Mrs. Bird mulled over the name. "Is Tag your real name?" she asked.

"No, my real name is Tyler Andrew Goo..." He hung his head in shame. "I've disgraced the name of my father, and I can never use it again. From now on my name is just Tyler Andrew."

"No, no, Tyler Andrew Goo... Your fader and moder, t'ey must know t'at you are now a Christian. You must tell t'em. You must go to t'em," she said, her eyes pleading.

"I can't, Mrs. Bird. I've done too much to them. I can never go back, never." His eyes misted, for he longed to be with them, but he thought they did not want him to come home.

When he was well enough, he moved in with the Birds. At first he was overwhelmed by all the people. There were still ten children at home, the oldest, Callen, being twenty-one, the same age as Tyler. Stacey, the youngest, was only five. Tyler learned to love them all, though he occasionally forgot a name. He became good friends with Callen.

In three weeks, Tyler was as good as new, and spiritually he was new. After getting saved, he felt the desire to read the Bible, pray, and go to church regularly. The Birds were so happy. They only wished he would tell his parents, but Tyler was obstinate. He still felt he had done them too much wrong for them to forgive him. Mr. and Mrs. Bird and Callen were talking about the problem one day when they decided on a plan of action.

"We've got to find out where his parents live," Mr. Michael Bird said. It was amusing to hear him and his wife talk together for his English was clear. The children, except the youngest, mostly spoke like he did, but once in a while one would say "Vill you come over?" instead of, "Will you come over?" Or "'appy" instead of "happy".

"Ya, but Tyler vill not tell us 'oo and vere t'ey are. 'Ow can ve?" Mrs. Bird asked.

"If I could find out where *The Mademoiselle Jewel* is, maybe Cecilia would tell me," Callen suggested. The Birds had known the Dunninghams for a long time. Mr. and Mrs. Bird had often tried to witness to them, but they would not listen. The Birds believed, however, that Cecilia had a tender heart, and their prayer was that she would get saved and lead her parents to Christ. Callen had a feeling that Cecilia was not in on the swindle and was probably mourning over it.

"How will you find out where they are?" Mr. Bird asked.

"Well, first I'll ask the sheriff if he knows. If he doesn't, I'll pray and ask God to lead me to them." He paused, and then asked, "Dad, do you think we should do that, though? I mean, what if Ty's right, and his parents really don't want him back?"

Mr. Bird looked lovingly at his son. He was glad that his son was not afraid to ask the questions that were troubling him. "Callen, Tyler says his parents are Christians. Now, not all Christians are willing to forgive, but the Bible commands it. I've prayed about this situation, and the Lord gave me this verse. Matthew 7:12, 'Therefore all things whatsoever ye would that men should do to you, do ye even so to them: for this is the law and the prophets.' If one of

my children would ever go astray, I pray that someone would help them see the truth and come find
me so I could welcome them back home."

Callen nodded in agreement. "When can I
start?"

They spent the next week in search of the riverboat and found that she was back in New Orleans, a
long way from the Birds' farm in Mississippi. Callen
wondered how he was ever going to get there. His
family did not have much money. Then one day as
he was sitting on his bed praying about the problem,
his parents walked in. Mr. Bird handed Callen an
envelope. In it was one thousand dollars.

Cal was stunned. He sat for a moment, wondering where the money came from. The answer
dawned on him and he exclaimed, "Dad, this is your
life's savings!"

Having had twelve children, very little money
ever went into the Birds' savings account. It had
taken most of his parents' lives to save this much.
"Are you sure you want me to use *this*?" Callen
asked.

"Yes, son. Your mother and I prayed about it, and
we decided that this was a good thing to spend the
money on. Take it and use all of it, if you have to."

Callen smiled at his parents. "You two are the
most caring people in all the world. With the Lord's
help, I'll find the Dunnighams."

At breakfast the next morning, Mr. Bird announced that Callen would be going away on a trip.

"Vere are you going, Callen?" Stacey asked. "Vill you be long gone?"

"Gone long," he corrected gently. "It's a surprise. I've got some personal business to attend to, and I'm not sure exactly how long I'll be gone."

The family prayed for Callen at the close of the meal. Then he went to saddle his horse. After tying his blanket and saddlebags onto the saddle, he mounted. Tyler filled two canteens from the pump and handed them to his friend.

"Take care, Cal. I'll be praying for you."

"Thanks, Ty, I'm going to need it." They shook hands and Callen galloped away.

The railroad station at Jackson was fifty miles from the town where Callen lived. His plan was to leave his horse there and take the train to New Orleans. His main fear was that the riverboat would leave before he got there. Speed was of the essence. Pushing as hard as he could, resting only when it was absolutely necessary, he quickly reached his first destination. The morning of the fourth day, breathing a sigh of satisfaction, he trotted into Jackson. His first stop was the livery stable.

"How much would it cost me to keep my horse here for two to three months?" he asked.

"Well, le' me see here," the old man said in a high-pitched voice. "Don't normally keep 'em that long. Oh, I'll settle for forty dollars. Sound fair?"

"Sure," Callen answered, chuckling. He led his horse into an empty stall and relieved him of his tack. "Thanks, Brownie. You got me here in good time." He patted the horse's neck. After paying the elderly man, he hurried over to the train station.

"When does the next train leave for New Orleans?" he asked, leaning on the counter.

"In one hour," the thin clerk said without looking up from his paperwork.

"I'd like a ticket please." Callen reached for his wallet.

This time the clerk looked up, revealing a rather odd face decorated with thick glasses almost dangling off his long pointy nose. He pushed the spectacles up and studied Callen through the half-inch lenses before asking, "Now, what would a country boy like you want in a high class place like New Orleans?"

"I've got business there."

"Yeah?" the clerk said, leaning one elbow on the counter. "You plan to hook up with a riverboat crew?"

"Why would you ask that?"

"Just wondered. I'm warning you to stay away from one riverboat called *The Mademoiselle Jewel*.

They're a rough bunch. I know, because I'm from New Orleans. If you ask me, there isn't a one of those riverboat men I'd trust. My advice is to stay away from all of them."

"Thanks for the advice, but don't worry. I'm only looking for some information from an old friend. Can I have a ticket please?"

"Sure."

# Chapter 9

# THE SEARCH

Callen boarded the train and settled into his seat. He watched the scenery pass by, but soon his thoughts concentrated on the task ahead of him. The Dunninghams may have pulled out; if so, he would have to track them down. Even if he found them, he knew it would not be easy to get the information from them. On top of it all, he would have to find Ty's parents and bring them to Mississippi. It seemed like an enormous task. Then he remembered the account of God speaking to Moses at the burning bush. Callen retrieved his Bible from his bag and turned to Exodus chapter three. Moses had told the Lord that he was not able to deliver the children of Israel. In verse eleven, he asked, "…Who am I, that I should go unto Pharaoh, and that I should bring forth the children of Israel out of Egypt?"

Callen knew the feeling. He knew he could not accomplish this task alone. The young man was thankful for the Lord's answer in verse twelve. "And he (God) said, Certainly I will be with thee; and this shall be a token unto thee, that I have sent thee: When thou hast brought forth the people out of Egypt, ye shall serve God upon this mountain." Though Moses was not able, God was.

Callen read a few more verses and found even more comfort from verse fourteen. "And God said unto Moses, I AM THAT I AM: and he said, Thus shalt thou say unto the children of Israel, I AM hath sent me unto you."

Moses asked God, "Who am I?" God said, "I AM." God gave Moses strength when Moses was willing to admit that he could not lead Israel without God's help.

"Lord," Callen prayed, "thank You for letting me try to help Tyler. I can't do it alone; I need Your help. Please, help me."

Callen's thoughts drifted back to Cecilia. *She must be heartbroken*, he thought and wished that things could have been different for her and Tyler.

Indeed, Cecilia was devastated. The night of the accident Agatha had taken her to her room and stayed with her until she had fallen asleep. She awakened some hours later only to find the boat far away from the town where Tyler was. Frightened, she raced to Tag's room. Her heart stopped when she saw that he was not there and all his belongings were gone. Feeling faint, she made her way to her parents' room.

"Where are we?" she cried. "Where's Tag? Why did we leave town? Why is his room empty?"

"Calm yourself, my dear," Dunningham said. He laid his hands on her trembling shoulders. "Tag decided that this life was too rough for him. Frankly, the attack scared him badly. He wished he could have seen you before we left, but you were asleep, and he was a little woozy from that bump on his head. He sent you his love and told me to tell you goodbye for him."

Cecilia shook her head. "That can't be. He couldn't have left us. Tag was going to buy a riverboat. He wanted to strike out on his own, and last night he asked me to marry him," she said, showing them the ring. "We, we were going to tell you this morning." She sank onto the bed, her body shaking with sobs.

Dunningham shot a surprised glance at his wife before approaching his daughter once again. "There's no need for tears, Cecilia. He didn't deserve you anyway; he must've seen that. You'll soon forget him." He smiled at her and said, "Your mother and

I have good news. We're getting a new riverboat. *The Jewel* was good to us, but it's time for bigger and better things. We've now got enough to buy the best there is."

Cecilia looked up at him and then at her mother. "Where are we getting the money?"

"Why, from all that good business we've had lately," he answered, still smiling.

She shook her head again. "I know you didn't have enough money to buy a better riverboat. You just told mother that we only had half of what was needed. Now all of a sudden we've got enough to buy one. Where did the money come from?" When they said nothing, she answered the question for them. "You stole it from Tag! You stole his money!" she screamed.

"Yes! Yes I did!" he shouted back. "No one will ever know. I made it look like he was in debt to me, that he lost all his money gambling. I did it for us, Cecilia. I did it for *you*. I want you to have so much more. This will be the last boat, I promise. In about five years we'll buy us some land and live there. I just need a little bit more money for *us*." His reason sounded good, but C knew that it was not true.

"That's what you said when you bought *The Jewel*, and you said the same thing when you bought *The Sailing Star*. I never wanted this. All I ever wanted was for us to be a family. I don't feel like I belong to anyone. Tag gave me the chance to have a family of my own, and that's all I want."

Cecilia left their room in tears. She knew they would not turn back, no matter how much she begged. She leaned against the rails of the boat and cried.

Weary from the long ride on horseback and then by train, Callen finally arrived in New Orleans. Tired as he was, he headed straight for the building marked "Marshal's office." Pushing open the door, he found a man sitting behind a desk, going through a stack of wanted posters. The man rose. "Hello son, my name's Martin Long. What can I do for you?" he asked cheerfully.

"I'm Callen Bird," he said, extending his hand. They shook heartily. "I'm wondering if the riverboat *The Mademoiselle Jewel* is still docked here?"

The marshal's face clouded. "Listen, Mr. Bird, and take my advice. Stay as far away from that group as you can. They're nothing but trouble. I don't care for any riverboat gamblers, but the Dunningham crew is the worst of the lot."

Despite the seriousness of the marshal's words, Callen grinned. "You are the fourth, no, fifth person that's told me to stay away from them."

"It wouldn't hurt for five more to tell you," the marshal said. "I'd hate to see another young man get mixed up in that mess."

"Don't worry. I'm not planning to join them." The marshal was so friendly and so obviously concerned that Callen told him the whole story. He ended with, "I've got to find out Tyler's last name and where he comes from."

"That's really Christian of you, son, and I'm glad to know that you're not aiming to lead their kind of life. The boat is down the road and to the left. It's the only boat at the docks right now."

"Thanks." Callen jumped to his feet, shook Long's hand, and dashed out the door. Jogging down the street, he mulled over the best approach to take. He decided that he had better try to find Cecilia first.

Upon reaching the boat, he made his way up the gangplank, alert for any sign of her. As he stepped onto the deck, he saw her emerge from the stairway.

"Miss Cecilia," he called. She turned and joy filled her face.

"Callen," she said, as he hurried over to her. She bombarded him with questions about Tyler and he held up his hand for silence.

"He's fine. In fact, he's far better than ever. He got saved. Miss C, I want to find his family, but he thinks they won't forgive him. He won't tell me what his last name is or where he's from. Do you know?"

Just then, Mrs. Dunningham appeared. She stopped short when she saw Callen talking with

Cecilia. "What are you doing here?" she asked coldly.

"Oh, hello Mrs. Dunningham." Callen was careful to be polite. "I'm trying to find out what Tyler's last name is and where he's from. I want to find his family and get them back together again."

"Why don't you ask Tag?" she wanted to know.

"Please Mother, let me tell him?" C begged, and Clara nodded.

"His last name is Goodton and he lived on a farm somewhere in Indiana. He has a brother named Samuel. That's all I know about him. Oh, I think he said he's been to Kentucky and Georgia." She paused, and then added, "Find them, Cal, please. Try to get them back together so that they can be a family again." His heart was moved at her pleading voice and eyes.

"I'll try, Miss Cecilia. I promise I will try. Thanks." He sighed as he watched her mother pull her away. Shaking his head and turning to walk back down the gangplank, he found himself face to face with Jack. The way the man was grinning sent chills down Callen's spine. He knew a fight was impending, and he was going to do everything he could to avoid it. Callen smiled back and tried to go around him, but Jack stepped back in front of him.

"Um, excuse me please," Callen said.

"What are you doing here? As I recall, your folks don't hold to riverboats and gambling and such," Jack said, folding his arms across his chest.

"I needed to ask Miss Dunningham some questions about a former employee. Now, if you don't mind, I'd like to be going." Once again Callen tried to go around him.

"Well, I do mind." Jack grabbed Callen's jacket with his left hand. "You listen to me," he growled, his voice low and menacing. "You stay away from Cecilia Dunningham, or else…"

"Or else what?" Callen asked. Two seconds later he was regretting that question. Jack's right hand shot out and landed a jarring punch to Callen's stomach. The suddenness of the attack caught him off guard and he toppled backwards. Jumping to his feet, he tried to tell Jack that it was too dangerous to fight on the deck of a boat. Jack paid his warning no heed and charged. Cal jumped aside and the gambler fell to his knees. Jack got up and charged again, managing to deliver a couple of stinging blows to Callen's face. His onslaught pushed Callen against the wall. Realizing that he was going to have to fight him, Cal let loose with a hard right to Jack's face and then, not giving him time to recover, he hit him with a left. Jack swung, missed, and Callen punched him twice. Jack went sprawling backwards. The deck was slippery and Jack slid toward the rail. He caught himself and staggered to his feet only to lose his balance again. Callen dove for him and managed to grasp his coat and keep him from toppling into the water. He helped the gambler regain his balance.

Spade and Duce rushed up to the two men as Callen let go of Jack's coat. The other two gamblers held Jack's arms to keep him from continuing the fight, and Callen left quickly. Once he was off the riverboat he walked back to the marshal's office. Martin Long had just come back from a routine check around town when Callen walked in, massaging his bruised jaw.

"What happened to you?" Martin asked. "Here, sit down and I'll get you some coffee." The marshal directed him to a chair and poured him a cup of strong coffee. Perching on his desk, he again asked Callen what happened to him. As Callen rubbed his sore hands, he told him.

"It wasn't a total failure, though. I found out what Ty's last name is. It's Goodton, Tyler Andrew Goodton. He's from Indiana, and he's got a brother named Samuel. He's been to Kentucky and Georgia. You wouldn't by any chance know anything about him, would you?" Callen asked, taking a drink of the steaming coffee.

Martin stroked his chin thoughtfully. "Le' me see here. Goodton," he mused softly. "The name doesn't ring a bell, but I *have* had a little experience with run away children. He probably came through those states you mentioned on his way to New Orleans. There's a chance his family tracked him to either Kentucky or Georgia, then lost his trail. I have a friend in Kentucky who might be able to find out if anybody by the name of Goodton came looking for a lost boy. I'll send him a wire."

"Marshal, Kentucky's a pretty good size state," Callen said, doubtful at the marshal's idea. "It would take a long time to check with every local sheriff and marshal there. Do you think it's worth the time or should I head straight for Indiana?"

Long chuckled. "You don't know my friend," he said simply. "Come and stay with us tonight. I'll go send that wire right now."

Much to Callen's surprise, in seven days a positive reply came. Martin came flying into the house on a Monday morning, shouting triumphantly. "Listen to this!" he cried.

Marshal Long:

Martin, I found out that five years ago a young man by the name of Samuel Goodton came to the state of Kentucky looking for his younger brother named Tyler Andrew, age sixteen. The latter had run away from his home in Indiana. I have enclosed the address below. I pray that it's the correct one.

Ike

The Marshal read the address and looked up at the astounded Callen.

"I can hardly believe it!" Cal exclaimed when he found his voice. "How did he find out so fast?"

"My friend happens to be a man named Ike Stagert, and he happens to be the best detective in the state of Kentucky. In fact, he's probably one of the top ten of all the detectives in the country. We grew up together."

"Marshal, you've been such a help to me. How can I ever thank you?" Callen asked.

Martin Long smiled. "I'll tell you, Cal. Just let me know how it all turns out, and that'll be all the thanks I need. Besides, I really didn't do anything. I'm glad the Lord let our paths cross, and I got to help someone out."

Callen left early the next morning on a train bound for Indiana. With Marshal Long's prayer ringing in his ears, he reread the address. "Clear Water," he mused. "It sounds like a small town. I wonder what his family is like." Weariness from the journey overcame him. He found a partially comfortable position and drifted off to sleep.

# Chapter 10

# REUNION

allen, his heart racing with excitement, stepped off the train in the town of Clear Water. His first stop there was Sheriff Maren's office, where he found the sheriff standing on the porch. Callen asked him if he knew of a family named Goodton. After studying the young man for a moment, Maren asked, "Are you coming peaceful, son?"

"Yes sir. My name is Callen Bird. I have some personal things to discuss with them, but I mean no one any harm."

"Okay. The elder Goodtons are away, but their oldest son lives on a farm 'bout ten miles out of town." After giving him detailed instructions, he said, "If he's not at the house, take the left trail to his field, and if he's not there, keep following that trail and you'll come to his best friend's house. If he's not there," he paused and shrugged, "I don't know what to tell you."

Callen laughed and thanked the sheriff. He rented a sorrel gelding and galloped his horse down the road. It did not take him long to find the house.

"Howdy!" Sam called out as the rider approached.

"Howdy!" Callen dismounted and ground tied his horse. Extending his hand, he spoke, "The name's Callen Bird. I'm looking for a man named Samuel Goodton. Would that be you?"

"Yes, and this is my wife Esther," Sam said, nodding toward Esther, who was by then standing on the porch. "What can I do for you, Mr. Bird?"

Callen took a deep breath. He had prayed for this moment, but now that it had arrived he was nervous. He was afraid that they might not want Tyler back. Pushing aside his fear and remembering the verses in Exodus, he began to speak. "I need to talk to you, Mr. Goodton, about some personal matters."

Esther smiled at the two men. "I'll leave you two to your conversation and start supper," she said, going back inside.

Once again, Callen took a deep breath. "This question may come as quite a surprise to you. Do you have a brother named Tyler?"

Sam's heart began to race. "Why? Do you know something about him?" In his fear and eagerness he had grabbed Callen's shoulders.

"Why don't you sit down? It's a long story." After Sam had seated himself on a log, Callen launched into Tyler's history for the past five years. When Callen spoke of Tyler getting saved, Sam buried his face in his hands and wept.

"Why didn't he tell us?" Sam asked, wiping the tears from his eyes.

Callen paused, choosing his words carefully. "Mr. Goodton, he's afraid. He's afraid that you and your family could never forgive him for what he's done. That's why I came here instead of Ty. He wouldn't even tell us his last name. I found out from Cecilia, the girl he was going to marry. I'm afraid that you're going to have to go to Tyler and show him that you'll forgive him."

Sam stood up. "I will. Just give me time to get my wife over to her mother and father's house."

After a quick supper, Sam and Esther packed a few things before he took his wife to the Makers' house.

"Oh, Sam," she whispered as he helped her out of the wagon, "I'll pray that all goes well."

"What's this?" Mr. Maker asked, stepping out on the porch. Sam gave him a brief explanation. "Oh my!" he exclaimed. "Sam, this is wonderful, and don't you worry about Esther and Matthew. We'll take good care of them." He took her bag and carried it to the house.

Before mounting his horse, Sam kissed his wife and held her for a few minutes. Then his kissed his one-month-old son.

"Take care, Samuel. Remember, I'll be praying for you," Esther said.

Next, Sam went to Tom's house and told him the news. Before leaving, he said, "Tommy, when Mom and Dad get back, would you tell them that I found out something about Tyler and that I went to investigate. Don't make any promises to them, though. Just ask them to pray, please."

"You know I will. Be careful, pal."

After Tom led them in prayer, Sam and Callen rode back to Clear Water. Sam stopped at his parents' house and brought Ace, Tyler's horse, with him to town. After leaving the three horses at the livery stable, they boarded the train for Mississippi.

On the way there Sam plied Cal with question after question about his brother. Callen was quick to answer each one and Sam absorbed every bit of information.

"I can hardly believe that I'm going to see him. It's been so long." Sam had to pause and wipe away some tears. "To know that he's been born again is such a relief to my heart." He checked his watch and sighed. "We've got a long ways to go yet. I guess we'd better try to sleep." Before he closed his eyes he had one more question. "Cal, once we reach Jackson, how far is it to your place?"

"Fifty miles," was the sleepy reply. Sam sighed again and pulled his hat over his eyes.

Reaching Callen's home state a couple days later, they picked up two horses. Brownie neighed and tossed his head in excitement when he saw Callen. The young man seemed just as happy to see his horse. After saddling Brownie and the rented horse, they stocked up with supplies, and started out on the last leg of the journey.

"There it is, Sam," Callen said when the farm came into view. "It's nothing fancy, but it's filled with the Bible and love. Come on. We'll ride in through the back way so no one will see us." Sam followed Callen as they made a wide circle and came in from behind the farmhouse. They tied their horses and headed toward the back door. An old hound dog got whiff of them and let loose with a chorus of deep barks. At a signal from Cal, the dog hushed.

"Vaht are you barking at, Bear?" little Stacey asked as she walked outside. Bear led her over to where Sam and Callen were hiding.

"Callen, you're 'ome!" she cried, running toward him.

"Shhh, Stacey," Callen whispered. He knelt and hugged her.

"I missed you," she said in a quiet voice.

"I missed you, Stace. Listen, I need you to do something for me. You see this man here?" She nodded. "His name is Samuel Goodton," he explained. "He's Ty's brother. Now, will you get Tyler to come out here without telling him why, please?"

"Sure, you yust vait 'ere." She raced back into the house. In a few minutes, she came out, leading Tyler by the hand.

"What is it you wanted to show me, Stacey?" he asked.

When Sam saw his brother, his heart almost stopped. He stood up from his hiding place.

"Ty, it's me," he said in a shaky voice.

Tyler's mouth dropped open. "Sammy?" He swallowed hard as tears fell down his cheeks. Sam ran toward him and threw his arms around his neck. They wept.

"Ty, I missed you so much," Sam said, hugging his brother tighter. As he did, he felt Tyler's arms tighten as well. Then Ty stepped back and looked up at his brother.

"I'm sorry, Sammy. I'm sorry for what I did. Can you ever forgive me?" he asked.

Sam smiled. "I forgave you a long time ago, Ty. I'm glad you're alright," he said, resting his hand on Tyler's shoulder. "God be praised for His mercy."

"How did you find out where I was?" Tyler asked.

Sam looked at Callen who was standing behind them. By this time the whole family had come out and was watching the two brothers. "I guess you could say 'A 'Bird' told me.'" He paused and then said, "Ty, come home with me."

Tyler shook his head. "I can't."

"Yes, you can. Mom and Dad miss you more than words can tell. They would've come with me, but they were away when I left. Come home, Tyler."

He looked away from his brother. "Sam, I don't deserve to be able to go back there. I've disgraced the name of Joshua Goodton. I'm not worthy to be called his son."

Mr. Bird, who had been quiet as the two brothers spoke, decided it was time to say what was on his mind.

"Tyler, you say your parents are Christians, right?"

"Yes, sir. They are."

"Well, they must not be very good ones," he said rather abruptly.

Sam opened his mouth to protest but caught himself. He saw where Mr. Bird was going, so he simply folded his arms and smiled.

Tyler did not catch on, and he did protest, politely yet firmly. "My parents are the best Christians in the world. No one ever possessed a more Christ-like character. They are obedient to God, kind, loving, longsuffering, gentle, forgi…" His voice trailed off as he contemplated what he had just said.

"Go ahead, Ty," Sam prodded. "Finish the sentence. You were going to say 'forgiving', weren't you?"

Tyler looked at his brother, then at the Birds, and then back at Sam. "When do we start home?" he asked softly.

"Tomorro' morning vill be a good time," Mrs. Bird said. "Your brother looks like 'e could use a good night's sleep and a varm meal. Come, dinner is almost ready."

Early the next morning, amidst prayers and many farewells, Sam and Tyler left. As they traveled, the two brothers told each other all that had transpired during the past couple years. It was a wonderful time that the two of them never forgot.

Upon reaching Clear Water, they went to the livery stable. When Ty walked in, he immediately saw the handsome bay. "Ace!" he shouted, running into the stall and petting the horse. "Ace, how are you? Did you miss me?" The bay whinnied in delight at seeing his master.

Sam leaned up against the wall and watched. Tyler turned to him, and said, "Thanks for bringing him, Sammy."

"You're welcome. Come on; let's get saddled up." Sam hoisted his saddle and laid it on Dusty's back. In five minutes they were on their way home.

When they reached the path that led to the house, Tyler stopped. Sam turned Dusty around and trotted up to his brother. "What's wrong, Ty?"

"Sam, I'm nervous. I'm afraid to face them." He hung his head in shame. "I was so wicked to them, and I don't have the right to ask them to forgive me."

Sam was silent a moment as he tried to think of something to say that would ease Tyler's fears. "Ty," he began slowly, "Mom and Dad love you, and you don't have to be afraid. I didn't tell you this before, but ever since you left there's been a place for you at the table. Every morning Mom sets a clean place setting out for you. It stays there all day long and they pray for you to come home every time they see it. They want you to come home, not so that they can get some sort of revenge, but so they can show you forgiveness."

Tyler's eyes misted. "Okay, I'm coming." Even though Tyler knew his parents would forgive him, the butterflies in his stomach grew worse the closer they got to home.

At the house, Josh was sitting on the porch, waiting. Ever since Tom had told him that Sam was going out to look for Tyler, Josh had spent most of his time watching the road, praying at each dawn that today would be the day his sons would come home.

Joshua's heart quickened as he saw two figures on horseback coming down the road. He stood and, shading his eyes from the sun, tried to discern who they were. Mary, who was feeding the chickens, followed her husband's gaze. Both of them recognized Tyler at the same time.

"It's Tyler!" they both shouted. Mary dropped her bucket of feed and rushed toward them. Josh followed her.

Ty saw them coming, and the yearning to reunite with them overcame his fear. He hurried Ace toward them.

Mary had a head start on Josh and she reached their prodigal son first. Tyler jumped off and pulled his mother close to him.

"Oh, Tyler, my son, my baby boy! You've come home! Praise God, praise His holy name!" She wept on his shoulders.

"I love you, Mom," he whispered. All those tears he had wanted to cry because he had missed them so much, but had held in, seemed to explode inside of him. He never wanted to let her go. He just wanted to stand there and feel the love in her embrace, but he still had to face his father. He stepped back and looked at Josh.

"Dad, I'm sorry, so very sorry." He had intended to say more, to tell his father that he did not deserve forgiveness, but "Dad, I'm sorry" was all he had time to say before Josh engulfed him in a loving embrace. Sam put his arm around his mother. Together they watched father and son cry away many years of grief and cry tears of joy.

"Welcome home, son," Josh said, once he was able to speak. He stepped back and looked at his boy. "I'm so glad you've come back. The Lord is so good. Come, let's go to the house." For the first time in almost six years the four Goodtons, hand in hand, entered their home.

"Well done, Samuel," Josh said, hugging his oldest son. "I'm proud of you."

"It was all the Lord," Sam said, putting his arms around his father. Sam did not want to leave, but it was getting late, and he had to go tell Esther. The following day was Sunday, and Tyler planned to go before the church and apologize, but Sam was going to tell Esther, her family, and Tom and Carol tonight. After a time of prayer and thanksgiving, Sam headed home.

Esther was sitting on the porch reading her Bible when Sam rode into the yard. Realizing how much he missed her, he lightly spurred his horse into a gallop.

His wife jumped to her feet and waved as Sam's horse came to a sliding halt in front of the porch. "Sammy, did, did you find him, and did he come home?" she asked as he ran to embrace her.

"Yes, praise God."

"Oh, Sam!" she cried, throwing her arms around him again. "Praise the Lord." He hugged her lovingly as they both cried.

Sam took Esther and Matthew home. Then he hurried to Tom and Carol's house.

Tom heard him coming and rushed outside to greet him. Sam dismounted, but was so overcome with joy he could not speak. He just nodded his head, and Tom shouted, "Hallelujah!" The two best friends knelt on the ground and praised the Lord. They both remembered the times they had knelt together and prayed for Sam's younger brother. The Lord had heard and answered their prayers.

Sunday morning was wonderful. Ty's grandparents were overjoyed, to say the least, when they saw him. The whole church began to rejoice. Tyler went before them all and apologized, and they welcomed him back.

# Chapter 11

# BACK TO NEW ORLEANS

Tyler loved Matthew, and Matt liked his Uncle Ty. It filled Sam's heart with joy to see his little brother playing with his son.

It was obvious that Tyler had changed. He worked hard at the farm with an enthusiasm his family had never seen. Josh and Tyler spent many happy hours together working in the fields. They prayed often for Cecilia, her parents, and the crew of *The Mademoiselle Jewel.*

In January of the following year, an announcement came. Sam and Esther were going to have another baby.

"Your mother told me the good news. Congratulations," Mrs. Pitt said to Esther one night after church. The Pitts, who had joined the church several years ago, were a singing family that traveled to different churches to provide them with good gospel music. Because they were often gone, the Goodtons and Sampsons had not been able to spend a lot of time with them. Still, they had come to love them dearly.

"Thank you," Esther said warmly.

Several evenings later, Esther asked, "Sam, I know you're tired, but could we pick out names for the baby after supper tonight?"

"Sure, sweetheart," Sam said. After drying his hands and face, he hung the rag on the peg and stepped up beside her. "Right after we eat, we'll pick out a name." He kissed her, and they sat down together and enjoyed a delicious meal.

While they ate, Sam listened as Esther told about her day. As she talked, he realized that lately he had not made much time to just sit and be with his wife. He and Tom were working on improving their farms, and though that was good, Sam had put it before the needs of his family.

*Lord,* he prayed silently, *please forgive me and help me to be a better husband. Please help me to think of her before I think of me. Amen.*

As soon as dinner and Bible reading was over, Sam sat down on the sofa. "Esther, leave the dishes for now. I'll help you after we're done."

She smiled, sat down beside him, and he led in prayer.

"Shall we do it like we did before?" she asked when he was done praying.

"Sure, if you want, but you go first this time."

"Well, it won't take me long to decide. I still like Mary Lisa. Do you mind?"

"No, I really like that name. Now let me see here." He thought for a few minutes. "How about Michael, after Mr. Michael Bird? We'll go with Thomas for a middle name. What do you think?"

"I love it!" she exclaimed.

Sam smiled at her exuberance and started to get up, but she tugged at his sleeve.

"Could we pick out *two* names?" she asked.

"Why?" he asked.

"I would like to. Please?"

He shrugged. "Why not?" He sat back down. "Okay, let's do it backwards. You pick the boy's name and I'll pick the girl's."

"Your turn to go first."

"We seem to be following a pattern of having a first name that starts with the letter *m*. In the Bible Mary had a sister named Martha so how about Martha Joy?"

"Wonderful. I like it." She leaned against her husband's shoulder, obviously deep in thought. "As you know, my mother lost two sons, both before me." Her voice quivered a little, and Sam slipped his arm tightly around her. She sniffled and brushed away a tear. "So," she continued, "I've always wanted to name one of my sons after them. It would mean a lot to my mother and father. The boys' names were Mac and Shane, but I can't decide which one to choose."

"Mac or Shane," Sam mused out loud. "Mac or Shane. Mac, Shane. That's it!" Esther jumped at his exclamation.

"What?" she asked.

"We'll call him MacShane, and Mac or Shane for short."

"Will that be his first name or both first and middle?" she asked.

"First name only. His middle name will be…"

"Tyler!" she finished for him. "Then he'll be named after my two brothers and your brother."

"Perfect."

Together they cleaned up the kitchen and turned in.

A few weeks later, Tom, Sam, and Tyler went into town for some supplies. As Sam and Tom bought the things they needed, Tyler went to purchase a newspaper for his father.

"Hi, Ty," Luke Neils greeted. He had been working at the newspaper office for two years and he loved it. "Want a paper? The latest story is fresh off the press."

Tyler chuckled. "Okay, you talked me into it." He tossed Luke the money, and the young printer handed him a copy. "Thanks, Luke." Ty walked outside and opened the paper. He read the headline and felt the blood drain from his face.

# Fire Rampages in The New Orleans' Dock.

## Riverboat Gambler, Archibald Dunningham, Loses Boat and most Possessions.

Fear gripped Tyler's heart. Was Cecilia all right? Agatha and Abel, were they hurt? Tears blurring his vision, he swiftly read the article. He breathed a sigh of relief when he read that no one had been seriously injured. The fire had been started by a drunken crewmember who had left a cigarette burning in his room. Clutching the paper, Tyler ran to his brother.

"Sam! Sam!" he shouted. Sam jumped off the sidewalk and hurried over to Tyler.

"What's wrong?" he asked in alarm.

"Read this."

After scanning the paper, Sam looked up at Ty. "I, I don't know what to say, Tyler." He could see that his little brother was quite shaken. "Let's go show it to Dad."

The two brothers went to their parents' house and stood quietly as their father read the article. "Sounds like they're in quite a mess," Joshua said. He looked straight at Tyler. "Maybe you and I ought to go down there and see if we can lend them a hand."

"Thank you, Dad," Ty said.

The next day they headed for New Orleans. Tyler talked of Cecilia the whole way there. His heart ached to see her get saved. Ty wanted her to know that the joy he now possessed was the joy they had both sought for. With the Lord's help, he was determined to try to show her and the others the truth.

After what seemed like forever, they finally arrived in the city of New Orleans. It brought back many sad memories to Tyler. He thought of the day when he had first entered this city and he was filled with shame as he thought of how his running away hurt his family. He thanked the Lord that God had brought him home.

Joshua and Tyler walked briskly to the docks. What was left of *The Jewel* was there. Ty could barely recognize the demolished riverboat. There was hardly anything left of her. Workers were everywhere, clearing away the rubble and searching for anything of value. Scanning the group, Tyler was surprised that he did not recognize anybody. None of *The Jewel's* crew was in sight. Where were they?

"I don't see anybody I know, Dad," Tyler said.

"Well, I think that man over there knows *you*," Mr. Goodton said. Tyler looked at his father then followed the older man's gaze. He was just in time to see a man duck back into an alley.

"Jack!" Tyler shouted. "Hey, Jack! Wait a second!" He sprinted toward the gambler.

"What are you doing here?" Jack growled when they caught up to him. "If you're coming to cause trouble…"

"No, Jack, I don't want any trouble. I read about the fire back home, and my father and I came here to see if we could be of any help," Ty explained.

"Yeah, I'll bet you did," Jack sneered.

At that moment, Mr. Dunningham came out of a store carrying some packages. He stopped short when he saw Tyler. "Wh, what are you doing here?" he asked. His face paled, but he quickly recovered. "What do you want?"

"I wanted to see if there was anything I could do for you and the crew. Also, I'd like to speak to Cecilia, if I could. By the way, where is everybody?"

"If you mean the crew, they're not working for me any more. Only Jack is still with me. All the others left."

Tyler thought that strange but said nothing about it. "What about Cecilia?" he asked.

"She's none of your concern, Tag!" Jack said. He lifted his head proudly. "She and I are going to be married."

"What!" Tyler cried. Sweet Cecilia and Jack the troublemaker were getting married? It could not be. At first he was angry and wanted to punch both Jack and Dunningham, but then he felt his father's hand rest on his shoulder. Tyler sighed. "Congratulations, Jack. When's the date set?"

"Just as soon as I can get her out of this religious thing she's in," Dunningham said.

"Religious thing?" Ty echoed.

"Yeah. She calls it being a Christian and being born again, or something like that," Jack explained. "Whatever it is, I'm sure it'll wear off. When it does, we'll get married."

Tyler wanted to shout for joy. Cecilia was a Christian! "If she has the same 'religious thing' that I have, and I pray she does, it won't wear off," he said.

"Nonsense," Dunningham argued. "She'll see it our way soon. Then she will consent to the marriage."

"Where is she? Can I talk to her, please?" Tyler asked.

"Sure, if you can find her," Dunningham taunted as he and Jack walked away.

"Nice people," Josh said sarcastically.

"Dad, I've got to find out what's going on. Could we walk around town for a bit? Maybe we can find a crew member, or anyone who might know something about Cecilia." That is what they did. Together they walked through town praying and keeping their eyes open for the girl or one of the crew. The Lord had the situation under control and one of the crewmembers found them.

"Tag! TAG!" Tyler whirled around to see Shotglass huffing and puffing to catch up to them.

"Shotglass!" Ty exclaimed. He and his father hastened over to him. "Do you know where Cecilia is?" Tyler asked.

"Yes, but, I need to talk to you first, Tag." He hung his head in shame. "There's, there's no reason for you to believe me, but I'm sorry about what happened. Not only about the money, but also the things I taught you. They were wrong." Again he paused, searching for the right words. "You may not understand this, but I received Jesus Christ as my Saviour."

Ty's eyes widened "Really?" Shotglass nodded. "So did I!" the young man said excitedly.

It was Shotglasses' turn to be surprised. "That's wonderful. So you're not here for revenge."

"No. I read about the fire, and my father and I came to see if we could help." He introduced his father to the ex-bartender. "Can you tell me where Cecilia is?"

"Yeah, she's staying with the Brownlys. He's the preacher that led all of us to Christ."

"What do you mean, 'all of us'?" Ty asked.

Shotglass explained that almost the entire crew of *The Jewel* had gotten saved after the fire! Pastor Jim Brownly and his wife Marie went to the scene of the fire and presented the gospel to the crew. The pastor had spoken of the fires of hell, the fires that could not be quenched, the fires that went on for eternity. He told them that the only way to avoid hell was to accept Jesus Christ as their personal Lord and Saviour. The Dunninghams and Jack were the only ones that did not listen to him.

The two Goodtons were so very happy. Their prayers were being answered. Blinking away tears, Tyler followed his new brother in Christ to where Cecilia was staying. On the way, Shotglass, whose real name was Peter Blake, told them that since Cecilia was of age, she had moved out of her parents' home. She had told her parents that she loved them but could not be a part of their wickedness anymore. The Brownlys had welcomed her into their home. Shotglass also told them that she had no intention of marrying Jack.

# Chapter 12

# A BRIDE FOR TYLER?

H ere we are," Pete finally said. He pointed to a small, quaint brick house enclosed by a white picket fence. Strains of piano music came from somewhere within the house and suddenly someone began to sing the hymn.

"What a lovely voice," Mr. Goodton said in admiration.

Once again tears spilled out of Tyler's eyes. "That was Cecilia singing," he whispered.

The three of them headed for the front door. Before they reached it, the music and singing stopped. Ty heard the back door open and he quickly made his way around the house. There he saw her. She sat down on the porch floor and began stroking the soft fur of a tiger colored kitten. A Walker coon dog came and stretched out beside her. Tyler's heart pounded in his chest. He could see that Cecilia was different. He had heard it in her voice as she sang, and now he saw it in her eyes. There was peace and contentment in her countenance.

"C," he called out.

She jumped to her feet and turned to face him. At first, her face lit up with joy, but then it clouded with uncertainty. He knew she was wondering why he was here and what it was that he wanted.

"How are you, Cecilia?" he asked.

"I'm better than I have ever been. Oh, Tag, I'm sorry for what they did…"

He held up his hand. "There's no need to apologize. I've already forgiven them. I got saved a few days after, after, after the, trouble," he finally said.

"Really? I thought Callen said you did, but I wasn't sure. I am now a Christian, too," she told him. All fear that he had come for revenge was gone, and she was happy to see him again.

It was then that Joshua joined them.

"Is this your father?" she asked, noticing the slight resemblance in them.

"Yes." Tyler introduced her to him and told her why they had come. "I saw what happened to *The Jewel*, and I heard that almost everybody got saved."

"Yes. All but Jack and my parents." She looked away to hide her tears. "We've been trying to witness to them, but..." Her voice trailed off.

Mr. Goodton stepped up beside her. "Don't give up, Cecilia. We prayed for many years for our boy, and look what God did. It may take time, but never ever give up."

"Thank you, Mr. Goodton," she said, a smile returning to her face. "With the Lord's help, I'll never quit trying."

Mr. and Mrs. Brownly invited Joshua and Tyler to stay for dinner. Much to the Goodtons' surprise, some of Ty's old buddies were there. Most of the crew, he learned, had gone back to their homes and families. However, Ace, Dice, Duce, Spade, and Duke were still there. Their real names were Richard Dikes, Clark Mason, Andy Blaker, Raymond Lakes, and Lee Blaker. Tyler found out that Duce and Duke were cousins. This astonished him, because the whole time they were on the boat they had fought. The cousins explained that there had been a falling out in their family, mainly between their fathers. By accident the two Blakers had joined up with the same riverboat. They had continued the family quarrel there, but since they had become Christians, they had put those differences behind them. Their families were furious with them for forgiving each other and had disowned them. For the time being, the two of them were staying in New Orleans, and together they were praying for their families.

The Brownlys' guests all had a good time but, even amidst the joy, was a burden for the three unsaved members of their crew. After dinner, much prayer was made for them.

"Dad, could you do something for me?" Ty asked, as they got ready for bed in their hotel room that night.

"Sure, son. What is it?" his father inquired.

"Well, I just found this in my pocket." He showed his father the diamond ring. "It's the one I gave Cecilia. She must have put it in there when my coat was hanging in the closet at the Brownlys'. She also left this note." He unfolded the letter and read it aloud.

> Tyler,
>
> I couldn't give you this in person. I didn't have the courage. So I'm leaving it here for you. I realize that the wedding has been called off. Thanks for being my friend, though.
>
> Cecilia

"Dad, I'm not sure if the wedding needs to be canceled. I still love her very much. Maybe we could get married now that we're both Christians and we're serving the Lord." He ran his hand through his hair. "I'm not sure, though, that it's God's will. In the note it sounds like she wishes we could get married, but I could be imagining things. I'm not sure what to do. Will you pray with me, Dad, please?"

"Yes, Tyler. Come, let's pray now." Together they knelt and prayed.

After a while Josh stood up. Tyler, still kneeling, looked at him.

"Ty," his father began, "even though I can pray for you, I can't make the decision for you. I suggest you read the Bible and pray. God will show you, but you have to listen to Him. He might not tell you what you would like to hear. Listen anyway. I'm going to lie down, but I'll keep praying. If you have any questions wake me up. Okay?"

"Okay. Thanks, Dad."

"You're welcome."

Ty stayed awake long into the night. He read his Bible, prayed, read, and prayed again. On and on it went. "God, please help me. I want to make the right decision," he prayed.

As he was turning the pages of his Bible, his eyes fell upon Proverbs thirty-one, the chapter that taught of a virtuous woman.

"Wow, C is already developing these traits. God has His stamp of approval on her." He closed his Bible and began to pray again, "Dear Jesus, I love C with all my heart. Tomorrow I'm going to ask her father, and if he says yes, then I'm going to ask her. If he says no, I won't go against him. I believe You want me to marry C and if the Dunninghams stand in my way, I know that in Your time, You'll change their minds. Amen."

The next day they searched out the Dunning-hams and soon found both of them. Tyler was extremely nervous. His father noticed and placed his hand on his shoulder. "Just follow the leadership of the Holy Ghost, and whatever you do, don't lose your temper." He punctuated his warning with a teasing poke in his son's ribs. Ty chuckled.

"Yes sir," he answered. They approached the Dunninghams. "Mr. Dunningham, may I speak with you for a moment, please?" he asked.

"Make it quick. We have work to do."

"Sir, first I would like to thank you for what you did that night I was shot. If you had not left me in that town, I would have never met the Birds. It was Mrs. Bird who helped me to see that I needed to be saved, and it was Callen Bird who helped me get back with my family. Salvation, sir, is a wonderful thing. All your sins washed away, a home in Heaven waiting for you, and the Holy Spirit living in you. I wanted to ask you, what made you turn that wonderful gift down?"

Mr. Dunningham's face reddened and his hands clenched. "What right do you have to tell me what I need to do? How dare you tell me what's right and what's wrong? You have no right! Now leave us alone."

"I have one more question, Captain." He tentatively cleared his throat. "I talked with Cecilia, and she does not want to marry Jack. She said she would not marry him. Would you permit me to ask for her hand in marriage?"

"She's too good for you."

"I know, sir. If I don't have your permission, I won't ask her. I apologize for not asking you first when I proposed to her some months ago. I *am* sorry. Please forgive me."

Mr. Dunningham was obviously confused at Tyler's honesty. He finally shrugged. "Yes, you can ask her. She's moved out of our house, so she can make her own decisions. If she wants to marry *you*, then fine. I could care less." The two Dunninghams abruptly turned around and walked away.

Ty was dumbfounded and saddened as well. Dunningham had said yes, but he had also said he could care less about his daughter's future. "Thank you both!" Tyler called after them, but they paid him no heed. *How sad*, he thought to himself.

"He could care less," Joshua echoed. "My, what an awful thing to say about your daughter."

"I agree."

"Well," his father said, suddenly grinning at him, "well done, Tyler. Now, why don't you go and ask the girl?" he suggested. Ty nodded and they headed for the Brownlys' house.

"Nervous?" Josh asked.

"You bet."

His father smiled. "Sam was the same way. Jumpy as a skittish colt he was, but the Lord helped him, and he lived through it."

Tyler smiled back. "Thanks, Dad. I've already done the hard part, and the Lord got me through it," he said, knocking on the door. Pastor Brownly opened it. The Goodtons could hear the laughing voices of three or four of the ex-gamblers coming from the living room.

"Mr. Goodton, Ty, come in."

"Thank you, sir," Josh said.

"What can I do for you two?"

"I'd like to speak with Miss Cecilia please," Tyler said.

"She's outside in the garden."

"Thank you, sir." As his father and Mr. Brownly went to join the other men, Tyler started toward the garden. Ty kind of wished he could have brought his dad with him, but he knew that it had to be this way.

*Lord,* he prayed, *thank You that Mr. Dunningham said yes. Please help me to know what to say to Cecilia.* He pushed open the back door and turned the corner to where Cecilia was working. She was singing and, since her back was to him, she did not see him. He stopped and listened. When she finished her song, Tyler squared his shoulders and made his presence known.

"Ty," she called out. He was delighted to note the pleasure in her voice. She sat up and wiped the dirt off her hands and skirt. "I love working in this garden. I've always wanted to have one. Mrs. Brownly is so nice to let me help take care of hers, and guess what," her eyes sparkled, "they have horses!"

He chuckled as he remembered her telling him about pretending her bed was a horse. He also remembered the real reason he was there. Taking a deep breath, he began to talk. "C, I, I just got done talking with your father, and," he said, taking another deep breath, "he gave me his permission to ask you to, to…" He knelt down beside her. "C, I know that you thought the wedding was off, but I never stopped loving you. In fact, now that I'm saved and I know what love really is, I love you even more. I'd be honored if once again you would accept this." He handed her the ring.

"Oh, Ty, I don't know what to say. I, I…"

"Would you like some time to pray about it?" he asked.

"Yes, I would, Tag."

He smiled and stood up. "Take your time, Cecilia." He walked back into the house. The young girl watched him, and then began to pray.

Before dinner, she asked Mrs. Brownly if they could talk while they made supper.

"Sure, Cecilia," she said. "What is it?" Cecilia poured her heart out to her and Mrs. Brownly listened intently. Together they talked and prayed. The food was in the oven when Cecilia made her decision.

The Goodtons and the former members of *The Jewel* had been invited to dinner again that night. Ty was tense and a little scared. He half expected her to say no, but she did not bring up the issue. Disappointed, Tyler and his dad went back to their hotel room. As Ty hung up his coat, he found a note pinned inside his collar. He had not noticed it before because the night had been warm and he had not worn his coat.

The note read, "Look in your pocket."

Raising his eyebrows, he reached into the pocket and found another a note. It said, "I will. Love, Cecilia."

"Yahoo!" he shouted at the top of his lungs.

"Shhh," Joshua commanded, not seeing the note. "You'll wake up everybody here." Then he noticed the glow on his son's face. "What are you so lit up about?"

Tyler handed his dad the short yet important note. "Aha! This makes me want to shout," Josh said. He hugged his son tightly.

"Oh, Dad," Ty whispered, tears streaming down his cheeks. "The Lord is good. I'm going to marry Cecilia."

Josh smiled, wiping away his own tears. "Thank You, Lord," he whispered. "Thank You."

*Chapter 13*

# A NEW FAMILY

---

Tyler and Cecilia were going over wedding plans in the Brownlys' living room when Mrs. Dunningham walked in. The color was gone from her face and she looked disturbed.

"Mother, what's wrong?" Cecilia asked, rushing to her side.

"C, may I speak to you, alone?" she asked.

Tyler knew that was his cue to leave. "Um, if you ladies will excuse me, I'll go get a glass of water." Tyler stood, nodded to both of them, and quickly left the room.

"What is it, Mother? Is there something wrong?"

Her mother opened her mouth but said nothing. Instead she turned and paced the room, stopping when she reached the big window at the far left side. Then she spoke. Her voice, normally cold and sharp, was unsteady. "I just saw something that I thought would never happen. I was at the café when Duke walked in. Duce invited him to sit with him. Those two used to hate each other, but today they prayed together and laughed and joked through the whole meal. I remember when those two couldn't say one civil word to each other, not one! They used to argue about absolutely everything. Today the only time they argued was when they both wanted to pay the bill, but it wasn't a mean quarrel. They acted like brothers and best friends. Did their getting 'born again' have something to do with that? Can accepting Jesus as your Saviour calm such bitter feelings inside you? Can the Lord help *me* like He helped the Blakers?"

Cecilia smiled gently. "Yes, Mother, He can. In II Corinthians, Paul said, 'Therefore if any man be in Christ, he is a new creature: old things are passed away; behold, all things are become new.'"

"I would like to become new. Can you tell me how?" her mother asked.

Cecilia picked up the Bible that was lying on an end table and turned to Luke 19:10, "For the Son of man is come to seek and to save that which was lost."

"Mother, Jesus left His throne in Heaven and came to earth so that He could pay for your sins. The God of the universe made Himself of no reputation and died on the cross for you. Christ said, I think it's in Matthew, 'Come unto me, all ye that labour and are heavy laden, and I will give you rest.' He wants to be your Saviour and free you from the burden of sin. When the angel spake of His coming, he said, 'And she shall bring forth a son, and thou shalt call his name JESUS: for he shall save his people from their sins.'"

"What must I do to be saved?" her mother asked.

"These are the questions that I had," Cecilia said. "Mrs. Brownly showed me that, in the book of Acts, someone asked the apostle Paul the same question. This is what Paul and Silas said. 'And they said, Believe on the Lord Jesus Christ, and thou shalt be saved, and thy house.'"

"That's all?" her mother asked. The girl nodded. Mrs. Dunningham knelt down by the window and began to pray. "Lord, I would like to accept this wonderful gift called salvation. I believe on the Lord Jesus Christ. Please Lord, save me from my sin and help me to be a changed person. Thank You. Amen."

"Mother, I'm so glad," Cecilia said, hugging her mother. "Now that you are saved, you are saved for eternity. I John 5:13 says, 'These things have I written unto you that believe on the name of the Son of God; that ye may know that ye have eternal life, and that ye may believe on the name of the Son of God.'"

"Cecilia," her mother began, "can you ever forgive me for all the wrong things I've done? I am so sorry. Please, forgive me, darling."

"It's forgiven, Mother."

Needless to say, there was much rejoicing after the news spread. The friends' hearts still ached for Mr. Dunningham and Jack, but the burden had been eased.

It had been four days since Tyler and his father had arrived at New Orleans. Now that C and Ty were engaged, there was some deliberation as to where to have the wedding. Should they have it in New Orleans or should they go back to Indiana? They decided to wait here for a few more days.

On the eve of the fourth night, Pastor Brownly's favorite mule, Bill, cut his foreleg going into his stall.

"The cut's not bad," the pastor said, after inspecting Bill's leg. "Mrs. Brownly, would you get me the liniment?"

"We don't have any left, Preacher," she told him.

"I'll get you some, Preacher Brownly," Ty volunteered. He was given directions and soon set off, whistling cheerfully. However, the more he walked, the less cheerful he felt.

*My it's dark,* he thought to himself. *Quiet too. Very quiet.* The stillness made him a little jumpy. The night held the assumption of impending danger. Tyler tried to shrug off the feeling, but to no avail. "You could almost imagine something getting ready to explode in your face," he whispered, though there was no other person in sight. Then it happened! The alley he was walking by *did* explode with life. Tyler could barely discern the four men who appeared to be fighting. The moon came from behind the clouds and he saw three men trying to rob Jack! For an instant, Ty froze, unsure as to whether he should run for help or stay and fight with Jack. Then he saw Jack get hit hard and slump to the ground. That was answer enough. Jack needed help, now! Tyler let out a war whoop that sounded part Indian and part wolf and charged. The element of surprise on his side, the thieves turned away from Jack as Tyler barreled into them. Jack, recovering at the sound of reinforcements, began to fight back.

Tyler had never really fought before. He was neither big nor very strong, but he *was* quick. He darted under their crushing punches and slithered through their clutching arms, all the while delivering fast punches to his adversaries. Still, it was the Lord Who was taking care of him. Even as he fought, Tyler prayed. Just when it seemed that Tyler would also succumb to their thievery, a voice shouted, "Break it up!" A gun barked as if to punctuate the command. The five men, bruised and bleeding, obeyed.

"That's better. Now what's going on?" the deputy asked. Jack, breathing hard, staggered to his feet and told the deputy about the three men jumping him.

"I was about done in when this fellow came to my rescue. Thank you…" Jack realized that Tyler had been the one helping him and his mouth dropped open. He tried to talk, but nothing would come out.

"I know these three rats," the deputy said, not noticing the trouble Jack was having. "They've been known to try this sort of thing before. I'll lock them up and tomorrow you can come to my office and sign the complaint. When Marshall Long gets back, he'll be glad to know we caught these men." He pulled handcuffs out of his pocket and secured the three outlaws. "Are you two going to be okay?" he asked Jack and Tyler.

The two men said that they were fine. "Well, I'd see a doctor before too long," the deputy admonished. "Come on you three troublemakers."

The young men watched the deputy herd the thieves toward the jail. When they were out of sight, Jack turned to face Ty. "Why?"

"Why what?" Tyler asked, puzzled.

"Did you know it was *me* they were beating up?" he asked.

"Yes."

"Then why did you help me?"

"You needed help and I was there. I just did what anyone would have done."

Jack shook his head. "Not me. If that had been you in trouble, I would have walked right on by and not given it a second thought. What made you risk yourself for me?"

*Please help me to say the right things, Lord,* Tyler prayed. Out loud he said, "I don't hate you, Jack. I'm ashamed to say that I did at one time, but that was before I was saved. After I accepted Jesus Christ as my Saviour, I learned to forgive. Hating someone doesn't hurt the one you're angry at; it hurts the person hating. God showed me that and gave me the grace to forgive. He also showed me how He suffered terribly for me, that He went to the cross and died a horrible death for me, and that He arose from the dead for me. After He did all that for me, I rejected Him and made myself His enemy, but He kept on loving me. He watched over me even when I ran from Him. Then He brought me to the place where I would listen to His Word. When I asked Him to save me, He did. How could I keep on hating when God was willing to forgive a wicked sinner like me?"

"So, you really do change after getting saved. I always thought that Christians were just a group of people who were trying to make themselves out to be better than everybody else. You're not like that. You, C, and all the others are not proud or hateful toward those that wrong you. I had you pegged wrong, Tag. There's something real about your Christianity." He hung his head and groped for words. "Would God save *me*?"

"Yes, He will. The Bible says that the Lord is 'not willing that *any* should perish, but that *all* should come to repentance.'"

"What do I have to do?" Jack asked.

Quoting verses from memory, Tyler went through the plan of salvation.

"Romans 3:23, 'For all have sinned, and come short of the glory of God;' Do you know that you are a sinner?" Ty asked. "Sin is the transgression, or breaking, of the law. This verse says everyone is a sinner. That means you, me, everyone."

"I know I'm a sinner," Jack admitted.

"Romans 6:23 says, 'For the wages of sin is death; but the gift of God is eternal life through Jesus Christ our Lord.' Everyone who sins must die," Tyler explained. "If you die without Christ you go to hell, a place filled with fire. It is eternal, forever."

"I don't want to go there," the gambler said, his face turning pale.

"No one does. That's why the last part of this verse is so wonderful. '… but the gift of God is eternal life through Jesus Christ our Lord.' The gift of God is salvation and Romans 10:13 says, 'For whosoever shall call upon the name of the Lord shall be saved.'"

"That's all I have to do?" Jack was amazed. "Such a wonderful gift, and all I have to do is ask. I'm not worthy of that."

"There is no one worthy of it, Jack, but God wants us to have it."

"Can I ask Him here and now?"

"Yes. The Bible says '… behold, now is the accepted time; behold, now is the day of salvation.'"

"What do I say?"

"It really does not matter what you say. What's in your heart is what counts. You have to believe with all your heart."

"How do I know if I believe with all my heart?"

"Let me tell you about a man in the Bible who believed with all his heart. A preacher named Philip was showing a man from Ethiopia the plan of salvation. They came to some water and the Ethiopian asked if he could be baptized. Philip said, 'If thou believest with all thine heart, thou mayest.' The Ethiopian said, 'I believe that Jesus Christ is the Son of God.' Philip stopped the chariot, they 'went down' into the water, and Philip baptized him.

"Baptism didn't save that man, and it won't save you. It simply shows others that you are now a Christian. The Ethiopian was born again when he believed on Jesus. Do you believe that Jesus Christ is the Son of God?"

"I do."

"Then tell Jesus what is in your heart."

Jack looked toward Heaven and began to pray. "Jesus, I've never prayed before in my life, so I'm a little shaky. I would like this gift of salvation. I know that trusting in You is the only way to be saved. I believe that You are the Son of God. I believe that there is no other way to be saved. You are the only One Who can do it. Please save me. Thank You, Lord."

Again there was rejoicing at the Brownlys' house. Jack, whose real name was Nick Whitland, was now a member of their Spiritual family. Everyone was elated.

During the middle of their rejoicing there was a loud knock at the door. Cecilia opened it and caught her breath. Mr. Dunningham was standing there.

"I was walking past the house and saw Jack through the window." He glared at the new Christian. "Don't tell me *you* got religion."

"No, I didn't get religion. I got saved, Captain," he replied. "We were wrong, sir. It's not a fake or a show. It's real. There is no need to fear it. God wants people to be saved. I found out that He loves me. He loves you, too."

"Don't you dare preach to me! I've heard it all before!" He slammed the door and left.

His daughter grabbed a shawl and ran after him. "Father! Father, please wait!" she cried. He stopped and waited for her. It was beginning to rain and was getting colder.

"What is it?"

"Father, please, listen to me. Mother told me that you used to go to church. What made you stop?"

"I, I started gambling and I got rich. I thought I didn't need God. I didn't think I was that bad, but now I don't know. Everything has hit bottom in my life."

"Jesus can help you, Father. He wants to help."

"I've rejected Him, Cecilia. He doesn't want anything to do with me." He turned to walk away, but she held on to his arm.

"Oh, Father, that's not true. Do you remember the rich young ruler in the Bible? He rejected Jesus, but Jesus still loved him. He still wanted the young man to get saved."

"I've lived so wickedly, though. I've cheated people and stole money; I ruined the happiness of my daughter. I'm so wicked."

"Father, that's just the kind of people that need to be saved. The Bible said in Luke that, '...the Son of man is come to seek and to save that which was lost.' Salvation is for those that sin. When the scribes and Pharisees murmured against Jesus' disciples because they ate with publicans and sinners, Jesus said, '...They that are whole need not a physician; but they that are sick.' In Matthew it was told that He was coming to, '...save his people from their sins.'"

"You mean God will save me even though I've done so many wicked things?" Mr. Dunningham asked.

"Yes, He will."

There in the rain, Mr. Dunningham fell to his knees and began to pray. "Oh Lord, have mercy on me. All my life I've lived contrary to Your will, and I don't want to do that any more. Lord, there's not much left of me. I've nothing to offer You except a broken heart and life, but, Lord, for some reason You love me. Please save me, Lord Jesus. Thank You. Amen."

"Oh Daddy, Daddy, I'm so happy," she cried, throwing her arms around him. For the first time in many years, he hugged her.

"You haven't called me daddy in a long time. I love you, Cecilia, and I'm sorry for all that I've done to you."

"I forgave you already, Daddy. Come on, let's go tell the others."

"Oh my, Cecilia, you'll catch your death out here in this cold rain." He wrapped his heavy coat around her, and together they went back to the Brownlys' house.

All *The Jewel's* crew who were still in New Orleans pooled their money so that they could go to Indiana for the wedding. Sam was Tyler's best man and C asked her mother to be her maid of honor. It was a grand wedding.

"You know what's so special about this marriage?" Clara asked after the ceremony was over.

"What?" Archibald asked. The two of them were relaxing on the elder Goodtons' porch.

"It's the fact that we are a new family in three different ways. One, we're all born again, so we're new creatures in Christ. Two, because we're saved, our family is closer. Three, we have a new member of our family."

"Yes," her husband agreed. "I couldn't be more pleased with the man who has married our daughter."

# Chapter 14

# DOUBLE BLESSING

L ife was beginning to settle down around the Goodtons' farms. Ty and Cecilia had a place of their own not far from Josh and Mary's house, and they were happy there. The Dunninghams had gone east, and *The Jewel's* crew had found work in various places of the country.

"Hey, Tyler!" Sam called as he rode into his brother's yard. "Guess what? There's going to be an auction a week after Saturday. Everyone else is going, and we're planning a picnic. Want to come?"

"Sure. Maybe I could find a horse for Cecilia," Ty said.

"I thought she has a horse," Sam commented, sliding off Dusty and heading for the well. "Can I have a drink?"

"Help yourself. I'll get a bucketful for Dusty." Tyler picked up a pail, filled it with water, and brought it to Dusty. His brother's little horse drank deeply. "C doesn't have a good horse all to herself," Tyler told his brother, returning to their first conversation. "I'd like to get her a real nice horse and I've been trying to find a special one just for her. You know how much she likes horses."

"Yeah, I know. It sounds like this auction is going to be big. You ought to find a good one there. Well, I got to get back to work. See you, Ty. Thanks for the water." He finished the water in the dipper then mounted.

"You're welcome." As Tyler watched his brother ride off, he began to pray. "Lord, thanks for my family. Please help me to find a good horse for Cecilia."

The day of the auction arrived and the crowd was in a festive mood. The Goodtons, Sampsons, Greys, and Makers found a nice spot for their picnic. After spreading several blankets to accommodate their large group, the three younger couples went to look at the horses.

"Look at that one," C cooed, pointing to a pretty sorrel mare. Cecilia was the only one in the family who did not know Tyler intended to buy her a horse today.

"She *is* pretty," Esther agreed.

"You've got a good eye for horses, Cecilia," Sam praised.

"Not a bad looking horse, but I kind of like that one over there." Tyler drew their attention to a beautiful, four-year-old black-and-white mare.

"Oh, she's simply gorgeous, Tyler," Cecilia said. "Look at those markings." The mare had black markings about her back, neck, and sides, and black mingled with her white mane and tail. She looked at the approaching group and, when they reached the corral, she loped up to them. As C pet the gentle horse, Tyler nodded at Sam. This was the horse for Cecilia.

Sam was thinking about the pinto mare when out of the corner of his eye he saw a black horse. He turned to look and thought he must have been dreaming. The horse was alone in a small corral, a rope attached to his halter. The man holding the rope was lunging him, an exercise where the handler stands the rope's length away from the horse and directs the animal in a circle, often changing the gait and direction. Some horses were so well trained that the handler used only voice commands and a whip to guide the horse.

"Tom, look at the way that horse moves. He's so smooth."

"Wow. Come on, let's ask about him," Tom said.

The trainer explained that he was a Tennessee Walking horse. "The horses are bred and trained to have a smooth gait and to walk with their forelegs extended," he told them.

"Thank you," Sam said to the trainer. As he and Tom walked away, Sam prayed silently, *Lord, one day I'd like to raise those, if it be Thy will.*

A large brass bell rang, its noise sounding out across the auction grounds. "Ladies and gentlemen," a voice boomed, "the auction is about to start. Please gather around the stage."

"Now, what am I bid for this fine sorrel gelding? He's five years old. Do I hear fifty dollars?" The auctioneer rattled off numbers and bids, and the price rose. After that horse sold, they led out another one, then another, and on and on it went. The last horse was the pinto mare. Sam inconspicuously mingled into the crowd. Tyler had asked him to do the bidding because he wanted to surprise Cecilia. Sam knew how much Tyler wanted to spend.

The bidding started. It seemed like everyone in the crowd wanted her, and soon Ty's limit was reached. Praying, he held his breath. Would he be outbid?

"Two hundred once…two hundred twice…Sold! To the gentlemen with the tan vest for two hundred dollars." The auctioneer pounded a gavel on the podium, and Ty let out his breath. Sam was the only person he had seen wearing a tan vest. The younger brother's eyes scanned the crowd. When he saw Sam, he raised his eyebrows in question. Sam nodded and grinned.

"Thank You, Lord," Tyler whispered.

Cattle were selling now. The three young men had decided to buy thirty head of Hereford cattle. When the thirty they had picked came up for bidding, they bought them.

Soon the auction was over and the people began to leave.

Sam, Tom, Tyler, Joshua, Joel, Mr. Maker and Mr. Grey had to herd the cattle to the pasture that the boys had fenced off for them. All the ladies went to the Makers' house to wait until they were done.

"What did you do with the horse, Tyler?" Joshua asked as they drove the cattle.

"Terry Carson had to deliver a message out our way, so he took the mare with him. He'll leave her in the barn at our place."

"I wish I could see the look on Cecilia's face when she sees her," Sam said. Just then, two yearling bulls broke from the herd and ran for the woods. Dusty and Midnight went after them. Josh and Joel watched as their sons herded the runaways back. It took them a while, for they were not experienced at working with cattle, but it was obvious that the two boys enjoyed it.

"Josh, I think that both our boys might turn out to be cowboys yet," Joel said.

"I think you're right, Joel."

That evening Tyler was bursting with joy. After the cattle were secured, he picked up his wife and headed home.

"Weren't those horses simply beautiful? That pinto mare was the best, I think." Cecilia chattered the whole way home, but Tyler was too excited to talk.

"Ty, is something wrong?" she finally asked.

"Oh no, C, I was just, um, just thinking. Now, um, what were you saying?"

When they finally got home, Ty reined in by the porch and helped his wife down. "I'm glad you had a good time, Cecilia," he said. "I'm going to put the horses away."

"Alright, I'll go make us some coffee."

The minute she disappeared into the house, he hurried into the barn, and put the team away. Tyler took a length of rope, made a halter, and slipped it on the pinto. After leading her out of the stall, he spent several minutes brushing her smooth coat and combing her mane. "There you are, Patches. You look great."

He peeked out from behind the barn door. Cecilia was still inside, so Tyler stepped into the yard.

"Cecilia, would you please bring the coffee out here?" he called.

"Sure, Ty, I'm coming." The door opened and she walked out onto the porch with a tray. "What a wonderful idea to drink it out here. It's such a lovely evening. Shall we sit on the porch and..." She stopped in mid-sentence. "Why that's, that's, it couldn't be, but it is. No, it can't be, but..." She was tongue-tied.

"She's for you, Cecilia," Tyler told her.

"Oh, Tag!" She ran toward him, still carrying the tray. Tyler took it from her so she could pet the horse. "Tag, thank you, thank you so much!" As she stroked her horse, she spoke softly to her. "You are such a beautiful girl. What am I going to call you?"

"Why not Patches?" Tyler asked, trying to balance the tray and maintain his hold on the lead rope. "It sure fits her."

"That's perfect! I'll call you Patches. Do you like that, Patches? Alright, then, that's what we'll do." Cecilia turned to face her husband. "Thank you, Tyler," she said, trying to hug him, the tray, lead rope, and all. Tyler set the tray down and returned her hug.

"You are welcome."

For a girl who had grown up on a riverboat, Cecilia had learned to ride quickly. She and Patches got along splendidly. The next day Cecilia rode her horse over to show the family.

"Look at her run," Carol said.

"Cecilia looks great on her," Esther added in admiration.

Esther's due date was approaching quickly. August came, and they were looking forward to a bountiful harvest. During the middle of the month, Esther went into labor. Both Sam's and Esther's parents were over eating supper. Esther stood up from the table and nearly passed out. Lisa and Mary helped her into the bedroom. Sam paced through most of the delivery and prayed through all of it.

When Mary came out of the bedroom, her face was beaming. "Sam, she had a…"

"Mary!" Lisa called, her voice filled with anxiety. Mary rushed back into the bedroom.

The three men looked at each other. What had happened? Were Esther or the baby hurt in some way? Mr. Maker led them in prayer. Twenty minutes later, Mary came out again.

"Mom, what's going on? Are they all right?" Sam asked.

"Yes, son, all three of them," she answered with a smile.

"Good," Sam said. Then his body went rigid. "Wait a minute! What do you mean by 'all three'?"

Mary laughed and hugged him excitedly. "Twins! She had twins, Sam!"

Sam began to sway and his father grabbed his shoulders to steady him.

"Congratulations, Sammy!" Mr. Maker boomed as he shook Sam's limp hand.

"Thanks," Sam said a little weakly. He stood up straight. "Can I see them?"

Mary nodded. Sam ducked through the door and stepped toward his wife. Lisa was tucking a blanket around her daughter. She smiled at her son-in-law and left the room.

Esther, a baby in each arm, looked up at her husband. "Sam, twins, twin boys. This one," she said, moving her right arm, "is Michael Thomas, and the other one is MacShane Tyler. Mike came first."

"How can you tell them apart?" Sam asked, still dazed.

"Easy. They're not identical. Mike looks more like your side of the family. His hair is brown and his eyes are a much lighter blue. Mac's hair is blonde like my mother's, and his eyes are deep blue. Also, Mac is heavier. Here, hold them and you can tell."

Sam was not sure if he could hold both of them at the same time, but Esther said he could. He sat down on a chair and let her place them in his arms.

"It isn't as hard as I thought it would be," he told her. "Now I can see the difference, and feel it, too. Isn't this something? What a double blessing. I never dreamed of us having twins."

When she said nothing, he looked at her. "Wait a second. Why did you want us to pick *two* names that night? Did you know?"

She laughed. "Of course not, but I had been praying for twins. So, you might say that it was an act of faith. Aren't they wonderful?"

"They sure are, Esther. I'm so blessed. I have a beautiful wife and now three fine sons."

"Three down and seven to go," she said. In response to his questioning look, she said, "We wanted to have ten children, five boys and five girls. We're getting closer to our goal."

# Chapter 15

# THE BIG RACE

E sther, I've been thinking and praying about something." It was the first of February, and Sam and Esther were sitting together by the fire.

"About what, Sammy?" she asked, leaning against his arm.

"Well, ever since I can remember, I've had a dream, a dream to have a ranch out West. Yesterday I read in the paper about the territory of Montana. Many people are going there. The wagon masters and the guides all say that it's a wonderful land. I think that God wants us to move there someday. I'm just not sure when."

Esther knew her husband well and deep down inside she had known that this moment would come.

A tear formed in her eye at the thought of leaving her mother and father, but she smiled bravely at Sam.

"If that's God's will, I'll be happy," Esther said.

He quickly turned sideways so he could face her. "Will you help pray with me, Esther?" he asked, grasping her hands. "I want to make sure that I'm making the right decision. I want it to be God's will and not just my dream."

"Of course I will." For two months they prayed. On a quiet April evening they discussed the issue once again.

"Sam, you know that I'll go whenever and wherever you believe God wants us to go. I have faith in your walk with God," Esther told him.

"I know that. At first I argued with God. I told Him that I couldn't take you away from your parents and all that you're familiar with, but in the end God won. The West needs families that serve Him. God needs regular people who will stand for the right even in a lawless area." He paused. "I still don't know exactly when we'll be leaving though. The Lord will tell me in good time."

"Well," Esther said, her eyes suddenly beginning to sparkle, "before you decide when, you might want to take into account that when we make the trip there will be six of us instead of five."

"Six? You mean…?"

"Yes, Sam, I'm going to have another baby."

"Oh my, I may have to build us a bigger house!" He kissed his wife. "Another baby. Why don't we pick out a name right now?" Sam prayed and asked for God's wisdom.

"We already have two wonderful girl names, but no girls," Esther said with a chuckle. "Mary Lisa and Martha Joy, but we had better pick out a boy name."

"Let's see here," Sam said, scratching his chin.

"Sam, if it's a boy, why don't we call him Montana? That way we'll always remember the night we decided to set out on this wonderful western adventure."

"Montana? Yes, I like it," Sam agreed. "What about a middle name? I know! How about Laramie, after your father?"

"Montana Laramie is perfect," Esther said. "Sam, when are we going to tell the folks that we will be leaving?" she asked with a catch in her voice.

"I guess when we find out when we're going. I'm sure it won't be before the baby is born. So, we've got a little while anyway." He wrapped his arms around her and kissed the top of her head. "It will be hard, I know, but the Lord will help us."

"I know," she said, peace filling her heart at that promise.

Some time later the Goodtons and Sampsons were in town on business when they were attracted to a flock of people gathered around a short man standing on a platform. Decked in red, white, and blue, he spoke in a strident voice that rang throughout the town.

"Come one, come all, to the horse race coming Saturday next! Everyone is welcomed to try for the thousand-dollar prize! The race will commence at three in the afternoon, and it doesn't cost anything to enter! Sign up folks! Step right up and put your signature in this here book!"

Three or four men were quick to sign up. Others crowded around the man who made the announcement to ask him some questions. The Fourth of July was coming up. Along with the yearly festival, this race was being held.

"What do you say, big brother? Are you going to enter it?" Ty asked.

"I don't know. Dusty is still fast and strong, but he's also eighteen years old. I don't know how he'd do with all those younger horses. What do you think, Tom?"

Tom shrugged. "It would be fun. I've always wanted to run Midnight in a real race. We don't have to sign up until Thursday. We could think about it."

"Good idea. Come on, we've got work to do at the farm." Sam picked up little Matthew, who was standing beside him, swung him onto his shoulders, and headed back to the wagon.

"A thousand dollars would really help us as we prepare to head west," Sam told Esther that evening as she was putting supper on the table.

"You do what you think, Sam. I've seen Dusty run and I know he's fast. I think that you would have a good chance. Matthew, please move over," she asked gently. "I can't get my work done with you standing there." She laid down the roast chicken and picked up her oldest son. He was a handsome boy, almost two years old, with dark hair like his mother, but he was built like his father. Matt was smart and his green eyes seldom missed anything. Already he was saying short sentences. Esther cuddled him for a minute then she set him down.

"Me help?" he asked.

His mother racked her brain to think of something that he could do. "Yes, get Mommy a towel to lay a hot plate on."

He quickly got the towel, laid it on the table, and then raced over to where the twins were playing. Duke, looking twice as big as normal standing beside the boys, nuzzled his hand. Matt flung his arms around the dog, and Duke wagged his huge tail.

Sam smiled at his three boys. He and Esther loved them very much and were thrilled that another child was on the way.

Sam and Tom prayed and talked about the race the next day as they worked. They decided to sign up. Every day they took their horses out for a good run to help them get in shape. Midnight and Dusty enjoyed the exercise. The two horses, used to being together, had been separated for a while. They were glad to be back together again.

"Hey, these old guys can still move," Tom said, his face aglow. He ruffled Midnight's mane. "I'd forgotten how wonderful it felt to ride him."

"I know, Tommy," Sam said, letting Dusty pick his own gait. "I've got those two three-year-old colts that aren't totally broke yet. I've been working with them a lot lately and I haven't had time to ride Dusty." The brown horse tossed his head and pranced about proudly. "Yeah, you're a good old guy, aren't you? Come on, let's see if we can beat this black monster to the trees."

"Oh no you don't!" Tom shouted gleefully. "After him, Midnight!"

Though the two horses were best of friends, each tried for dominance. Powerful muscles rippled under their satiny coats as they raced across the open field. A tangle of fallen trees and limbs lay directly in front of the racers. Dusty swerved and avoided it. Tom was going to do the same, but Midnight resisted his pull on the reins.

"All right, jump it if you want, you crazy horse," Tom whispered. The big black stallion flew over it easily. In a few bounds he was at Dusty's side again. The two reached the trees together.

"Sammy, I think you and I are going to have to split that prize money if we win. Never yet has one horse beaten the other," Tom said.

"That suits me fine. Well, see you tomorrow, Tom. Come on, Dusty, let's go home."

The day of the race came and spirits were high. The sidewalks were filled with onlookers, each cheering on one of the fifteen contestants. The Goodtons, Makers, Greys, and Sampsons were all there, giving their support to Tom, Sam, and Tyler. Ty had decided to try the race as well with his new appaloosa, Fireworks.

"Gentlemen, you all know the rules and the path you are to take," the Mayor began. "The race starts here and will go out of town to the Lace farm. There you will circle the pole and come back. The first one to cross this line," he stopped and pointed to the finish line drawn in the dirt, "is the winner. There will also be a second and third place winner. Good luck!" The crowd cheered loudly.

The contestants gathered at the starting line. Sam found himself next to Tim Lard, who was astride a sturdy looking mustang named Stormy. "Good luck, Tim," Sam said.

"Same to you and your little whirlwind," Tim said, speaking of Dusty. People often jeered at Sam's small horse, but they always had to take back their taunts when they saw him run.

"Gentlemen, are you ready? On your mark, get set, GO!" The starting gun sounded and they were off. They flew through the main street then headed down the road toward the farmhouse.

"This is the part that I don't like," Mary said after the racers had left town. "We can't see them," she explained with a chuckle. All the others nodded in agreement, except Esther. She looked peaked, and both Lisa and Mary noticed.

"Esther dear, are you all right?" her mother asked, slipping her arm around her daughter.

"What, oh yes, Mother. I think I'm just tired," Esther answered. Lisa glanced at Mary. Both were wondering if Esther was right or if something more serious was wrong.

About a mile down the road, the race was starting to get interesting. Sam and Tom, though on different sides of the road, were running neck-and-neck. Bart Simms had held the lead so far on a speedy roan Quarter Horse. Hans Blaker, in second, was mounted on a red Morgan. Three other riders were in front of Sam and Tom, and four were between them. The two young men were waiting for the roan to tire. He had been running full out, and they knew he could not keep that pace the whole time.

Sam and Tom were saving their strength until they needed it the most.

They reached the farm and rounded the pole. Tim Lard was advancing on the Morgan. His horse, though not exceptionally fast, had stamina and could run far before tiring. Tim made it into second place.

After another mile, Sam gave Dusty more head, but the horse was still not running all out yet. They had another mile to go, and Sam was patient.

They had not gone far when they encountered a near disaster. A rabbit ran across the road right in front of four horses! Squealing in fear, the horses plunged, reared, and kicked. Tom, trying to get his horse out of the way, failed to see a hole by the road. Midnight fell, throwing his rider to the ground. Sam reined in to help his friend.

"Go on, Sam! We're fine!" Tom yelled above the noise of the pounding hooves. Both he and Midnight were back on their feet.

Sam paused, nodded, and urged Dusty into a fast gallop. Tom made sure his horse was not hurt; then he mounted. He intended to take it easy on the way back, but Midnight had other plans. Before Tom had settled in the saddle, the horse took off.

"Hey, what are you doing?" Tom cried. He tried to rein the horse in, but Midnight pulled at the bit.

He wanted to race. "Well, if you want to," Tom said. "Come on, catch Dusty." Midnight fairly flew after the racing horses. Leaning low on the saddle, Tom was amazed to see how fast they were gaining on the pack.

Meanwhile, Sam and Dusty were challenging the leader. The roan had fallen back and a stranger on a paint had taken the lead. They topped a hill and could see the town. It was time to let Dusty completely have his head. Sam touched Dusty's shoulder with his left hand. Dusty knew that meant he would soon be free to run as fast as he could.

"Get ready, Dusty," Sam whispered. "Now!" He emphasized the command with a light tap from his spurs. Dusty was racing with everything he had. The paint put on a new burst of speed, but he could not match Dusty's pace.

"That's it!" Sam praised as Dusty pulled into first place, but at that moment Sam heard another horse coming up on his right. At first he was apprehensive, but he heard Dusty whinny. Sam smiled. Even without looking, he knew that Tom was by his side. "Fine. Come on, Dusty, let's give them a workout!"

"Ha, ha, caught you!" Tom shouted. "Keep with him, Midnight!"

They were entering town now. The two horses ran as if they were tied together. They were almost to the finish line and the crowd was cheering wildly. Then, as if they had planned it, both Sam and Tom reached over and shook hands. They crossed the finish line, as best friends should, together.

*Chapter 16*

# THE LITTLE
# EARLY BIRD

The onlookers began to cheer even louder. Never before had they seen such a race.

C and the Goodtons clapped for joy as Ty finished second, and the Lards for Tim, who came in third.

"Well folks, I guess we have two first-place winners," the Mayor said, once the crowd quieted down. "Sam Goodton and Tom Sampson, I'm honored to present both of you with five hundred dollars. The second place prize of two hundred dollars goes to Tyler Goodton, and this handsome saddle goes to third place winner Tim Lard. Gentlemen, we thank you all for your participation."

"Nice ride boys!" Joel boomed, slapping them on the back. Carol came running, threw her arms around Tom, and kissed him.

"Man, I'll win a few more races just for that," he teased. He knew she would have been just as pleased even if he had not won.

Esther hurried over to her husband and kissed him. "That was a wonderful race, Sam." He smiled and gave her a hug. Then Matt ran up to him.

"Daddy won! Daddy won!" he cried. Sam, his face flushed from the thrill of the race, laughed. Holding his arms out to the boy, he caught him and swung him around.

"Yes, the Lord helped Daddy, Uncle Tom, and Uncle Tyler to win," Sam explained.

It was soon evening and time for everyone to go home.

"Goodnight, Mom and Dad," Sam said, kissing his mother and hugging his father.

"Goodnight to you, and congratulations," they said. As Josh went to say goodnight to his grandsons, Mary pulled Sam off to the side.

"It may be that I'm a nervous mother-in-law, but I think Esther might not be feeling very good. Keep an eye on her, Sam," she advised.

"I will. Thanks for telling me, Mom."

"You're welcome, son. Just watch her."

Sam did as his mother advised. When he told Tom about his mother's fears, Tom was quick to lend a hand. He did much of the farm work alone, leaving Sam more time to spend with Esther. Sam did the housework, giving her the opportunity to rest. Her due date was the twenty-ninth of October, and by the first of August she seemed to be doing better.

It was a warm day on August the seventh. Sam, Esther, and the boys had breakfast and did their morning Bible reading. Sam read a chapter from the book of Psalms, as was their habit in the mornings. They also wanted to read through the Bible, so they would read one chapter from another book at night. Already they had read Genesis through Deuteronomy. Tonight they would read Joshua chapter one.

"I best be headed for work," Sam said to Esther.

"Daddy, play go seek?" Matt begged, pulling on Sam's pant leg. His eyes looked pleadingly at his father.

"Well, alright. I think I have time for one game," Sam agreed. Having to say goodbye to his family every morning was something that Sam dreaded. He would rather have stayed home and played "go seek".

Sam closed his eyes and started counting to thirty as Matt scurried off to find a good hiding place.

"Twenty-eight, twenty-nine, thirty! Ready or not, here I come!" Sam had a pretty good idea where Matthew was, but he did not let on that he knew. "Now, let's see, where could he be?" He looked behind the couch. "Nobody back there. Under the table maybe? Nope, not there. In the closet? No, he's not there either. My, my, where could he be?"

Duke barked and walked into the kitchen. Sam followed him. The dog clawed at the pantry door and barked again. Sam peeked in. "Aha, there you are!"

"Duke found me," Matt moaned. Duke, sensing that he had displeased his young charge, dropped his head. Matthew crawled out and hugged him. "It okay, Duke," he said.

Chuckling softly, Sam went to say goodbye to Esther and the other boys.

His wife was in the living room getting ready to pick up Mike. She started to stand up, but groaned.

"Esther, what's wrong?" Sam cried, rushing to her side. He took Mike, sat him on the floor, and then carried Esther to the bed. She was gasping for breath.

"Esther, what is it?" he asked.

"Sam…I…think the…baby." She was struggling to get the words out.

"It's too early," he said, on the verge of panicking.

"I...know...but...get my mother...your mom..."

"Lord, help me please," Sam prayed. "I can't leave her alone. What can I do? Duke, I can send Duke. Duke! Come here, Duke!" In three bounds the dog was at his side. Sam found a piece of paper and a pencil and wrote a note to his mother.

Mom,

Esther thinks the baby's coming. Please come, and send for the doctor. Please hurry!

Sam

He folded the note, and using a piece of yarn tied it securely to Duke's collar. Holding the dog's huge head in his hands, he spoke. "Duke, take this to Mom. Take this to Mary. Understand? Quickly, Duke." He opened the door, and the dog took off down the trail. "Please let him make it in time, Lord," Sam prayed. He put the twins in their crib and went back to Esther. He sat down beside her and grasped her hand.

"Don't...worry...Sam. Be...awhile yet," she said, but he knew she was worried. He began to pray with her. Then he saw Matt standing in the doorway, his eyes big and his face white. Sam remembered the time when his own mother was sick and how frightened he had been. Though Matthew was not old enough to understand exactly what was going on, he did know that something was very wrong.

Sam held out his arms and Matt ran to him. His father pulled him close and continued to pray.

Meanwhile, Duke was covering the ground fast. Though he did not understand what was wrong, he knew he had to get to Mary. He broke off from the main trail and cut through the woods. The route was covered with thorns and tangled shrubs, but Duke could make it.

Mary had just come out of the house, bearing a tray of lemonade for Tyler and Cecilia, when Duke burst out of the trees. His normally spotless black coat was covered in burs and his front right leg was bleeding.

"Duke!" the three of them shouted in unison. By the time Tyler and Cecilia stood to their feet, Duke had made his way to the porch.

"There's a note tied to his collar," Tyler said, rapidly untying the yarn. He read the note aloud.

"Oh my! Ty, please, hurry and go for the doctor," Mary instructed, untying her apron.

"Yes, but with Dad out in the field, who will take you over to Sam's place?" Tyler asked.

Despite the serious situation, Mary smiled. "I'm not so old that I can't ride by myself. You go get the doctor."

"Yes ma'am." He jumped off the porch, swung into the saddle, and raced toward town.

"What can I do, Mrs. Mary?" C asked.

"Do you know how to get to the Makers' house?" Mary inquired. When C nodded in affirmation, Mary continued. "Go get Mrs. Maker and tell her what's happening."

"Okay," she said, running over to where her pinto was tied. Cecilia mounted and rode toward the Makers' home.

Mary darted back inside and hastily changed into riding clothes. She grabbed her hat and raced to the barn, pulling her gloves on as she went. She bridled Cocoa, her chocolate colored mare, and led her over to a hay bale. "No time for a saddle," she explained to the horse and the dog as she climbed on top of the bale and then mounted. "Come on, Cocoa, Duke! Let's go! Lord, please help me." The three of them raced down the trail.

Sam, still trying not to panic, was praying. "Lord, please help them to get here soon." Esther's pains were coming more quickly. Just when he thought he was going to have to deliver the baby himself, he heard Duke barking.

"Thank You, Jesus," Sam cried. He ran to the door and flung it open. He felt an overwhelming sense of relief at the sight of his mother.

"How is she?" Mary asked, even before her horse had stopped completely.

"I think she's getting close, Mom," Sam said.

They both hurried into the bedroom, and Mary could tell that Esther was indeed getting close to giving birth.

"Sam, if the doctor doesn't get here soon, you'll have to help me deliver the baby," Mary said. "Just do as I say, alright?"

"Okay, Mom, I'll try," Sam said, feeling twice as nervous.

"Oh, Mrs. Mary…it's so early. Am…I going to…lose…the baby?" Esther asked, her voice weak and her face turning gray.

"I don't know, Esther dear," Mary answered honestly but tenderly. "I *do* know that God can save this little early bird. Sam, would you please pray?"

During the middle of the prayer they heard Tyler and the doctor galloping in. The Makers were right behind them. A few minutes later Josh and Cecilia came in. After telling the Makers what was going on, C rode to the field and got Joshua.

The men went out to pray in the living room. Tyler slipped his arm around his older brother, and Sam mustered a smile of gratitude for Ty's support.

An hour later the doctor came out of the bedroom, his face grim. "Well," he began, addressing the group. "They're both alive. The baby was breech. Came out feet first. It was too early for him to be born, so he might not be fully developed inside. To be honest, I don't know if he will live." He turned to Sam with a look of compassion. "Sam, I've seen God miraculously heal people in worse condition than your baby. I'd say that if he can make it though the night, he might make it completely."

"How's Esther?" Sam asked.

"Fine, but exhausted."

Sam's normally erect shoulders drooped. Then they straightened up again. "He? Did you say *he*? You mean, it's another boy?"

"Yes. Sam, I delivered Esther, and I've never seen two babies that looked more alike than Esther and your new son," the doctor said, a smile lighting his tired face. "He definitely looks like the Maker side of the family."

"Then I guess we named him right." Sam turned to Mr. Maker. "With your permission, we were going to call him Montana Laramie."

Tears formed in Mr. Maker's eyes. "Yes, yes, that would be fine."

By that time the whole family was there, including Tom and Carol and their families. Round-the-clock prayer and care were given to Montana. As the night wore on, his condition worsened. Around midnight they were sure that they were going to lose him, but they continued to pray. Then, around two in the morning, he began to improve. He took the milk that was offered him, and his stomach was able to retain it. In the morning, he was better.

Sam embraced his father after watching the sun come up. Josh whispered, "'And the prayer of faith shall save the sick, and the Lord shall raise him up...'"

"'...The effectual fervent prayer of a righteous man availeth much,'" Sam whispered in return.

"Yes, son," Josh said. "God's promises are true."

# Chapter 17

# TOM AND CAROL'S WISH

H e's so small!" Sam said, wondering at their newest son. "I thought Matt was little, but Montana isn't half as big as he was."

Esther sat rocking the tiny boy. "Yes, he is small. The doctor said that when he gets older he might have trouble with physical labor. He probably won't be as strong as the other boys."

Montana had finished his bottle and was starting to fall asleep. Everything about him, his hair, his eyes, and the shape of his face, reminded Sam of Esther. When he smiled, Sam could see Esther's smile.

"Daddy, will baby get bigger?" Matt asked. He had climbed onto a stool and was gently rubbing Montana's head.

"Well…" Sam's voice quavered and his and Esther's eyes met. They both knew that Montana was still fragile, that at any moment he could relapse and they could lose him. "He's still sick, Matthew," Sam continued. "We need to pray for him and take very good care of him." Matt nodded. He had already been helpful, keeping the twins occupied and happy while Mommy and Daddy took care of the baby.

"Yes, Daddy." Matthew kissed Montana and his mother and jumped off his perch. He plopped onto the floor and laid his head on Duke's stomach. They had groomed all the burrs out of the dog's coat and had tended to his cut. The bandage was almost ready to come off.

Leaning back in his chair, Sam looked at his family. Precious Esther was sitting across from him holding Montana. Mike and MacShane, almost inseparable, were playing with toys. Matthew was curled up with the dog. *God, You are so good to me*, he prayed silently. *You gave me good, godly parents and a wonderful wife. You brought my brother back to me. Gave me a sweet sister-in-law. I have a great best friend. He has a wonderful wife, and I have four great sons. Thank You so very much.*

Sunday morning the Goodtons piled into a wagon and off to church they went. Pastor Luke Carson was aging, and his health was not good. He was planning to resign and let his son Terry take over. Terry had already been doing a lot of the preaching.

After the congregational singing and a few special songs, Terry went to the platform. "That was wonderful singing, folks. I appreciate the special music. It touched my heart. Now please turn in your Bibles to Luke 17:11-18." When the pages stopped rustling, Terry began to read.

"'And it came to pass, as he went to Jerusalem, that he passed through the midst of Samaria and Galilee.

'And as he entered into a certain village, there met him ten men that were lepers, which stood afar off:

'And they lifted up their voices, and said, Jesus, Master, have mercy on us.

'And when he saw them, he said unto them, Go shew yourselves unto the priests. And it came to pass, that, as they went, they were cleansed.

'And one of them, when he saw that he was healed, turned back, and with a loud voice glorified God,

'And fell down on his face at his feet, giving him thanks: and he was a Samaritan.

'And Jesus answering said, Were there not ten cleansed? but where are the nine?

'There are not found that returned to give glory to God, save this stranger.'"

Terry finished reading and looked up at the congregation. "I want to preach on the subject, 'Jesus and the Lepers'."

Sam listened as Terry reminded the congregation of the time that only one leper came asking Jesus to heal him in Mark 1:40-45.

"Jesus touched him," Terry said, "and told him, 'I will; be thou clean.' Now, there are *ten* lepers, but that does not overwhelm the Lord. It is wonderful to know that Jesus is never overcome by trouble. He already knows about it, and He always has the right answer. It does not matter how big the task or how many workers He has."

Terry said, "Sometimes I think to myself 'I'm just one man. How can I do anything for God?' Then I remember the little boy who gave his lunch to Jesus in John chapter six. The boy only had five barley loaves and two small fishes, but he was willing for Jesus to use them. Because of his willingness, five thousand people were fed. God can use small things to accomplish His plan. He never gets overwhelmed."

The second point brought conviction to the hearts of the people. "The Lord is never overwhelmed, but He is often overlooked. Notice," Terry pointed out, "that all the lepers cried out for healing, but even though Jesus healed all ten, only one came back to thank Him for what He had done."

Terry's eyes filled with tears. "I am often guilty of failing to thank God. Sometimes it's easier to pray than it is to praise. Sometimes it's easier to want than to worship, or to get than to give. Let me give you some verses that teach and command us to praise the name of Jesus Christ.

"In Ephesians 5:3-4, Paul says, 'But fornication, and all uncleanness, or covetousness, let it not be once named among you, as becometh saints;

'Neither filthiness, nor foolish talking, nor jesting, which are not convenient: but rather giving of thanks.'

"In Philippians 4:6-7, he says, 'Be careful for nothing; but in every thing by prayer and supplication with thanksgiving let your requests be made known unto God.

'And the peace of God, which passeth all understanding, shall keep your hearts and minds through Christ Jesus.'

"In Colossians 2:7, he says, 'Rooted and built up in him, and stablished in the faith, as ye have been taught, abounding therein with thanksgiving.'

"Lastly, John says, in Revelation 7:12, 'Saying, Amen: Blessing, and glory, and wisdom, and thanksgiving, and honour, and power, and might, be unto our God for ever and ever. Amen.'

"You might ask me, 'What is the will of God for my life?' I Thessalonians has the answer. 'In every thing give thanks: for this is the will of God in Christ Jesus concerning you.'

"As you can see," Terry said, stepping to the side of the pulpit, "God puts a lot of value on praise. We read that the occupants of Heaven spend a lot of time praising God. So, let's get practiced up for Heaven by praising the Lord down here.

"Finally, this morning," the preacher continued, "I would like to say that Jesus *can't* be overvalued."

At this statement, several people shouted, "Amen!"

"Look here in verses fifteen and sixteen of our text, 'And one of them, when he saw that he was healed, turned back, and with a loud voice glorified God,

'And fell down on his face at his feet, giving him thanks: and he was a Samaritan.'

"I like that part about glorifying God with a *loud* voice. You'll notice that Jesus didn't say, 'Shhh, don't make a scene. Won't you be quiet?' Jesus wasn't amazed that this man was praising Him. In fact, in verses seventeen and eighteen, He asked where the rest of the lepers were. 'And Jesus answering said, Were there not ten cleansed? but where are the nine?

'There are not found that returned to give glory to God, save this stranger.'

"Let me say one more thing, and then I'll be done. God takes special care to tell us in verse sixteen that this one leper was a Samaritan. In verse eighteen Jesus calls him a stranger. The Jews looked down on Samaritans and treated them like dirt. Their logic would say that this man had no right to worship the Saviour. I'm glad that Jesus didn't mind. Someone may tell you that you've been too wicked to worship Christ. Don't you believe it! All you need to do is come back to God. If you've never been saved, come to Him this morning. Ask Jesus to forgive you of your sin and save you. Put your trust in what He did for you on Calvary. The Bible says in Matthew 11:28, 'Come unto me, all ye that labour and are heavy laden, and I will give you rest.' It also says in John 6:37, 'All that the Father giveth me shall come to me; and him that cometh to me I will in no wise cast out.'

"If you are a Christian, but have backslidden, you can come and get forgiveness. Jesus forgave Peter, even when Peter denied that he knew the Lord. Won't you come, please?"

People flocked to the altar at the invitation. Two people accepted Christ as their Saviour and many Christians made the decision to praise the Lord.

"That was a good message, Terry. It really helped me," Sam said afterwards.

"Thank the Lord, Sam," Terry said. He and his dad were at the door shaking peoples' hands.

"Hello, Pastor Carson. How are you feeling this morning?" Esther asked, addressing the elderly pastor.

"I'm doing better than I deserve, and how is this little one?" He reached a crippled hand out to touch the baby's hand. Montana's small fingers wrapped around the pastor's first finger.

"He's doing great," Sam answered.

"Yes, the Lord's been so good to him," Esther said. "I've never seen a baby with a more determined spirit. I know the Lord has given it to him. He's given Montana a soldier's determination."

"That's wonderful," he said.

A month passed and Montana's health improved. By the beginning of December he was doing much better than anyone could have imagined. Though frail, he was alert and happy.

As usual, a big Christmas party was planned. It was going to be at Tyler and Cecilia's house this year.

"Ty, how are we going to fit twenty-*six* people in here?" Cecilia asked, looking at their living room. It had always seemed spacious to the two of them, but C was not sure if they could fit the whole family in it.

"Twenty-six?" Ty echoed. "Are you sure that's how many are coming?"

"I think so." Cecilia picked up a piece of paper and began to read names.

"My parents are coming. That's two. Your parents will be here; that makes four. Joel and Virginia make six. Mr. and Mrs. Maker make eight. Then Mr. and Mrs. Grey, Melissa, Tessa, Tiffany, Leah, and Jane make fifteen. Add Tom and Carol and you have seventeen. Sam, Esther and the boys make twenty-three."

Tyler was counting names in his head. "I thought you said twenty-six people were coming. Add you and me to that list and that's only twenty-five."

She smiled. "The twenty-sixth is on the way."

Tyler looked at her for a minute, contemplating what she had said. "Cecilia! You mean it?"

"Yes, I'm going to have a baby. I found out yesterday."

"Oh, C!" he cried as he hugged her. "I've been praying we would have a child. Thank You, Jesus. I can't wait to tell everybody!"

Christmas day all the guests somehow managed to find a comfortable seat in the house. Once everyone was settled, Tyler told them the good news. Sam bounded from his chair to congratulate his little brother.

"I'm so happy for you, Ty. I can't tell you what joy my four boys have brought me." As he spoke, Sam saw Tom's shoulders sag, and he saw him reach over and squeeze Carol's hand. No one else seemed to notice.

*I wonder what's wrong,* Sam thought to himself. Tom and Carol were smiling now and congratulating Tyler and Cecilia.

Even as the party reached the climax, Sam could not help but worry about his best friend. He wished he knew what the problem was so that he could help.

It was the beginning of March. Sam still wondered about Tom and Carol. He had not seen them show any sign of being sad or hurt since the Christmas party, yet Sam was concerned.

"Sam." He jumped as Esther's voice interrupted his thoughts. He laid down the ax he was sharpening and looked up at her.

"I didn't hear you and Mom come back from town," he said, grinning at her.

"I'm sorry. I didn't mean to startle you."

"That's okay. I was done anyway. Did you need something?"

"No, not really," she answered. "I just wanted to tell you something."

"What's that?" Then it hit him. He recognized the warm smile that was on Esther's face, and they both began to chuckle. "I can't believe it!" he said.

"Me neither, but it's true. I'm going to have *another* baby!" Esther said. Hand in hand, they walked to the porch and sat down. Finally, Esther spoke.

"God is so good to me. In Psalms 127:3-5, the Bible says, 'Lo, children are an heritage of the LORD: and the fruit of the womb is his reward.

'As arrows are in the hand of a mighty man; so are children of the youth.

'Happy is the man that hath his quiver full of them: they shall not be ashamed, but they shall speak with the enemies in the gate.'

"I always wanted a lot of children," she said. "I remember two girls I went to school with. All they ever talked about was marrying a rich man and having things. One day they asked me what kind of life I wanted. I told them I wanted to marry a godly man, raise a bunch of children, and serve the Lord. They thought I was crazy. They told me I'd miss out on life, but I wouldn't trade what I have for anything. *They're* the ones who have missed out."

"Do the boys know another one is on the way?" Sam asked.

"No, let's go tell them." They went into the house and assembled their little troop.

"Boys, your mother is going to have another baby," Sam said. Matt's face lit up.

"Really, Daddy?" Sam nodded and Matthew hugged his mother. "I am happy, Mommy. I'll help you with him."

"It might be a girl, Matthew. We already have two girl names picked out. Would you like to help us pick out a name for a boy?" Esther asked.

"Yes!"

They let Matthew pray before they started. It touched their hearts to hear their young son pray for his Mommy and the baby.

"Now, what are we going to call it if it's a boy?" Esther asked. "It has to start with the letter *m*."

"That's right. Let's see..." Sam began to think of all the people who had helped him along in life. He remembered Callen Bird telling him about Martin Long, the marshal who had helped Callen find Tyler.

"How about Martin for a first name?" he asked.

"I was thinking about that name," Esther said. She also knew of the part Martin Long had played in the finding of Tyler.

"Martin William," Sam said. He was not sure where William had come from. It just seemed to fit.

"I like it!" Matthew exclaimed. Sam and Esther laughed and hugged him affectionately. Then he ran off to play with his brothers.

The next morning Sam could hardly wait to tell Tom about the new baby. Calling goodbye to his family, he and Dusty galloped to the field. Tom, already there, waved and laid down his tool.

"Hey, Tommy, guess what?" Sam said, sliding down.

"What?"

"You're never going to believe it." Sam uncinched the saddle and flung it over the corral.

"What?" Tom asked again.

"It's so amazing," Sam said, letting his horse run in the fenced in area.

"What is the news?" Tom demanded with a grin as he cornered Sam.

"We're going to have another baby!" Sam expected Tom to react as he had when he found out about the four other boys, but there was no shout of joy. Instead, a look of sadness crossed his face as his smile disappeared. Sam had seen the same reaction at the Christmas party.

"That's wonderful, Sam," he said, but his voice held a catch.

Sam studied his friend's countenance, noting the pain that was there. Tom was rarely despondent, even when faced with trials. Something was terribly wrong with the man Sam had grown up with.

"Tom, is there something wrong? I noticed that at Christmas, when Ty and C said they were going to have a baby, you seemed sad, and you looked that way just now. I don't mean to meddle but…" He paused, unsure of how to continue. He wanted Tom to know that he was willing to listen.

Tom took a deep breath, and tears began to fall down his cheeks. "Sam, I owe you an apology. I've been jealous of you and Esther. Carol and I have been trying to have children ever since we got married. Next June will be five years. I know that's really not very long, but when you want a child so bad, it seems like forever. You know, we took that trip two weeks ago? Well, we went to see a doctor in Indianapolis. Doctor Ron was concerned and he suggested it. The doctor in Indianapolis said that…" He stopped and tried to control his emotions. "He said that he doesn't think we'll be able to have children."

Sam felt as though he had stabbed him in the heart. He remembered all the times he and Tom had talked about the children they wanted, and about their children playing together. They had hoped that each one of them would have a son and that their sons would be best friends. Those dreams were now shattered.

"I'm so sorry, Tom," Sam said softly. He put his arms around Tom, and Tom cried on his shoulder.

After a few moments, Tom stepped back and dried his eyes. "I never thought that anything would encourage me to be angry with you. You have been more than just a friend to me. You've been like a brother, but, when you and Esther started having children, I got jealous. It wasn't so bad at first, but with Ty and Cecilia expecting, and Terry and Abby Carson having the two girls, it's hard. Hearing the doctor's report was almost more than we could handle. Both Carol and I were getting angry." He smiled ruefully. "God began to get after us. We realized that really we were mad at Him and that's why we thought we could not bear the trial. We weren't gleaning His strength because we were fussing with Him. It was affecting everything that we did. I couldn't pray. I couldn't enjoy the services at church. I couldn't do anything. Neither could Carol. So, last night we both prayed and told God that if He sees fit not to send us any children, we'll keep on serving Him. God has already been so good to us. Even if He never does anything else for us, we're going to try to serve Him to the best of our ability. Will you please forgive me for being envious?"

"I forgive you, Tom."

"Thanks, and thanks for listening to my problems," Tom said.

"Don't mention it. Besides, what are best friends for?"

*Chapter 18*

# THE LAST TIME

H ow are you feeling, Esther?" Sam asked her one August afternoon.

"Not very good, Sam," she replied from the bed.

Sam was worried. Esther had been terribly sick during most of the pregnancy. Since she was nearing her due date, she and Sam had spent the month with her parents so her mom could care for her. The boys were with Grandpa and Grandma Goodton.

Sam took Esther's hand in his. With his other hand he carefully tucked a blanket around her. "Do you realize that if you have the baby this month all five of our children will have been born in August?"

She smiled weakly. "At least it will be easy to remember their birthdays. I need to rest, Sam. I'm so tired."

"Okay, honey," he said, his free hand caressing her pale cheek. "I'm going to check on the boys. I'll be back soon." He kissed her and stood to his feet.

"Sam, tell them I love them, please. Give them all kisses from me and see how the little soldier is doing." Esther had nicknamed Montana "Soldier" because, though fragile, he kept fighting to stay alive. He was only a year old, but had been through a lot.

"I will," he assured her. Sam made his way to the barn. Dusty snorted and pawed at the ground at the sight of his master and Sam rubbed the pony's small head. "Good boy," he said softly. He pulled his saddle off the rack and laid it on Dusty's back. When he tried to put the bridle on, Dusty playfully fought it. The horse had not been ridden much lately, and he was frisky.

"No!" Sam said, more sharply than he had meant to. Dusty stopped immediately and opened his mouth wide to accept the bit. Sam's shoulders drooped. "I'm sorry, Dusty. I didn't mean to snap at you." The brown horse's ears perked up, and he nuzzled Sam's hand. "Good boy," Sam said again. He mounted and headed towards his parents' house.

Both he and Esther hated having the family separated. The boys had been staying with them at the Makers', but last week they had gone to the Goodtons'. Sam had prayed about the change, and he thought it would be better for the boys. He hoped that it would not be for long.

As he rode, Sam thought about Ty and Cecilia's baby. Ellen Joy had been born in June. *Thank You, Lord,* he prayed, *that all went well with her delivery. Please help Esther and our new baby.*

"Daddy!" MacShane cried when he saw his father ride in. The two-year-old leapt off the porch with Duke at his heels and ran toward his father. Sam dismounted and pulled the boy close. Mac was a husky fellow with blonde hair and blue eyes. Because of his stocky build, his grandpa Maker had given him the nickname "Lumberjack." The most adventurous of the four boys, he often got into things that he should not, usually through curiosity rather than naughtiness.

Mike's personality was the opposite of his twin's. Though he enjoyed adventure, his favorite pastime was to lie by the fire and listen to someone read. His favorite book was *The Sweet Psalmist*, a book of poems about the life of King David. It belonged to Mrs. Goodton, who would often read it to him. Mac, never very interested in books, would rather play and explore. Though they were different, the twins were best of friends. When one needed help, the other was always right there. They would often call each other by their middle names. Sam did not know how that got started, but he and Esther did not mind. It seemed to be something special between the twins.

Matthew was growing taller every day. Even at age three he loved to help with the work on the farm and with looking after his little brothers.

Montana never seemed to get any heavier; he just grew taller. Though his health was good, he was still weak. He did his best to keep up with the other three, though he often had to stop and rest. Matt kept a close eye on him, making sure that the others did not play too hard with him or push him beyond his limits.

The four of them were soon crowded around their father, all trying to hug him at the same time.

"Daddy, how's Mommy?" Matthew asked when they all settled on the living room floor.

"She's still not feeling good, son," Sam said, leaning back against the couch.

Matt's shoulders drooped at his father's answer. Sam knew that he wanted to go home. He hugged him encouragingly. "The baby should be coming anytime," Sam said, trying to make him smile. It worked. Matthew could hardly wait for the baby to be born.

"Really?" he asked.

"Yes, sir, and after it's born it shouldn't be long until we're all back at the house again."

"Good!" Mike exclaimed.

"Good," MacShane echoed. He had climbed up on the couch and had wrapped his arms around his father's neck. Mike and Matt were sitting on either side of Sam, and Montana had crawled onto his lap. Duke lay at his feet.

They sat for a few minutes, glad to be together. "Hey, you boys want to play a game?" Sam asked.

"Yes, sir!" they shouted.

"All right. Go hide."

Josh and Mary were watching them from the kitchen. They laughed as the twins went streaking up the stairs to find a good hiding place. Matthew had taken Monty by the hand, and they went to find a place in Sam's old bedroom.

Twenty minutes and seven games later, Sam was saying goodbye. Though reluctant to leave the boys, he wanted to get back to Esther.

Two days passed and Esther went into labor. She was very weak and the doctor feared they might lose both of them.

After many anxious moments, Martin was born. Much to the doctor's surprise, the boy was healthy. This time it was Esther who was sick.

After a week of illness, she began to recuperate, but the doctor had sad news. He told Sam and Esther that they should not have any more children.

"Sam, we've had to stop halfway," Esther told him one afternoon. She was sitting up in bed and looked much better. They were waiting for Josh and Mary, who were bringing the boys over to visit their Mommy.

"How's that, honey?" Sam asked. Martin was resting contently in his arms, his shock of red hair looking even redder in contrast to the white blanket.

"We were going to have ten children, remember? I'm content with my five boys, though," she said.

"I am too," Sam agreed.

"I miss them all. Doctor Ron says I'll be able to go home at the end of this week. Then we can all be together again." She paused to take a sip of tea. "Sam, I know we had decided to call the baby Martin William, but could we change the middle name?"

"To what?"

"Well, he looks so much like you. Could we call him Martin Samuel?"

Sam smiled. "If that's what you want, that's what we will do." So, Martin William became Martin Samuel.

There was a knock on the door. "Come in," Esther called out. The door opened and three boys rushed into the room.

"Mommy!" they cried. Bed springs squealed as the boys jumped onto the bed and hopped around, trying to get close enough for a hug.

"Easy boys, easy," Sam admonished, a grin on his face. They quieted down but still pressed up to their mother's side. She smiled and hugged each one.

"Matthew, I can't believe how you've grown, even in these last few weeks," Esther said, slipping her arm around him. "I hear that you've been helping Grandpa a lot on the farm."

"I try. I like it," he answered, leaning against her shoulder.

"Good. How are you, Michael?" she asked, squeezing his hand.

"Miss you," was the answer.

"I miss all of you, too. Mac, are you staying out of trouble?" she teased, ruffling his sandy hair.

He nodded and Esther chuckled. "Wonderful. Where's Montana?"

"Right here, Esther," Josh said, setting him on Esther's lap. He had carried the boy in to avoid any chance of him getting accidentally stepped on.

Montana threw his small arms around her neck and she hugged him gently. Neither Sam nor Esther had any favorites among their children. They loved them all equally, but because of the constant care that Montana had needed when he was a baby, a special bond had formed between him and his mother.

"Daddy, I please hold the baby?" Matt asked. His father put Martin in Matthew's arms, but Sam kept his hands under the baby to support him. Matthew gently rocked his new brother. "Thanks, Dad. Hi, Martin, remember me?" It appeared that Martin *did* remember him. He smiled and waved his arms at the sound of his older brother's voice. It was then that Sam told them about the name change.

All too soon it was time for the boys to go back to the Goodtons' house. After many hugs, kisses, and tearful goodbyes, they headed back, but they did not have to stay there long.

Early Monday morning, Sam drove the wagon over to his parents' house, threw the reins around the fence post, and hurried into the house.

The boys were sitting at the table eating pancakes and sausages for breakfast.

"Daddy!" they shouted, napkins and forks flying across the table as they dropped whatever they had in their hands then scampered to him.

"Guess what, boys," Sam said gathering them around him. "Today, we get to go home!"

They stood for a minute, speechless.

"Mom too?" Matthew finally managed to ask.

"Baby?" the twins added hopefully.

"Yes, *all* of us are going home," Sam answered.

"HURRAY!" the boys cried.

It was such a joyous time when all seven of the Goodtons were home and everyone was well.

# Chapter 19

# PLANS ARE MADE

Happy birthday!"

Two years had passed. It was the seventeenth of August, and the family was celebrating the boys' birthdays. Instead of having five different birthday parties in the same month every year, they celebrated all five birthdays on one day. Matthew was five, Mike and Mac were four, Monty was three, and Martin was two.

"Blow out the candles," Mary said. Each grandma had baked two cakes. The twins had asked if they could share one. Each of the other three boys had a small cake of his own with the appropriate number of candles on it.

"This cake is good, Grandma," Mike said to Lisa.

"Why thank you, Michael. I'm glad you like it." She gave him a hug.

"It *is* really good, Grandma!" Mac said. As usual, he had more cake *on* him than he did *in* him. Nevertheless, Lisa hugged him, cake and all.

"Now, let's open presents," Mr. Maker said after the cake had been eaten and the boys cleaned up.

Everyone was there, including Tom and Carol and their families. Sam and Esther loved this party. It felt almost like Christmas. With their arms around each other, they watched the boys tear open their packages.

Night was approaching. The boys had long since fallen asleep and had been carefully tucked into their beds. The visitors were gone, and Sam and Esther found themselves alone.

"That was a wonderful party," Esther said, bringing some coffee into the living room.

"It sure was," Sam replied, lifting the steaming cup to his lips. "Umm, you make the best coffee."

"Thank you." She sat down beside him, cup in hand, and gazed into the fire.

"Esther, we need to talk."

"About what?" she asked, turning to face him.

"About going west." Because of the many different events of the last two years, they had not discussed the subject. They had thought about it, and all the extra money they got was set aside for it, but nothing definite had been decided.

"West," she echoed. "Doesn't the very word thrill you? It sounds inviting, yet challenging."

"Yes, it does," Sam agreed.

His wife looked straight into his eyes. "You've decided on when we're going to leave, haven't you?" Even though she was excited about the "adventure," as she called it, she dreaded leaving her family.

"Yes, I have. Not this summer, but the next. I read in the paper that a year from next April a wagon train will be heading west to Miles City, Montana. The wagon master is one of the best. His name is Ricky Daniels, but he's earned the nickname 'Trail Blazing' Daniels. He'll be a good man to ride with."

"When will we tell the family?" she asked softly.

"After this Christmas." He took her hand in his. They both knew it was going to be hard on everyone. The Makers, Greys, Sampsons, and Goodtons were all very close. It would break many hearts, but God would mend them again in time.

Esther squeezed Sam's hand, stood up, and went to their piano. She sat down and played a nameless tune.

"I'll miss hearing you play on the trip," Sam told her. He stood up and walked over to her. "When we get settled in Montana, we'll have to find us another piano."

Esther stopped her trills and scales and began to play a song. Sam knew he had heard it before, but he could not think of what it was.

"Recognize it?" Esther asked, after she had played a verse and a chorus.

"Yes and no. What is it?"

"It's my arrangement of the new hymn 'At the Cross'," she said, changing keys and playing it an octave higher.

"Okay. I recognize it now. You play it slower. A lot slower."

"Right." She changed to a lower key. "Can you sing it there?"

"I think so. If I can remember the words." He took a deep breath and began to sing it at the slow and soothing tempo Esther had arranged.

"Alas and did my Saviour bleed?
And did my Sovereign die?
Would He devote that sacred head
For such a worm as I?"

Esther added the harmony on the second verse.

"'Was it for crimes that I have done,
He groaned upon the tree?
Amazing pity! grace unknown!
And love beyond degree!"

Esther changed keys and sang the last verse in a lovely soprano while Sam sang the harmony.

> "But drops of grief can ne'r repay
> The debt of love I owe:
> Here, Lord, I give myself away,
> 'Tis all that I can do!"

"That's beautiful, Esther," Sam said. "You think about the words more at that speed." He brushed a tear from his eye. "The cross and its message amaze me. To think that the God of the universe, the God Who created everything, left Heaven and died on the cross for *my* sins. All I had to do to receive His forgiveness was ask."

"God's grace is beyond our human understanding," Esther added. "Why would He love us so?"

"We may never know, but I am sure glad He does," Sam said.

"Me too."

Sunday came and the families all headed to church. The minute Sam saw Tom, he knew something good had happened. Tom had that look about him. Sam caught Tom's eyes and lifted his hands in a questioning gesture. Tom smiled wider and shook his head. Sam would have to wait.

"What was that all about?" Esther asked, after seeing the silent conversation between the two best friends.

"Tom is up to something," he answered, helping her down.

"Isn't he always?" Esther teased. Sam grinned and began the chore of "unloading" his five sons. The twins took flying leaps off the back of the wagon, landing safely in their father's outstretched arms. Matthew climbed down in his quiet, sure way and went to stand by Mac and Mike. Monty and Martin had to be lifted down. With Sam holding Martin, Mike and Mac holding tightly to Matt's hand, and Monty with his mother, they entered the church.

Sam had just gotten everyone seated when the Greys and Tom and Carol came in. Once again, Sam gave Tom a questioning look. Tom pointed to Melissa Grey.

"What?" Sam mouthed.

These words formed on Tom's lips. "Wait and see."

Sam did not have to wait long. As always, the service started with prayer, and Tyler was called on to pray. For a few minutes, Sam forgot about Tom's surprise. Hearing his little brother publicly announce his need for God's help and his love for God always lifted Sam's heart.

"Thank you, Brother Ty," Terry Carson said when Tyler had finished. "Now folks, I believe Miss Melissa Grey has something she would like to tell you all. Miss Grey."

"Thank you, Pastor," she said as she stood up.

Sam's mind quickly returned to the day Carol's parents had adopted four young Indian girls whom they named Melissa, Leah, Tiffany, and Jane. Melissa had been four years old. She was now a beautiful young woman almost twenty-three years old.

"As you all know, I have been working with our Indian friends, Brother Caleb Running Deer and his family, at the Indian reservation. The Lord has allowed us to see many souls saved over the past two summers." She spoke perfect English with a pleasant trace of her Indian accent. "God has used that ministry." She paused and smiled warmly. "Yesterday, Brother Running Deer's son Joah asked me to marry him." As she spoke, she lifted her left hand. Rays of sunlight streaming in from the stained-glass windows glistened off a lovely diamond ring. The whole church clapped and cheered.

"I wish to thank you all for your love to my sisters and me. You took us in and cared for us when no one had the right to ask you to do so. I want you to know that we do not take that lightly." Her voice choked with emotion. All the ladies in the church were digging through handbags looking for hankies.

"Please, dear family in Christ," she continued, "pray for Joah and me as we strive to serve the Lord in the reservations. Thank you all."

Sam grinned at Tom; the latter gave his friend the thumbs up.

After church, Sam and Esther were among the first to congratulate Melissa Grey.

"Where are you going after you get married?" Esther asked.

"There is a large reservation in Georgia where we will be working. Jane is coming with us," Melissa said.

"We'll miss you both very much," Sam told her.

"We will miss all of you."

Only two weeks later Todd, by way of letter, proposed to Tessa Grey. He also sent money to Terry and Abby, Sam and Esther, Tom and Carol, and all the Greys so that they could go to Maine for the wedding.

"Ah, smell that air," Sam said as the buggy rolled to a stop in front of Todd's parents' house. The others all took deep breaths of the rich sea air.

"You sound like a sailor, Sammy," Todd said, looping the reins over the post. He led the group of twenty-one people into the house.

The next day, as everyone was enjoying the scenery, Sam pulled Todd off to the side. "I need to talk to you, Todd," he said. Todd nodded and together they walked down the shore.

"What is it, Sam?"

"Well, it's good news, and yet it's sad news. Esther and I have been praying, and we know that the Lord wants us to go west."

His friend smiled. "That is wonderful! I know that you have wanted to do that for a long time." Then his smile faded as he realized what Sam was saying. He hung his head. "So, the bad news is that you probably will never come back to Maine, right?"

"That's it. We're going to Montana. Nobody else knows about it yet."

"Not even Tom?" Todd asked.

"Nope. We're going to tell them after Christmas. I wanted to tell you now, since this might be our last visit."

Todd shuffled his feet in the sand for a few minutes then gazed out to sea. "You know, Sammy, I do not see how people can live without the hope of Heaven." He turned to face his friend. "Even if we never see each other again on this earth, we do not have to fear. We will be together again in Heaven for *eternity*."

"That's a wonderful truth," Sam agreed. "I'm glad that this life is not all there is. The Bible says, 'If in this life only we have hope in Christ, we are of all men most miserable.'"

"That is the truth." They walked in silence for a few minutes then Todd spoke. "Sam, I am happy for you. I really am, and, one more thing. I would like to thank you for being my friend. I do not know how I would have made it if God had not put you and Tom in my life. One of the things that helped me when we moved was the fact that I knew both of you were praying for me."

"Thank the Lord. He knew that Tom and I needed *your* friendship." Sam stopped and looked around. "Hey, where are we?"

Todd looked about him. "Close to a mile from Mom and Dad's house. I did not think we had gone this far. Come on. I know a shortcut back."

The group was eating breakfast the next morning when Todd came in.

"Hurry up everyone! Today we are going sailing!" he cried.

"What?" they asked.

"Listen, I want you guys to spend some time out on the ocean before you have to leave." He cast a meaningful look at Sam, but the others were too excited to notice.

Soon they were boarding one of Todd's smaller ships, *The Midget,* to spend the day at sea.

"Cast off!" Eugene Lark bellowed. "Hoist the sails!"

Todd surveyed the activity with a practiced eye. "Look alive down there!" he commanded a pair of mates who were not performing their duties accurately. They quickly put some vigor into their work. "That is much better, men," Todd praised.

Todd's friends watched him. He handled his authority well. He commanded with fairness, always listening to both sides of the story. He was quick to lend a hand to a sailor who needed help, and he never made himself out to be better than his men. They did not fear him; they respected and honored him. They knew that he was a born-again believer, and many of them had accepted Christ as their Saviour because of his testimony and actions.

The wind filled the sails and the boat glided through the water. The newcomers stood in awe on the decks.

"Well, what do you all think?" Todd asked.

"I feel like I've got the world at my fingertips!" Tom exulted.

Eugene Lark laughed heartily. "Those were Captain Leonard's exact same words when his uncle asked him that question years ago."

"Come on, Mr. Lark. I am not old enough for it to be 'years ago'," Todd told his first mate.

"Aye, Captain, if ye say so." Smiling, he walked away.

"Eugene Lark and his wife Pat are precious Christians," Todd said with admiration. "He is also the best sailor that I have ever met. He has helped both my uncle and me keep this business going."

Todd stopped talking and watched his friends enjoy the ride. His gaze focused on Matthew. "Do you like it, Matthew?"

"Yes, sir! It's very beautiful!"

# Chapter 20

# TELLING THE FAMILY

I do not want to hear one wisecrack out of any of you," Todd warned Sam, Tom, Terry, Joah, and his other brother-in-law Joe Lance, as they were getting ready for the wedding.

His friends winked at each other.

"Why, whatever do you mean?" Tom asked innocently.

"You all know quite well what I mean. I told all of you at your weddings that the groom is not supposed to be nervous." He grinned. "Now I am scared to death!"

"Take it from some guys who have been through it, you'll live," Joe comforted. "One look at your bride and all worry vanishes."

"I hope you are right, Joe," Todd said nervously.

Joe was right. When Tessa walked down the aisle, Todd lost thought of everything but her.

"That was a beautiful wedding," Esther said to the newlyweds, and the others agreed.

"Thank you all for coming," Todd said.

"Thanks for inviting us, Todd. We're very happy for you and Tessa," Tom told them.

"It was wonderful that you all were able to come," Tessa said. She looked lovingly at Todd, and he put his arm around her.

All too soon it was time for the guests to go back to their homes. The farewells were more heartfelt this time. The Leonards had been told that this was probably Sam and Esther's last visit. Though saying goodbye was hard, they were glad that the young couple wanted to serve the Lord out West.

"Here Esther, Carol, we bought you these," Candice said as she and Abigail handed each of their friends a box. Candice, Abigail, and Todd were triplets. When the Leonards had lived in Indiana, Candy and Abby had been close to Esther and Carol. Even though they had parted, they still were friends.

Inside the boxes were lovely necklaces decorated with seashells.

"Oh, they're beautiful!" the girls exclaimed. "Thank you both so much." They lifted the necklaces from their boxes and helped one another put them on.

"Boys, these are for you." Todd reached into a bag and handed each of Sam's boys a large seashell. "These are all from different countries. This one is from China." He handed it to Matt. "This one, Mike, is from the coast of Australia. Mac, this one is from Canada. Monty, yours is from South America. Martin's is from the coast of Africa."

"Thank you, Uncle Todd," the boys chorused.

"You are quite welcome. Terry and Abby's girls each have one too. Joan and Jenn, do you remember where yours are from?"

"Yes, Uncle Todd," Joan said. "Mine is from Japan."

"Mine is from the coast of Europe," Jenn said.

"Right." Todd picked up two ornate boxes and handed one to Sam and the other to Tom. "These are for you guys," he said. Inside the boxes were two small, identical daggers handsomely studded with emeralds.

"Todd! We can't take these! They must have cost a fortune," Sam told him, admiring their beauty and elegance.

"No, please, take them. I have one just like them. I bought them in China. I wanted you both to have one as a reminder that we are still best friends." Earlier he had bought daggers for Terry, Joe, and

Joah. Terry's was studded with rubies, Joe's with diamonds, and Joah's with sapphires.

"Thank you, Todd," Tom said, placing the dagger back in the box.

"Yes, thank you." Sam knelt and showed his sons the weapon.

Four days later saw everyone back home. It was not long until they were getting ready to celebrate Christmas.

"Daddy, how long before Christmas?" Mac asked.

"Three days, MacShane," was the reply. "Are you getting excited?"

"Yes. I can't wait."

"Well, you won't have to wait too much longer," Esther said, continuing to rock Montana. He had a slight cold. It seemed that he was more prone to illness in the winter months.

"Here, Mom, let me hold him please," Matthew said. Esther placed Montana in his arms. "Thank you, Mommy. I'm looking forward to Christmas, too. I love it when everyone comes over, and I like it when we all sing. I like all the presents the best though!"

Sam smiled. "Presents are fun, but remember, Matthew, Christmas is really about when Jesus came to earth. That's the real reason for Christmas."

"Daddy, guess what," Mike said, sitting down beside Sam.

"What?" Sam put his arm around the boy.

"Grandma Maker said she's going to make her special cass, cass…"

"Casserole," Sam finished for him.

"Yes, that's it. Casserole."

"Good, I like her casserole," Sam said.

"Me too."

"Me three!" Mac added.

"Me four," Matt put it.

Later on that night, Sam could not sleep. Carefully, so he would not wake Esther up, he made his way to the kitchen. Thoughts of going west filled his mind. So much had to be planned; so much had to be done. Where did he even begin? His mind would not stop spinning.

"Lord," he prayed, "please calm my head and my heart." To take his mind off the journey, he began to pray for and think about his sons. How he loved those five boys and many wonderful memories were associated with each one. There were also some hard memories, like the times when Sam and Esther had to discipline them. Matthew had been ten months old when he got his first spanking. In the middle of the night, he began to scream. Sam, sure that someone was trying to strangle the boy, had raced into the bedroom only to find Matthew giggling. Since he had told a lie, Sam spanked him.

Mike was one-year-old when he first had to be spanked. His mother had told him to sit down and in anger he hit her. She had to spank him.

Mac's first experience came when he was eleven months old. He pushed his brother and Esther had told him no. He did again and once more she told him no. He clearly knew what "no" meant, because he had obeyed her at other times. When he pushed Montana for the third time, Sam spanked him.

Perhaps because he had been too ill to misbehave, Montana was nearly a year and a half old before his first spanking. Esther and he were alone at the house and she asked him to go play so she could start supper. He put his hands on his hips and said, quite firmly, "No!" Esther told Sam later on that it was so funny that she was tempted to laugh, but knowing he had to be taught that he had done wrong, she spanked him.

Then there was Martin. Sam shook his head. He was sure he could count on two hands how many times the others had needed to be spanked, but that was not the case with Martin. He was the youngest, only six months old, when he was first spanked. Sam remembered well how it took three swats to stop the boy's angry screams and bring genuine tears. The incident took place when Esther had tried to put him to bed and he put up a fuss. Nothing was wrong; he just did not want to go to bed.

Martin was much more active than the other four. He seemed unable to sit still, and quite often his liveliness got him into trouble. He wanted to do everything and try everything. Sam thought about the time that every day for a week Martin had been spanked for the same offense. How it hurt Sam and Esther to have to spank him so often. Finally, Martin stopped his misbehavior.

Sam hated spanking his children, as did Esther. They knew, however, that if they did not discipline them now, there would be no telling what would become of the boys. If they were allowed to lie, they might move on to stealing. If as children they were allowed to hit their mother in anger, as teenagers they might seriously injure or even kill someone. Sam knew that some people did not believe in the importance of discipline, but Sam had read Proverbs 22:15, "Foolishness is bound in the heart of a child; but the rod of correction shall drive it far from him."

Sam was not foolish enough to think that God wanted him to beat his children with a rod. Such harsh punishment was based on a misinterpretation of the Bible. God does, however, advocate spanking when done with love and consistency. The Bible teaches that all are born sinners and that is why children do wrong. Discipline, done God's way, will teach a child what is right and what is wrong and will eventually show them their need of a Saviour.

Sam and Esther knew that they had not done everything right so far in raising their children. Still, it was obvious to those around them that there was a difference between these five boys whose parents were consistent and those children whose parents were not—parents who would discipline their children for a certain wrong only once and let them get away with it the second time, who would cruelly beat their children, or who never disciplined at all. The Goodton boys were well-behaved most of the time, polite and pleasant to be around. They loved their parents, partly because Sam and Esther took the time to teach them and discipline them. The boys were learning that Mom and Dad did certain things because they loved them.

"Lord," Sam prayed again, "Thank You for helping us. Please continue to guide and lead us so we will raise our children as You want us to. Lord, Your way is the best way."

Christmas came, bringing with it a pile of snow. Bundled up like Eskimos, the families made their way to the Makers' house.

Christmas melodies were coming from the house as Sam and Esther pulled in. Before the boys were out of the wagon they began to sing.

Esther listened to her five sons and could tell that each one would one day have a good voice. Silently she prayed that they would always use whatever talents God gave them for His glory alone. She often wondered about their future, taking into account the characteristics that they already had. Would Matthew grow to be a strong and faithful leader? Where would Mike's love of books take him? Would Mac travel in search of adventure? What would Montana be strong enough to do? What would be the energetic Martin's life? Esther shook her head in amusement. She knew whatever happened would, at the very least, be far from dull.

Soon they were gathered around the table eating Christmas dinner. Next came the presents and then, evening fell, and the families had to bid goodnight to each other

Two days later Sam went to talk with his father.

"Dad, there's something I have to tell you," Sam announced, walking into his father's barn.

Josh laid down his hammer and nails and turned to face him. He studied his son's expression and noticed the tension. "Sit down, Sammy boy."

Sam lowered his tall frame onto a hay bale. Josh sat down beside him, and looked at him for a few seconds. "What is it, son?" Joshua asked quietly, when he saw that Sam was struggling for the right words.

"Dad, Esther and I have been praying, and we believe it's the Lord's will that we…" He paused and looked at his dad. He knew that Josh would not be angry, that he would want Sam to do God's will, but it would be terribly sad to have to say goodbye. "We're going to move west." He told his father all the details.

Josh's mind went back to the time that the wagon train had come by their place. He remembered how Sam had cast dreamy looks toward the West ever since then. Josh nodded. God had been preparing Sam for this time.

"Son, I've never known a finer young man, one that loves the Lord as you do. I'm not saying that because you're my boy. I'm saying it because it is true. I know you walk with God and that you have made sure that this is God's will."

"We've tried to make sure, Dad. Esther and I have fasted and prayed. It is God's will."

Joshua and Sam stood up and once again Josh nodded. Father and son found themselves in a warm embrace. The tears began to spill down their cheeks. It was a bittersweet moment for both of them. The father was proud that his son was willing to follow God, and the son was glad that he had his father's support, but they would miss each other.

Sam finally stepped back and he noticed his mother standing in the barn door. She had apparently overheard, for she kept brushing away tears.

Sam turned toward her and held out his arms. She ran to him and hugged him tightly.

"May God go with you, my son," she whispered.

Sam rode away with half of his heart singing and the other half broken. He had his parents' blessing, but he would miss them.

Sam headed the horse and buggy toward the Makers' house. Esther had wanted to tell her parents herself, so he had dropped her off there before going to tell his parents.

Mr. Maker was on the front porch when Sam came in. At first, Sam wondered if he was angry, but he quickly dismissed the thought. Jumping out of the buggy, he looped the reins around a small tree and then stepped up on the porch.

Mr. Maker was silent for a few minutes. When he spoke, it was with genuine love. "I'm proud of you, Sam." Sam was somewhat surprised at his choice of words and wondered what he meant. Mr. Maker explained. "It takes a man to do what you're planning to do. It's not easy to take a wife and five children west. Most men wouldn't even try it, but you are willing to go because it is God's will. I'm proud of you," he said again.

Sam and Esther found it difficult to hold back the tears during the evening meal. The food, though delicious, seemed to only choke them. Finally, Sam laid down his fork and reached for the Bible.

"Are you done already, Dad?" Matthew asked.

"Yes, son. You keep on eating and I'll read from the Bible. I'll start in Psalms thirty-one. 'To the chief Musician, A Psalm of David. In thee, O LORD, do I put my trust; let me never be ashamed: deliver me in thy righteousness.'

"Verse two, 'Bow down thine ear to me; deliver me speedily: be thou my strong rock, for an house of defence to save me.'

"Verse three, 'For thou art my rock and my fortress; therefore for thy name's sake lead me, and guide me.'"

He stopped and contemplated the last verse. "'Lead me, and guide me'," Sam mused aloud. He looked up at Esther and smiled. She nodded, her lips forming a smile as well. They both knew that God wanted them to make this trip and that He would guide them.

The next day Sam was at the field early. He wanted to tell Tom before they began work. Deep in his heart was a hope that maybe Tom and Carol would come with him. He knew, however, that it was a selfish desire. Some of the people in town wanted Tom to get involved in local politics. A few had even suggested that he run for mayor in the next election. Tom had made no definite decision, but Sam knew that if he did run he would probably be a cinch to win. Sam thought that Tom and Carol would be better off staying in Clear Water.

Sam was diverted from his thoughts by the sound of an approaching horse. Tom was riding toward him. "Howdy, partner. You're here early," Tom said cheerfully, jumping down off his horse.

"Yeah, I needed to tell you something."

"What's that?" Tom asked, leading his mount to the corral.

"Well, it's…" Sam stopped, his mind racing to find an easy way to say what he had to say. Tom, sensing that bad news was coming, stopped walking, tightened his hands on the reins, and turned to face his friend.

"Esther and I are moving west," Sam said rather abruptly.

Tom's jaw dropped, and he let the reins fall to the ground. His mouth moved as he tried to say something, but nothing came out.

"We've prayed about it Tom, and we know it's God's will," Sam explained. "We plan to leave next spring."

Tom recovered, took a deep breath, and forced a smile. "I guess I shouldn't be surprised. That's been your dream ever since I can remember. I'm glad that the Lord saw fit to let you fulfill it. It just kind of shocked me at first. I wasn't expecting to hear that, but you're my best friend, and I'm glad you're seeing a dream come true." Tom walked over to him and they embraced.

Sam, his arms around his best friend, had to bite his tongue to keep from saying, "I always thought we would do it together, with our wives and families. What about the promise we made to always be there if the other one needed help? How can we keep that promise if we're miles away from each other?" Instead of speaking these words, he choked back his tears and prayed that God would keep their friendship strong even though they would be miles apart.

In a few weeks everyone knew of Sam and Esther's plan. A few of the townsfolk thought they were crazy, but the majority were pleased to see the young couple willing to obey the Lord. Matthew and his brothers took it pretty well.

"All of us go?" three-year-old Monty asked, fearing that maybe one of his parents or brothers would be left behind.

"Yes, Montana. Your mom, your brothers, and I will go," Sam assured him.

"What about Duke?" Mike asked, his small hand closing tightly over Duke's collar.

"We wouldn't think about leaving without Duke," Esther promised, reaching out to pet the dog.

"What about Grandpa and Grandma Maker, Grandpa and Grandma Goodton, Uncle Ty and Aunt C, and Uncle Tom and Aunt Carol?" Mac wanted to know.

"Well, they're going to stay here," Sam told him.

Matthew was having the hardest time. Sam pulled him close to him. "God will take care of us and our family. I know it's hard right now, but one day God will bless us for obeying His word. I can promise you that."

In the middle of the night, Sam awoke with a start. *What woke me up?* he wondered. He listened intently but heard nothing. Sam was about to go back to sleep when he thought he heard someone crying. It sounded as though it was coming from Matt's bedroom. Sam quickly got up, put on his robe, and tiptoed out, trying not to wake Esther. Going to Matthew's bedroom and quietly opening the door a crack, he peeked into the room. His son was sitting on the bed crying and holding on to Duke. The dog whined softly and nuzzled his arm.

"Matthew," Sam called gently.

"Co…come in… Dad," Matt answered between sobs. Sam sat down on the bed and hugged his oldest son.

"Are you scared about moving?" his father asked, still holding the trembling boy.

"A little bit," came the whispered reply.

"That's not the reason you're crying, is it?"

"No, sir. I'm gonna miss everybody. What if I never see my grandparents again, or my aunts and uncles, or cousin Ellen?" Matt buried his face in his father's shoulder and cried.

That same fear had gone through Sam's mind hundreds of times. It was frightening for him, let alone a five-year-old boy. Then he remembered what Todd had said after being told that Sam was leaving. "You know, Matt," Sam began, "we can all be together again some day. The Bible says that if we get saved, we can go to Heaven. There we will never be separated again."

"Daddy," the boy said, fear in his voice, "I'm not going to Heaven. I'm not saved."

"Would you like to be?" Sam asked.

"Yes, sir," Matthew answered, looking up at his father.

"Let me get the Bible." Sam picked up Matthew's Bible and opened to John 3:3. "'Jesus answered and said unto him, Verily, verily, I say unto thee, Except a man be born again, he cannot see the kingdom of God.'"

"How do I get born again?" Matthew asked.

"Jesus tells us in verse sixteen, 'For God so loved the world, that he gave his only begotten Son, that whosoever believeth in him should not perish, but have everlasting life.'

"Matthew, do you know why Jesus had to die?" Sam asked.

"Yes, sir. Everyone's a sinner and we must pay for our sins. Sin is the bad things we do, like lying and stealing. Jesus didn't want us to have to pay for our sins, so He did. That's why He died."

Sam nodded. "Are you a sinner?"

"Yes."

"Do you believe that Jesus died and rose for you?"

"Yes."

"Then all you have to do to get saved is believe on Jesus and ask Him to save you."

Matthew jumped off his bed and knelt down beside it. "Dear Jesus, I want to get saved. In the Bible it says I have to believe. Even though I'm little, I understand and I believe. I want to go to Heaven someday. Please save me. Thank You, Jesus. Amen."

Matthew stood up and smiled at his dad. "I can sleep now, Daddy. Jesus is with me, and He will never ever leave me."

# Chapter 21

# FRIENDS FOR THE JOURNEY

O h, Sam, I'm not sure what else to do," Esther said plaintively. Though it was only the beginning of July, she had already begun packing.

"Esther honey, we've still got nine months," Sam soothed. He took her hand and led her to the couch. "Now, sit down for a few minutes and take a break. You're going to run yourself ragged." He sat down beside her and put his arm around her.

She relaxed. "You're right, Sam. I'm so excited about this trip, but I want to make sure we don't leave anything important behind. I also want to make clothes for the boys, and you could use some more as well. Also, what we don't need we should sell. It won't bring a lot of money, but it will help.

Some of our things I'd like to leave with my parents. Then…" She paused and pressed her hand to her forehead. "My, listen to me chatter along, and I haven't even asked how your planning is coming."

He smiled and began to softly rub her arm. "Well, I'd like to sell most of the stock and get four good horses for the wagon. We'll take my saddle horse Sunny and your horse Carmel."

"What about Dusty?" she asked.

"I haven't decided what to do with him. Dad said he would keep him so I won't have to sell him. I'd like to take him with me, but he's almost twenty-three years old. I don't know if he could stand the trip, but he might go crazy if we're separated. I'll pray about it."

At that moment, Monty came running into the living room. "Uncle Tom is here," he announced.

"Thank you, Montana," Sam said, rising from the couch. On the way out the door, Sam poked Monty in the ribs. The boy giggled and darted toward the kitchen. Sam chuckled and went outside.

"Hi, Sam." Tom had already dismounted and was tying his horse to the hitching post.

"Hi. What brings you out here at this time of the day? Normally you're foaming at the mouth, waiting for Carol to serve you supper," Sam joked.

"Right now I have something far more important than supper to discuss."

Sam leaned against the side of the house. "What might that be?" he asked.

Tom responded with a poem.

"Within my heart was a struggle:
Which way would I go?
Where fame and fortune were sure to be,
Or where I would really find peace for my soul.

One way offered worldly goods,
The other way was God's will.
I decided that money would fade away,
But God's reward for eternity never will.

So I took the way God chose,
Which, to be honest, I'm glad to do;
For deep down inside it's what I wanted,
Because I get to be with my friend so true."

Sam grinned. "I like it, but I have no idea what you're talking about."

"It's like this. You know how everybody wants me to get involved in politics? I've been praying about it, and I know that it would *not* be God's will. Frankly, I'm glad about it. Anyway, the Lord began to deal with me a year and a half ago about doing something else besides farming here in Indiana, but I wasn't sure what it was He wanted me to do. I think He was testing me to see if I was willing to be obedient. Now, however, I know beyond a shadow of a doubt." He looked Sam in the eye, and grinned. "Sammy, would you mind some company on your trip west?"

Sam snapped to attention. "Tom, do you mean it? Are you serious? You're coming with us when we leave? On the same wagon train?"

Tom shrugged. "Well, if you don't want us, we could always go on the next wagon train." He tried to pull off his joke, but he was so full of joy he could not do it. This is what they had talked about when only little boys playing under their favorite tree. They were going West.

"Can you believe this?" Tom said, as he gave Sam a brotherly hug.

"Oh, Tom, I can't. I had *hoped* that you and Carol might come with us, but..." Sam stopped, the tears streaming from his face. "Maybe we'll be mightily used of God out west. Come on, let's go tell Esther."

The two young couples had much work to do. They sold all the animals and possessions that they did not need. Sam and Tom tried to give the land back to their parents, but they refused. The elder Goodtons and Sampsons insisted the young men sell the land and use the money to help finance the trip. Tim Lard bought the land, agreeing to take possession after Sam and Tom had left.

"Sammy, what about your bear rug?" Mary asked one night. Sam, Esther, and the boys had eaten supper with Josh and Mary so that they could spend more time together.

Sam glanced toward the fireplace where the old rug lay. When he and Esther had moved into their house, they had decided to leave the rug with Sam's parents. Sam could hardly remember how the living room looked without the big rug. He still liked to lie on it and lean his back against the massive head. His boys loved it as well.

Sam pondered the question for a moment. Should he try to take it with him or leave it with his parents?

"I think it needs to stay with you and Dad," Sam finally said. "The house wouldn't look right without it. Besides, maybe out West we'll get us another one."

The boys' faces lit up with excitement.

"Could we help you make the rug, Dad?" Matthew asked.

"Sure, you all can."

August came and the yearly party for the boys was held. At six years, Matt was tall for his age and the image of his father in build. His hair was black like his mother's and he had his father's green eyes.

Mac, with blonde hair and grayish blue eyes, was at least an inch taller than his older twin. He was stocky, much like Esther's grandfather, while Mike, with his brown hair and brown eyes, favored Mary.

Montana looked like his mother in every aspect. They both had jet-black hair and soft green eyes.

Martin was built like his Uncle Tyler, but his face was a duplicate of Sam's. He had his father's fiery-red hair and deep green eyes. There was almost always a look of mischief about him. Esther lovingly called him "the Tornado," and he liked the title.

The next day Sam decided what should be done with Dusty, his trusted companion.

"We're going to take Dusty with us," he told the family. His sons cheered. Sam hardly rode the old brown horse anymore because he was afraid to work him too hard, but the boys spent many hours on him. He was perfect for them. "I decided," Sam continued, "that he would be much happier with us. Also, I found out that Tom's bringing Midnight. I don't think Dusty could stand being away from both me and Midnight."

"I think that's a good idea," Esther agreed.

"Dad, what're we going to do when we get to Montana?" Monty asked.

Sam was taken aback at the question. He realized that he had not shared his dreams with his sons. "Well, the Lord willing, I'm going to buy some land, and we will build a house and barn, corrals, and things like that. Then we'll get some cattle and horses and start building a real ranch. What do you think of that?"

"Sounds good to me," Monty said.

"Do you think we'll see any Indians on the way there?" MacShane asked, short of breath from a friendly tussle with his twin.

"Probably, Mac." The Indians along the route called the Bozeman Trail had been on the warpath. However, small clans of Sioux Indians had been talking of peace and had promised safe travel for those who would take a new trail, which had been named the Sioux Pass. Sam wondered how long these Indians would stay peaceful. The thought of his family being attacked by savages was one of his greatest fears. He was always able to calm his fears with Isaiah 41:13, "For I the LORD thy God will hold thy right hand, saying unto thee, Fear not; I will help thee."

It seemed as though Christmas was just a few days later. Everything happened so fast. The crops were harvested and all the stock sold. Sam and Tom each bought four good horses and a wagon. The things that they wanted to keep but could not take with them were carefully boxed up and taken over to their parents' houses. One day, if the railroad ever went out to Montana, those items would be sent out to the younger Goodtons and Sampsons via the iron horse.

Soon all that remained to be done was the buying and packing of the things they needed for the trip.

"Can I have everyone's attention?" Josh said. His booming voice silenced the talkative crowd at the Greys' house on a lovely Christmas day. All eyes turned on him. It was obvious he was trying to hold back a flood of tears. "As you all know, this will be the last time, at least for a couple of years, that we can all be together for Christmas. So, we want to make this a very special day. We'll start with games, and then we'll eat. After that we have some special presents to hand out, and we'll have a little family singing. Let's have both Tom and Sam pray for us to start our day."

The day was filled with joy. The games played both inside and outside were filled with friendly competition.

Mealtime was always a big thing at Christmas. There was hardly enough room on the table for all the food, enough to feed a crowd of people whose vigorous activity that morning had made all of them hungry. They had ham, roast beef, fried chicken, carrots, peas, potatoes and gravy, corn, green beans, casserole, and fresh homemade bread. For dessert they had homemade ice cream and four different types of pies: apple, pumpkin, cherry, and peach.

"It's time to read from the Bible," Joshua said. Everyone gathered in the living room. Josh handed Tom the family Bible, an heirloom Josh had given to Sam, that they still took turns reading from at Christmas time. Tom opened the old but precious Book.

"If it's alright," he began, "I'd like to read Luke 1:35-37 instead of Luke 2:1-14. There's something I'd like you to see." The others said that was fine.

"'And the angel answered and said unto her, The Holy Ghost shall come upon thee, and the power of the Highest shall overshadow thee: therefore also that holy thing which shall be born of thee shall be called the Son of God.

'And, behold, thy cousin Elisabeth, she hath also conceived a son in her old age: and this is the sixth month with her, who was called barren.

'For with God nothing shall be impossible.'

"Now," Tom said, "did you notice the phrase, '...who was called barren' at the end of verse thirty-six? Elizabeth was an old woman, and all those years she had never been able to have a child, but God chose to bless her, and in her old age she bore John the Baptist. I believe the Lord was trying to teach us a lesson in soul winning in this passage.

"Paul sometimes referred to those he had led to the Lord as his children. I Corinthians 4:15 says, 'For though ye have ten thousand instructers in Christ, yet have ye not many fathers: for in Christ Jesus I have begotten you through the gospel.'

"Many Christians today are spiritually barren: they are not leading people to the Lord. When I think of the word 'barren' I think of the word 'misery'." His voice quivered and he brushed a tear from his eye. He and Carol knew what it was like to be barren physically. "In First Samuel 1:11, Hannah was praying for a child. She considered it an *affliction* to be childless. Here is what she said. 'And she vowed a vow, and said, O LORD of hosts, if thou wilt indeed look on the affliction of thine handmaid, and remember me, and not forget thine handmaid, but wilt give unto thine handmaid a man child, then I will give him unto the LORD all the days of his life, and there shall no razor come upon his head.'

"If we would learn to weep and be heartbroken over spiritual barrenness, then we would see more people saved. In Proverbs thirty, God compares barrenness to the grave, a drought, and a raging fire. Verse fifteen says that they 'are never satisfied' and that they 'say not, It is enough.'

"Notice the word 'called' in our passage," Tom said, looking down at the Bible. "That means that everyone knew Elizabeth was barren. We could say she was 'marked'.

"When people are marked with barrenness several things can happen. We learn from Sarah that you turn to foolish things. Rachel and Jacob fought because Rachel was barren, and Hannah forfeited her rightful place when she was barren. As Christians, we will face these things if we stop winning people to God. We won't lose our salvation, but God's hand of blessing will no longer be upon us.

"Best of all, I like the word right before 'called.' It is the word 'was.' That's the 'miracle'. God worked a miracle in Elizabeth's life and she had a child. Now she cannot be called barren. God can work a miracle in our lives and help us to lead others to the Lord.

"There are three steps to bearing spiritual children. First, beg God to help you. That is what Hannah did, and God honored her request.

"Second, get someone to pray for you. Genesis 25:21 says, 'And Isaac intreated the LORD for his wife, because she was barren: and the LORD was intreated of him, and Rebekah his wife conceived.'

"Third, tell everyone you meet about the blessed Lord Jesus and how He will save their soul. We learn that from the lives of Abraham and Sarah. They went for years and years without having a child. Then one day God told them He would give them a son, but it didn't happen right away. Though it seemed that God was not going to do what He said, Abraham trusted God. They just kept on trying and God did exactly what He said He would do.

"God often took a barren woman, worked a miracle, and gave her a son that changed the course of history. Abraham's wife bore Isaac, the promised son. Isaac's wife bore Jacob, the progenitor of the twelve tribes of Israel. Jacob's wife bore Joseph, the provider for Israel. Elkanah's wife bore Samuel, the prophet of Israel. Manoah's wife bore Samson, the protector of Israel. Zacharias' wife bore John the Baptist, the preacher and the man who prepared the way for the Lord Jesus Christ.

"Pray for yourself, ask others to pray for you, keep on telling, and I am done."

The others sat in silence, contemplating what they had heard. It stirred their hearts, and they knelt to beg forgiveness for their spiritual barrenness.

After spending some time in prayer, they prepared to hand out presents. The family asked if they could hand out their special gifts for the younger Goodtons and Sampsons last. Neither couple minded. Twenty minutes later, Joel turned to Sam and Tom.

"We wondered what we could get you two that would be practical and helpful on your journey. We hope these will do." Joel and Josh stood up and went to the closet, opened the door, and pulled out two Winchester rifles of the best make and design. Sam and Tom had never owned such fine rifles.

"Thank you, Mom and Dad," Sam said hugging his parents. Tom did the same. The young men knew that these weapons would be used a great deal. After the couples had expressed their thanks, Mr. Maker stepped forward.

"We, Josh and Mary, Joel and Virginia, Henry and Susie, Lisa and I, got together and decided that the Goodtons and Sampsons would buy gifts for Tom and Sam, and the Greys and us would buy something for Esther and Carol." With the help of Josh and Joel, Mr. Maker and Mr. Grey carried in two large but lightweight trunks. They were exactly what the young couples needed to carry their clothes.

"Oh Dad, Mom, they are perfect," Carol cried as she and Esther embraced their parents.

"Yes, they are," Esther agreed.

Tyler spoke up. "C and I had no idea what to get you," he said, looking first at Sam and then at Tom. "Then Dad solved our problem. It's not a normal Christmas present," Ty grinned, "but I think you'll use it." He handed each of them a large sack tied with green ribbon. The sacks were filled with shells for the rifles. The others laughed.

"Thanks, Tyler and Cecilia," Sam said, still chuckling.

"Yes, thank you. A gun's no good without ammunition," Tom added with a grin.

"Now we have gifts for our little boys," Mary said smiling affectionately at her five grandsons. The boys' faces beamed back at her.

"We're going to give you boys things that will remind you of us and our love. We'll start with the youngest," Mary continued. "Here you are, Martin." She handed him a box wrapped in tissue paper. The three year old tore off the paper and shouted happily when he saw the belt-buckle that his grandfather always wore when he worked. It was made of brass, and engraved on it was a deer bounding over a fence. Martin loved to hold and play with it.

"Thank you!" he said emphatically and bounded over to hug them. Then Grandma Maker handed him their gift. It was the bright red neckerchief that belonged to his Grandpa Maker. Marty had always wanted one. "Thank you!" he cried again, and punctuated his words with hugs.

"You're welcome," they replied.

"Montana," Mrs. Maker said, "I wasn't sure what you would like. Then I remembered this." She handed him a box. Inside was the heavy quilt blanket that Monty always slept with when he stayed at their house. For some reason, that quilt was his favorite, and no other blanket would do. From his other grandparents he received a small statue of a rearing horse that belonged to his Grandpa Goodton. Montana was elated as he hugged his grandparents.

"This is for you, MacShane," Mary said. He quickly opened his present and smiled when he saw his grandpa's old pocketknife. When Josh and Mac had worked outside together, Josh let him hold the knife until he needed it. Though he was only five, Mac knew better than to play with knives and promised that he would be very careful with it.

"While you're working at your ranch out West, you might want to wear this," Mr. Maker said. He reached behind the couch, picked up his hat, and handed it to Mac. The boy was speechless with delight. His thanks were manifested in big bear hugs.

"Mike, I know you like this picture," Lisa Maker said. "So I think you ought to have it." She gave him the pencil drawing of a mule pulling a plow. Mike's excitement was doubled when Mary gave him the book that he loved to have read to him, *The Sweet Psalmist*. He hugged both sets of grandparents.

"Matthew," Josh began, "I want you to have this." He handed Matt the fancy silver pocket watch that his oldest grandson had always admired.

"Grandpa, I can't take your special watch," Matt said, knowing how much his grandpa liked the watch and how expensive it was.

"Yes, you can. I want you to have it as a reminder of the good times we had together."

"Thank you, Grandpa," Matt whispered, his eyes brimming with tears.

"You're quite welcome, Matt."

"This is from us," Lisa said. Matthew grinned when he opened the package containing his grandfather's spurs.

"Thank you," he said, hugging them all.

"This is for all five of you," Cecilia said. She and Tyler handed them a brand new saddle. It was made for a child and was the perfect size for them. They were thrilled.

There were more gifts of blankets, clothing, tools, dried food, spare harnesses, and other necessities.

Then, after singing for an hour, the families went home.

*Chapter 22*

# SAYING THEIR FAREWELLS

---

I t was the first of March and pleasantly warm. All the preparations had been made and all that remained was the waiting.

Tyler was so engrossed in his work that he did not hear Sam ride in.

"Hey, Ty," Sam said, still sitting on his horse. His brother looked up at him and grinned.

"Didn't hear you ride in. What are you up to?"

"Nothing much. I just wondered if you'd like to go fishing. It's a great day for it. What do you think?" Sam asked.

"Fishing? Sammy, are you sure you got time for fishing?"

"I do."

It dawned on Tyler that what Sam really wanted was for the two of them to spend some time together.

"Sure, I'll go fishing with you. Give me a minute to tell Cecilia and get my horse." Five minutes later they were headed for their favorite fishing spot.

After baiting their lines, they settled down to wait for the fish. All was quiet for a few minutes. Only the sound of flowing water, birds, and the splash of an occasional fish jumping could be heard. Then Sam spoke, "I sure am going to miss you, Tyler."

Ty looked down at his pole and then up at Sam. "Same here." He choked back some tears. "When I think of the years I wasted, it tears me apart. I could have spent all that time with my family, and I used up those precious days on wicked things. I, I'm so sorry, Sam."

"I'm glad you got saved and came home. Just think how God was able to turn that situation around. You know, if a person will get right with God, He can take their past failures and bring honor and glory to Himself. God did that with Bathsheba. She committed adultery and God punished her, but she got right and she taught her son Solomon how to find a virtuous woman. It says in Proverbs 31:1, 'The words of king Lemuel, the prophecy that his mother taught him.' I believe Lemuel was Bathsheba's pet name for Solomon. This chapter teaches us about the virtuous woman, and it says that Bathsheba taught these things to Solomon. Many lives have been rescued and changed because of the truths taught in that chapter," Sam said.

"I see what you're saying," Tyler said. "After I got saved and started serving God, the crew got saved and God gave me a wonderful wife. He turned that whole situation around for good."

"Exactly! Now, never in a million years would I encourage anyone to sin. However, if you find that you've strayed from God, come back to Him and He will help you." Sam smiled as he thought of how God had helped his family down through the years. "He sure is a good God."

"Yes, He is," Ty agreed. Once again silence settled over the little stream. This time it was Tyler who broke that stillness.

"Sam, did Dad tell you about the letter I got from Mr. Dunningham yesterday?"

"No, I didn't see Dad yesterday. What did it say?"

"Well, as you know, his manufacturing business is really booming. God has blessed him, and he's thinking about starting up an extension of his business in Clear Water."

"Really?" Sam asked.

"Yeah, and he wants me to be the manager," Ty said happily.

"That's great, Ty!" Sam exclaimed.

"I know. It is a wonderful opportunity. Who knows, maybe in a couple years I could start a business of my own, one I can leave to my children." Tyler's whole countenance brightened. "I've prayed about it, and I believe it's God's will."

"It sounds great!" Sam said again. Then he realized that Tyler had said "children" and not "child". "Tyler, is Cecilia…?"

Ty grinned. "I told Father, and I thought he had told you. Yes, we're going to have another baby."

"Wonderful! Have you picked out any names yet?"

"Yes. If it's a girl we'll call her Clarissa Marie. If it's a boy we thought about Archibald Samuel, if you don't mind."

"Of course I don't mind."

"Thanks. Since your middle name is Joshua and so is Matthew's, we thought it might get confusing if three people in our family had the middle name Joshua. So we decided on Archibald, after C's dad, and Samuel, after you."

They talked and prayed most of the afternoon. Around five they decided to go home. Pulling in their lines, they were shocked to see that their bait was gone.

"How do you like that?" Sam showed Tyler the wormless hook. "We've been robbed!" he said, trying to hold back his laughter. "This calls for some serious fishing. No fish does that to me."

The brothers baited their hooks again and cast them into the water. When they left they had three fish apiece.

Ten days after Sam and Ty's fishing trip, the church held a farewell party for Sam and Tom and their families.

"We are gathered tonight to say our goodbyes to Sam and Esther and the boys, and to Tom and Carol," Terry Carson said as the service began. "Well, it's really not 'goodbye'. 'So long' would be a better term. For those of us who have trusted Christ as our Saviour, there is coming a day when we will all be together in Heaven for eternity. Until that day, we wanted them to know that we love them, we'll miss them, and most importantly, that we'll pray for them. Let's begin the service. Luke Neils, will you pray for us?"

After Luke prayed, Terry asked the two young couples and their families if they would sing. When their song was through, Terry opened his Bible to Genesis 32:1-2. "Is everyone there? Alright, let's read. 'And Jacob went on his way, and the angels of God met him.

'And when Jacob saw them, he said, This is God's host: and he called the name of that place Mahanaim.'

"You all know what has happened previous to this chapter," Terry said. "Jacob stole his brother's blessing and had to flee for his life. He went to his uncle Laben's house and abode there many years. Now God has told him to go back to his father's house. So, he gathers together his family, servants, and flocks and he is heading home. He knows that sooner or later he is going to have to meet Esau, his brother. Verse six says, 'And the messengers returned to Jacob, saying, We came to thy brother Esau, and also he cometh to meet thee, and four hundred men with him.'

"Get this picture in your mind," Terry continued. "Here's Jacob with his little helpless caravan. He thinks that Esau is bent on killing him. We find out later that Esau had forgiven Jacob, but Jacob doesn't know that yet. Let me remind you of something. Esau was a wicked man yet he forgave his brother. You and I, as born again children of God, ought to be willing to forgive.

"Can you imagine," he continued, returning to the message, "how scared Jacob must be? I can imagine him constantly looking all around, wondering if Esau was waiting just over that next rise. However, God wants Jacob to know that He is with him. I like what it says in the latter part of verse one, '...and the angels of God met him.'

"Who are these angels? These are not beings that we should worship. They have two purposes. One is to honor and glorify God, and the other is to minister to those that are saved. Hebrews 1:14 asks, 'Are they not all ministering spirits, sent forth to minister for them who shall be heirs of salvation?'

"Now that we know who these angels are, I'd like to show you what they can do. In II Kings nineteen we see that the Assyrians have God's people surrounded. The King of Israel prays and God sends one angel to wipe out the enemy. Verse thirty-five says, 'And it came to pass that night, that the angel of the LORD went out, and smote in the camp of the Assyrians an hundred fourscore and five thousand: and when they arose early in the morning, behold, they were all dead corpses.'

"One angel, just one, was able to defeat the enemy. Imagine what a troop of angels can do," Terry said in wonderment.

"Those angels that came to Jacob represented and were the help of God. God was saying, 'You're not in this alone, Jacob. I will be with thee.'

"I want to preach to you tonight on, 'The Help of the Lord.' My first point is that the help of the Lord will meet you on the dusty roads of common life. No matter what the situation is, God cares, and He will help you if you'll trust in Him.

"My second point is that the help of the Lord will meet you at the right time. We see this illustrated in the lives of Lazarus and his two sisters. In the eleventh chapter of John, Lazarus is sick. His sisters sent for Jesus to come heal him, but Jesus tarried and didn't come immediately. While Jesus tarried, Lazarus died. After he had been dead four days, Jesus finally came. Mary and Martha, Lazarus' two sisters, cannot understand why Jesus did not come right away, but Jesus planned to raise their brother from the dead. In waiting, He was able to show them a greater miracle than they had expected. God is not on the same time schedule as you are. Be patient and wait on the Lord.

"Point three is that the help of the Lord will come in the exact shape that you need. When Elijah was hiding from Jezebel, the last thing he needed was a host of angels arrayed for battle. It would have scared him to death. So the Lord came to him in a still small voice. I Kings 19:12, 'And after the earthquake a fire; but the LORD was not in the fire: and after the fire a still small voice.'

"When Joshua was at Jericho, he needed a warrior with a battle plan. The help of the Lord came to him in Joshua 5:13-14, 'And it came to pass, when Joshua was by Jericho, that he lifted up his eyes and looked, and, behold, there stood a man over against him with his sword drawn in his hand: and Joshua went unto him, and said unto him, Art thou for us, or for our adversaries?

'And he said, Nay; but as captain of the host of the LORD am I now come. And Joshua fell on his face to the earth, and did worship, and said unto him, What saith my lord unto his servant?'

"Over in the New Testament we find John exiled on the Isle of Patmos. What he needed was companionship. In Revelation 1:9-11 he found it. 'I John, who also am your brother, and companion in tribulation, and in the kingdom and patience of Jesus Christ, was in the isle that is called Patmos, for the word of God, and for the testimony of Jesus Christ.

'I was in the Spirit on the Lord's day, and heard behind me a great voice, as of a trumpet,

'Saying, I am Alpha and Omega, the first and the last: and, What thou seest, write in a book, and send it unto the seven churches which are in Asia; unto Ephesus, and unto Smyrna, and unto Pergamos, and unto Thyatira, and unto Sardis, and unto Philadelphia, and unto Laodicea.'

"When John was alone and needed someone to talk to, God Himself came to him and communed with him. We could go on and on, but all I'm trying to show you is that the help of the Lord will come in whatever shape you need."

"Finally, the help of the Lord in your life will leave a legacy that will help someone else down the road. Jacob named this place Mahanaim, a word that means 'two camps'. Turn with me, if you will, to II Samuel 17:24. The Bible says, 'Then David came to Mahanaim. And Absalom passed over Jordan, he and all the men of Israel with him.' When David needed a place to hide from his son who was trying to kill him and take away the kingdom, he went to Mahanaim. Could it be that he remembered hearing how God had helped Jacob here? David says in Psalms 22:4, 'Our fathers trusted in thee: they trusted, and thou didst deliver them.'

"Have you ever considered that God may use your trials to help someone else who is struggling?" Terry asked, closing his Bible. As he looked out over the congregation, his eyes rested on Sam and Tom. He spoke directly to them. "You are about to set off on a very long journey. Both of you are doing what you know is the Lord's will. When the trials come, remember that the help of the Lord is coming and God may use your problems to help another person." Then he spoke to the congregation. "These truths apply to all that are saved and trying to serve God. Let's ask God to help us trust in Him, no matter what the situation. Let's pray."

After the sermon, the congregation surprised Sam and Tom and their families by taking up an offering for them. The two couples knew how blessed they were to have such a wonderful church family.

After the service, refreshments were served.

"Know what this reminds me of?" Sam whispered to Tom as they found a place to sit.

"The farewell party we had for Todd and his family," Tom answered quietly.

"Yep. Never thought that there would be one for us."

"Me neither," Tom said, his gaze sweeping over all their friends. "It all seems like a dream."

Later that night, after the boys had been put to sleep, Esther and Sam decided to stay up and talk. Coffee cups in hand, they sat down in the living room.

"That sure was nice of the church to have a party for us and to give us that money," Sam said. Esther nodded, and Sam noticed that something seemed to be bothering her. "Esther honey, are you all right?" he asked. Tears welled in her green eyes and spilled down her cheeks. Her husband sat down his cup and held her tenderly. She wept on his shoulder.

"Oh, Sam," she cried, "I'm sorry. It's just all hitting me right now. The trip will be so long and dangerous. I fear that Montana may get ill on the way, and I'll have no way to care for him. Then, I'm going to miss my parents so much."

Sam held her lovingly. He realized how much of a strain all this had been on Esther. She had been so supportive of him all this time, always there for him. Not only that, but she was there to soothe her children's anxiety. She was so willing to give of herself and to bear the burdens of others. Now she needed someone to help lift her up.

Esther finally sat up and began to dry her eyes. "I'm sorry," she said again, looking away to hide her tears. Sam cupped her trembling chin in his hand and turned her face until she was looking at him. He kissed her.

"No need to be sorry," he said gently. "This has been hard on you, hasn't it?"

She smiled. "No, not really. I want to do this, and I know this is God's will. He will give me the grace to make it. Still, every once in awhile I get a little overwhelmed. When we women get overwhelmed, we tend to cry a bit," she informed him with a shaky laugh. "I'll be all right." She leaned against him.

"Just think," she said, "in a few days we'll start on our adventure. I often wonder what it will be like. I often dream of the place where we will live. I wonder what our house will look like and what kind of friends we will make, but most importantly I wonder who we will be able to witness to."

Sam smiled and laid his cheek against the top of her head. He knew he was blessed to have a wife like Esther. She loved God with all her heart, and she loved Sam and the boys. Her desire was to see their family serving the Lord in whatever area that He wished them to serve.

"I wonder those things, too. One thing's for sure, it won't be dull," Sam said. Esther nodded in agreement. Sam took her hand and looked into her eyes. "Esther, I want you to know that I think you're the greatest wife a man could ever have. You have such a giving spirit and loving attitude, and I know that you long to serve the Lord. In fact, do you know when God began to really draw me to you?"

"No, when?"

"It all started that day when Tom and I helped you carry those things you had brought for the Greys' little girls. You did everything you could to help those Indian girls. I saw people who said they were Carol's friends turn away from her when their family adopted Melissa and her sisters, but not you. You accepted them and welcomed them with true Christian love. That's one of the things that drew me to you." He grinned then said, "It did help a lot that you were the prettiest girl I had ever seen." They both chuckled. "I want you to know that I love you, and if you ever feel 'overwhelmed,' remember that I'm here for you." He kissed her again.

# Chapter 23

# WESTERN HORIZON

The normally quiet town of Clear Water now seemed to be exploding with life. It was the day before the wagon train was to leave, and people had come from miles around to send off family and friends.

"Look at all the people, Tommy!" Mac exclaimed, using his twin's middle name. He peeked out of the back of the wagon. The Goodtons, Makers, Greys, and Sampsons had just arrived at the bustling town.

"Wow, Tyler!" Mike's wondering eyes expressed the words better than his vocal chords.

"I didn't think this many people could fit in Clear Water," Matt said.

"We could get lost easily," Montana observed.

"That's why everyone stays in the wagon, right?" Sam asked.

"Right," five little voices chorused.

Luke Neils had told the group that they could stay in his large house for the evening. He and his wife would sleep in the print shop that he now owned.

After getting their families comfortably settled, Sam and Tom went to make sure everything was fixed with the wagon master and the people financing the trip. Josh, Joel, and Tyler went with them.

"My, this is quite a sight," Tom said, looking all around him. The others agreed. Everywhere folks were laughing, talking, and passing out gifts and advice. Strangers who were going to make the long trip together were getting acquainted and lending each other a helping hand. The air was filled with adventure, and everyone was busy. Some men were checking their harnesses and wagons while others were studying a large map. Women hurried about gathering last minute items, except for one lady who declared she was going to have her "last cup of social tea." Children and teenagers scurried about, some causing mayhem, others saying tear-filled goodbyes, and still others, with an air of seriousness about them, seeking to purchase some needed article.

Talk of the trip was mentioned in all the conversations. Some people boasted of their abilities as pioneers, some spoke of it in terrified whispers, and some were praying for strength. It was indeed an unforgettable sight.

The five men made their way to a makeshift building with the sign "Wagon Train Headquarters" hanging above the entrance. Since it was already filled to near capacity, Sam and Tom were the only ones of their group to go inside. After waiting in line for twenty minutes, they finally reached the desk. An older man with blue eyes and a radiant smile greeted them.

"Good day, my friends, and didn't the Lord send us a fine one. I was fearful that perhaps the day might be filled with rain or snow, but the Lord spoke to my heart, and said, 'Never fear, Jim. Just turn all your cares to Me and I'll take care of you.' My friend, He did, and I feel right sick that I spent all that time worrying."

Sam and Tom laughed along with the friendly man. They were glad that he was willing to share with them the blessing that God had given to him. It helped ease their fears.

"By the way, my name is Jim Pryce. What can I do for you gentlemen?" the man behind the desk asked.

"Do you know Luke Carson?" Tom asked. Sam glanced at his friend, bewildered. What did their pastor have to do with the wagon train or this man?

"Yes, I do," Brother Pryce said. "Luke and I have been friends for years. We've preached together more times than I can count. Are you boys members of his church?"

"Yes sir," Sam said, now remembering that their pastor had often spoke of his good friend, Jim Pryce.

"Glad to hear it. Another good friend of mine is financing this trip, and he asked me if I'd come and see the train off. I told him I'd be glad to. When I got here, I found out that he needed a man to work this desk, so I volunteered."

"We sure are honored to meet you. Our pastor speaks highly of you. I'm Tom Sampson and this is my partner, Sam Goodton. We should be registered in that book you have on the desk."

Brother Pryce shook hands with them and checked the large book in front of him. "It's a pleasure to meet you young men and, yes, you are in here. You have been assigned the positions of sixth and seventh place in the train. Here are the papers you need. There will be a meeting at five for the men, and the wagon master will speak to you. Then at eight there will be a time of prayer for the whole family."

"Thank you, sir," Sam and Tom said.

At five sharp, Ricky Daniels addressed the group of men seated before him. He was a tall man with a reserved demeanor, but he spoke with a sureness gained from experience.

"Men, I won't lie to you and say that this trip will be easy. It will be nothing of the sort. Who knows what obstacles we'll have to overcome. There will be mountains and flooded rivers to cross. We may face hunger, thirst, heat, and storms, but I can promise you one thing. I promise that I will seek the Lord's will and do what I believe is best for the train. You won't wake up one morning and find me gone. I promise to stay with you all.

"One more thing. I've guided many trains out West, and I've seen this problem over and over. People are not willing to lend their neighbor a hand. If we're going to make it, we need to be ready to help others. If someone needs water, let them have some of yours. If they're sick, fix them a meal or help with their stock. There's no room for stingy people. Do you understand me?"

The men all nodded in agreement.

"Thank you. Okay, we will leave at 8:00 tomorrow morning. Once on the trail, we'll be leaving earlier, but I want to give you time to say goodbye to your families and friends and to get anything you might need. I suggest that you go over your supplies carefully and make sure you're lacking in nothing. That will be all for now. Be sure to come to the prayer service tonight."

All the families did gather for a time of prayer. Not all the folks traveling were Christians, but all came—some out of need and desire, others out of curiosity.

"Folks," Brother Pryce began, "we've come tonight to pray for safety on the upcoming trip. If you are going to make it on this trip, you are going to have to have God's help. The Bible says in Matthew 7:7-8, 'Ask, and it shall be given you; seek, and ye shall find; knock, and it shall be opened unto you:

'For every one that asketh receiveth; and he that seeketh findeth; and to him that knocketh it shall be opened.'

"Folks, those verses are written to those that are saved. If you are lost, I beg you to give your life to the blessed Redeemer. It is not a hard thing to do. Just recognize that you are a sinner and that Jesus is the Saviour. Then ask Him to save you. John 6:37 says, 'All that the Father giveth me shall come to me; and him that cometh to me I will in no wise cast out.'

"Now, for those of you that are His children, it is time to pray and publicly show our need for God."

As the folks knelt down on the grass, Brother Pryce began to pray. "Dear Lord, we come to You tonight on behalf of these precious people. They are about to embark on a dangerous journey and they need Your help. The truth of the matter is, we need You for every second of our lives. I pray, Lord, that

You would put Your hand of protection upon this wagon train and the people in it. May You guide Ricky Daniels and give him the wisdom that he needs. Please supply their every need, whether it is food, water, medicine, whatever it may be. Please keep these folks safe from natural disaster and from attacks from Indians or white men. Help them as they scale mountains, cross the plains, and ford rough waters. Lord, I pray that if anyone on this train is lost, that they will get saved before it is eternally too late. We thank You for all that You have done and what You are going to do. In Your most precious and holy name I pray. Amen."

A few left as soon as Brother Pryce was finished, but the majority stayed. Weeping, with their faces buried in the grass, they begged the Gracious Almighty to be with them on their perilous journey.

Near midnight the Goodtons and Sampsons and their families and friends finally went back to the Neils' house.

Early the next morning Sam and Tom got their horses hitched up and finished packing the wagon. Then came the goodbyes.

"Well, Ty, I guess this is goodbye for now," Sam said, tears streaming down his cheeks. "I sure am going to miss you, little brother." They hugged and Sam silently thanked God that He had brought his brother back to their family.

"Me too, Sammy," Tyler said, brushing back his tears. "Thanks for everything."

Sam nodded and then hugged Cecilia. "Keep him out of trouble will you, C?"

Cecilia, choking back tears, said, "I sure will try, but you know Tyler."

"Yes, I do." Sam picked up Ellen and swung her in the air. "Goodbye, Ellen, and be good, and farewell to you, little one on the way."

Sam turned to the Grey family. "Brother and Sister Grey, take care. It's been such a pleasure to have you as part of the family. Leah, Tiffany, keep on serving the Lord," he admonished.

"Yes, sir. We'll pray for you," Leah said.

"Yes, we will," Tiffany told him. Then the Greys went to say goodbye to their daughter and son-in-law.

The Makers were tearfully embracing their daughter. Esther was wrapped in her mother's arms, and Mr. Maker was hugging them both.

"Sam," he said, trying to smile, "take care. You've got some mighty precious people traveling with you."

"With the Lord's help, I will," promised Sam, his voice deep with emotion. "Thank you, Mr. and Mrs. Maker, for allowing me to marry your daughter."

"We've been blessed to have such a fine son-in-law. You've been just like a son to us," Mrs. Maker said. Her husband nodded in agreement.

"I love you both very much." He then turned to say goodbye to Joel and Virginia.

"Uncle Joel, Aunt Virginia, thank you for all you've done for me." Sam hugged Virginia and shook Joel's hand.

"Like the Makers said, you've been just like a son to us," Joel said.

"Yes," Virginia said, smiling lovingly at him.

"I think myself blessed to have had such fine people to look up to," Sam told them.

It was now time for him to say goodbye to his father and mother. He pulled his mother close to him and hugged her. He could hear her whispering prayers for him and his family.

After Sam and Mary had hugged for about five minutes, Sam reluctantly let her go. With tears flowing freely down his face, he and his father embraced.

"We sure are going to miss you, Sammy boy." It was all Josh could do to get the words out, he was crying so hard. "Son," he continued, "I want you to know something. Out there in the West, you may come across some thing that can't be licked.

The Lord in His infinite wisdom may see fit to send you and your family a very hard trial. Your mother and I want you to understand that if the time ever comes where you feel you can't go on, our home is always here for you. Don't think that because you're making this trip our house will no longer be open to you if you need it. If it's God's will for you to come back and start all over again, we'll do our best to help you."

Sam's tears began to fall afresh. He had such wonderful parents. He had always known that if he ever needed them for anything they would always try to help. They were so godly, giving, forgiving, and obedient to God's will. Sam hugged them both again.

The time came for everyone to get in the wagon. Sam helped Esther up into her seat, and then lifted four of the boys into the back. Matthew was going to ride Dusty.

Sam got in his seat and headed his team to his assigned spot. As he rode, he let his eyes sweep over the town he knew so well. Memories flooded his mind. Beside his wagon was the corral where they had first seen Midnight. To the left was the field where he and Tom had beat the Bensen brothers in the three-legged race. The church was just beyond that, and beside it was the place where they had always had their Sunday afternoon picnics. To his left was the spot where the horse race had begun, and on down the road was the place where the finish line had been drawn in the dirt. Around the corner was Luke's print shop, and beside that stood the sheriff's office. Then they passed the tree where Sam had proposed to Esther and the place where they were married.

Then he began to see not places, but people. There were the Bensen boys. They ran a general store together.

Sam saw Brother and Sister Carson. They were both old and feeble and rarely came out of their comfortable home, but on this special day they had come out to give their blessing and support to the wagon train. Right beside them stood Terry and Abby Carson, their two girls close by.

Sheriff Maren and his family were waving at them and the Goodtons waved back.

Sam saw Luke and his wife and Tim with his fiancé. Beside them stood both Jones families.

The Pitts were there as well. The two oldest girls were married and serving the Lord as missionaries on a foreign field. The youngest was engaged to a pastor from Delaware.

There were so many more, many who had somehow been associated with Sam and Tom.

Sam looked at Esther and saw that she, too, was surveying the crowd and looking at familiar people and places. He took her small hand in his big one and squeezed it gently. She smiled and squeezed back.

"Are you ready, Esther?" he asked.

"Yes."

"Are you sure?"

"Yes, Sam, I am ready." She kissed him.

After everyone was in line, Jim Pryce was called on to pray one last time. Then the train began to move. Josh, Joel, Ty, Mr. Maker, and Mr. Grey were going to ride a mile with the train. All too soon that mile ended.

"Goodbye, Sam, Esther, and boys," Joshua said, his horse galloping alongside the wagon. "I reckon it won't be too long before the railroad extends to Montana. When it does, maybe we can plan a few trips to visit you. Until then, or the Second Coming of Christ, we'll be praying for you." He waved goodbye, his eyes brimming with tears. He turned his horse and headed back to town. The others did the same.

"Goodbye, Dad," Sam called. "I love you!"

For the first time in his life, Sam felt alone. His heart ached at the memory of the last sight of his mother and the sight of his father and brother disappearing from view.

Then he remembered that he was not alone. He had God living in him. He had Esther, the boys, Tom, and Carol. He looked back at Tom and their eyes met. Tom brushed away a tear and nodded to his friend. Sam nodded back. They were all in this together, and with the Lord's help they would follow the pull that was leading them toward the western horizon.

*Chapter 24*

# THE FIRST OBSTACLE

They had been on the trail only four days when they came to the first major problem.

They heard the rushing water long before they could see it. When they saw it, their hearts filled with fear. The river was flooded, fed by the melted snow. White water surged downstream and took no pity on anything that stood in its way.

"Folks, this river is called 'Last Chance' by the pioneers," their wagon master said. "Up until now we've had it easy, and there was always a chance to turn back. This river, though, is the test to see how many of you are really serious. Those that plan to turn and run at the slightest problem should not even attempt to cross it." He was blunt but compassionate. "If you don't think you can make it, you just head on back until you're truly ready for this trip. Nothing bad will be said about you."

Daniels sat tall and straight on the back of a big chestnut called Charlie. Charlie was a half Arabian, half Quarter Horse stallion with one white sock on his left hind leg. All of sixteen hands high and powerful, he loved taking his place at the front of the train or cantering ahead to scout the trail.

Beside Charlie, panting from his long run, sat a black wolf-dog, Rocky. Ricky Daniels and some others had been scouting around in the Rockies when they came upon a male wolf that had paired off with a female German Shepherd. In panic, Daniels' associates fired, killing the male, female, and all but one of the pups. Daniels had stopped them before they shot Rocky. He rescued the pup, intending to one day release it into the wild; but Rocky had developed a love and devotion for Ricky and a close companionship with Charlie. The three were inseparable.

The moment when Duke and Rocky met had been interesting. Duke, younger and bigger than the wolf dog, saw Rocky as a threat to his family. Rocky had the knowledge, the skill, and the instincts of a wolf; Duke was invading his territory. With teeth bared and heads down, they began to circle each other, snarling and growling. Only sharp commands from their masters had stopped them from attacking each other.

"Fine dog you got there," Daniels said, riding up beside the Goodtons' wagon.

"You too, Mr. Daniels," Sam answered with his hand tightly closed over Duke's collar. "Think they'll learn to get along before the end of the trip?" he asked, grinning.

"Maybe, but as long as they don't tear each other apart, I'll be happy," he said, amusement filling his face at Rocky's dislike for the other dog. "Come on, Rocky." Daniels wheeled Charlie around and galloped back to the front of the line.

The first four days had passed without an incident between the two dogs. Though they were by no means friends, at least they no longer growled every time they saw each other. Now, as the pioneers prepared to ford "Last Chance," dogs were the farthest thing from their minds.

"Matthew," Sam called. When the boy came, his father said, "Tie up Sunny and Carmel to the back of the wagon like I showed you. We'll let Dusty cross at his own pace. Esther, please get the boys settled in the wagon."

"Yes, Sam," Esther said, getting up from her seat and going to the back of the wagon.

"Hey, Sam!" Tom called. "We'll take the twins if you want."

"That would be a good idea. Thank you." He took Mike and Mac and got them settled in Tom's wagon. "It's going to be all right," he reassured them. "You just pray and sit tight. We'll meet you on the other side."

"Okay, Daddy," they said in unison. Sam smiled and patted their hands. He knew that they would not be too scared as long as they were together.

"I tied up the stock, Dad," Matthew said.

"Good boy. Now get in the wagon and keep Monty and Martin still."

"What about Duke?" Esther asked, once again sitting in the front of the wagon.

"He'll be all right. He and Dusty and Midnight are crossing together."

After making sure everything was secured, Sam climbed into his seat. He took the reins in his hands and waited. The five wagons ahead of him passed. Then it was his turn. The two families had already prayed together, but Sam whispered another prayer as he headed his team into the water.

The train had found a relatively safe place to cross where the white water was not as rough. Still, the wagon shook violently at the first impact. The horses shied in fear but, knowing they could trust their master, plunged ahead. Sam had never been so scared. One of the horses could stumble at any moment and cause the whole team to fall. They could be stranded in the middle of the river or hurled into its foaming path, but the horses did not stumble. They pressed on, soon reaching the middle of the river, the most dangerous spot. The water was almost up to the horses' chest, and it leapt greedily at the wagon bed. The horses stopped, afraid to go any farther.

"Come on, Bill, Sally, pull!" Sam encouraged them over the roar of the river. "Hup, Kate, Red, hup! Come on, let's go!"

Bill, the lead horse, put out one foot cautiously. Sally, beside him, did the same. Then they lowered their heads and began to pull. Kate and Red followed, and soon they were on the other side.

Sam jumped off and untied the two horses that were behind the wagon. Out of the corner of his eye he saw Dusty, Midnight, and Duke safely make it to shore. "Matthew, go check on Dusty and the other two," he instructed.

"Yes, sir," Matt said as he jumped down and ran over to the three animals.

Sam turned his attention to Tom and his wagon. Esther came and stood beside him, and he grasped her trembling hand. What if…? No, they could not even think about the "what ifs." Instead they prayed. Tom and his crew made it safely to shore.

The danger was not over yet. Six more wagons had to cross. All went well until the last wagon, carrying the Tad family, reached the middle. The horses balked and reared, tipping the wagon and throwing the man, his wife, and their two little girls into the water. Amazingly, the wagon righted itself, and the horses made for the shore.

Ricky Daniels dove into the water and swam out to the family. Sam and Tom were right behind him. The father had managed to get a hold of his wife and was pulling her to shore. Tom swam over to assist him. Ricky allowed the current to carry him to the youngest girl, and Sam went for the oldest. She went under before Sam reached her. Sam dove and felt around blindly. When his hands brushed something soft, he hauled it to the surface. To his relief, it was the girl. Cupping her chin in his hand, he started swimming toward shore, but he had just passed the middle when he felt his strength began to fail. Just when he thought he could not make it, he heard Matt yell, "Dad, the rope!" Lifting his head, Sam saw Duke swimming toward him with a rope in his mouth. Giving a powerful kick, Sam reached his dog and tied the line around the girl's waist. By that time some men on shore had gathered around Matthew and were helping him haul the swimmers in. Sam, holding the girl afloat with one hand and grasping the rope with the other, was pulled to shore. As his feet finally touched solid ground, his first thoughts were for the others. Struggling to his feet, he looked back across the river. His heart stopped when he saw no one, but then he realized that they were all safely on the bank.

"Sam," Esther sobbed, throwing her arms around him. He hugged her tightly. When she stood back and looked proudly at Matthew, Sam turned to face his son.

"You should have seen him, Sam," she said, brushing back her tears. "The minute the wagon tipped, he grabbed three ropes and tied them to trees. He gave Duke one and sent him after you. He tied another one to Rocky, and Rocky swam out to Mr. Daniels. Then he threw a line to Tom and the parents. Everyone else, including me, stood there in shock, but not our son. He knew exactly what had to be done, and he did it."

"Well done, Matthew," Sam said, pulling the trembling boy close. "Thank You, God, for my precious family. Thank You for helping us. Thank You," Sam prayed.

# Chapter 25

# ON THE TRAIL

---

Since everyone was too tired to go on, they made camp by the river's edge.

Early the next morning, the train resumed its journey. The trail was beginning to get rough. For the next week they made their way through dense forests, sometimes only traveling seven miles a day. There were times when the men had to clear away trees to make a path wide enough for a wagon to pass. Travel was treacherous.

On the second day of the third week, they entered Illinois, its flat plains a welcoming sight. For the moment there would be no more forests to conquer, but by the end of the week the travelers were wishing for some trees to shade them from the intense sun.

"My, it's hot," Matthew said that Monday morning as he and Sam were feeding their animals.

"Yes, it is, but at least we have plenty of water." Just then Martin came running up to tell them that breakfast was ready.

The days had now formed into a pattern. Everyone was up before dawn. The men would feed and check the stock while the women cooked the morning meal. When the food was ready, the people cleaned up as best they could and ate breakfast. They would hitch up the horses and, with their wagon master leading the way, start on their journey. They would travel until noon, stop long enough to eat a cold lunch and rest the horses, and then take off again. They would go as far as they could and then try to find a suitable camping spot. Once they found one, the women would start cooking while the men took care of the stock. After the evening meal, some would try to get better acquainted with their neighbors. Often the women would mend clothes by the light of the campfire, and the men would repair broken equipment.

The McBride family was traveling with the train. Scott McBride was a preacher. A friend in Miles City had sent him a letter telling him about a handful of Christians who were trying to start a church. They already had a building picked out, and they needed a pastor. The friend had wondered if Brother McBride would pray about coming. He did, and believed it God's will for him and his family to go.

All four of the McBrides sang and played instruments. Scott played the fiddle; his wife Cheryl played the guitar; Ann, thirteen, played the banjo; and Kay, ten, played the mandolin. At night they would often sit around the campfire and sing hymns. Others would gather around and sing with them.

When the train reached central Illinois, trees once again sheltered them. Everyone was in good spirits. Except for the trouble at Last Chance, the trip had really gone well. There had been no major accidents or illnesses, but circumstances were about to change.

The first problem was the water supply. Daniels informed them that the water hole where they were camping was the last one they would come to for five days at least. He advised them to fill everything they could with water and to use it sparingly. "Now," he said, "I hope you remember what I told you before we left. There's no room on this train for misers. Some of you don't need as much water as others. Be willing to share. These next few days may be rough. Not only will we not have water, but we'll be out on the plains again with very little shade. The temptation to use more water than you need will be hard to resist, but please, go easy on your water. Otherwise… I think we all know what can happen if we run out." Once he was done giving out instructions, the train began to move, leaving the water hole behind.

The morning of the third day one of the wives went to get water for cooking.

"Robert!" she screamed. "The water, it's gone!"

Once the others discovered what had happened, they quickly checked their water. Two other barrels were empty. Unbeknownst to the families who had neglected to check them carefully, the water barrels had been leaking.

After the men had repaired their barrels, the other folks shared their water with the three families. A whole day had been lost, and they were forced to camp in a none-to-perfect spot.

A crowd of over thirteen families will normally include at least one hothead, and the wagon train was no exception. Their troublemaker was Mr. Fred Trenton. He was always questioning orders and was quick to lay blame on the nearest person if he felt his safety was at stake.

"Mr. Daniels, why are we stopping here? It's not a suitable place. There is hardly enough fuel around here for a fire," Mr. Trenton complained.

Ricky and some of the other men were looking over a map. Before he could answer Trenton, a young man by the name of Ralf Raff spoke up.

"There's plenty of fuel, Mr. Trenton, if you know where to look," he said, trying to lighten the situation with a little joke.

"Oh, and what might you be talking about?" the arrogant man asked.

"Why it's all around you, sir. See all these black piles. They're called buffalo chips. They make an excellent fire…"

Mr. Trenton's face turned red. He knotted his fists and spoke through clenched teeth. "If you are suggesting that I walk around this camp looking for and picking up those, those *things,* you've got another thing coming."

"Hold it! Hold it both of you," Mr. Daniels demanded. Raff looked at him, his countenance apologetic. He had meant no harm. The wagon master nodded that it was all right. Then he turned to face the other man. "Mr. Trenton, I don't like camping here either, but we have no choice. So let's make the best of it."

Mumbling something about the unprincipled way he was being treated and the ridiculous way the train was being directed, he walked away.

Two days later, they faced more trouble. Raff and another man known only as Clint went out to scout for water. Both were young cowpunchers making the trip out west alone. Though very different in personalities, the two had developed a close friendship. Together they made a dependable scouting team.

"Let's see here. According to this map the water hole should be right over here," Raff said, directing his horse toward the north. "Hey, Clint, are you coming?"

Clint, looking uneasy, was gazing into the sky. Raff also looked up and shuddered. Four huge vultures were circling the area where the water should be.

"Let's look," Clint said. With a sinking feeling, they headed toward the birds. As they rounded a corner, their worst fears were confirmed. The water was stagnant. Surrounding the pool were the carcasses of animals that had died from the poison water. With heavy hearts, they returned back to camp.

"Whatever shall we do?" a woman wailed when she heard the news.

"We'll never make it," one teenage boy moaned.

"Now wait a minute, folks. Wait a minute," Daniels said, trying to silence the panicking crowd. "Please, listen to me. I know it seems bad, but let's not give up. This trail to Montana hasn't been here long. There may be water holes that others have missed. Even if there aren't, with the Lord's help we can make it."

"How? The nearest water is all of fifty miles away!" a voice from the crowd shouted.

"We'll have to ration the water that we have left. Use as little as you possibly can. Ladies, try to fix meals that don't need much water. Instead of every family making coffee in the morning and evening, let's only make a few pots of it and share it around. Now, everyone check your water supply and report to me how much you have." As the wagon master walked back to his animals, Mr. Trenton followed.

"We wouldn't be in this mess if those three families had not been so careless with their water," Mr. Trenton said bitterly.

"How do you figure that?" Mr. Daniels asked patiently.

"Well, we wouldn't have had to share the water that we had with them," he replied.

"Things like that happen on the trail, Mr. Trenton," Ricky said politely, though he was quite irritated with the man. "What do you want me to do? Kick them out of the train? As I recall, Mr. Trenton, you never gave them one drop of water. In fact, all you've done this whole trip is complain." Ricky Daniels never raised his voice, nor did he seem angry. Still, the authority in his voice hushed the man momentarily. However, he soon found something else to criticize as Daniels measured out water for his horse and dog.

"Mr. Daniels, what are you doing!" the man cried. "You're wasting precious water on worthless animals!"

"Mr. Trenton," Ricky said coolly and calmly. "This horse has carried me all day today in this blazing heat. I think he deserves some water. As for the dog, there may come a time when I run out of food and I'll need Rocky's help in finding and shooting something to eat. He also alerts me to danger. Without this 'worthless' horse and dog, I'd have a hard time doing my job, which happens to be taking care of you. If you don't mind, I gave the entire train, including you, an order. I wish to see that order carried out."

*Chapter 26*

# SICKNESS

S am, we don't have much water left," Esther
told him one day. The eleventh of May found
the train still many miles from the next water
hole.

"What do we have left?" he asked.

"Less than a fourth of the barrel."

Sam sighed, removed his hat, and wiped the
sweat from his brow. "Well, keep using as little
as possible. We need to keep praying and trusting
God." He took her hand and pulled her close to
him.

"I love you, Sam," she whispered.

"I love you too, Esther honey. You've done such
a good job with the water. We've even been able to
give some away."

Esther smiled at him and then went into the wagon where the boys were resting.

"How you doing, Sammy?" Tom asked, coming over from his wagon.

"Bad. We've got less than a quarter of our water left. What about you?"

"We got about half. If you run out, let me know, and we'll give you all we can."

"Thanks, Tom."

The next day was Sunday. The train took time to worship the Lord that evening after they had made camp.

"Folks, we have reached a very hard time," Brother McBride said. "The Lord is still with us, and He can help us get out of this terrible situation. I wondered what to preach to you this evening. I wanted to give you something that would encourage you. So, with the help of the Lord I would like to preach on the subject, 'Let not your heart be troubled.' Please turn in your Bibles to John 14:1. You all know the setting here. In chapter thirteen, Jesus and His disciples have finished the Passover meal and Jesus washes their feet. When we come to the first verse in chapter fourteen, Jesus says these words: 'Let not your heart be troubled: ye believe in God, believe also in me.'

"What were the disciples troubled about?" the preacher asked. "They worried about the same things you and I often worry about. The Bible narrows them down to three things: goals, grief, and guilt. In this passage Jesus gives them an answer to every one of those worries.

"The first thing they were worried about was their goals. We often find the disciples arguing over who would be the greatest. Mark 9:33-34, 'And he came to Capernaum: and being in the house he (Jesus) asked them, What was it that ye disputed among yourselves by the way?

'But they held their peace: for by the way they had disputed among themselves, who should be the greatest.'

"They were concerned about their goals," Brother McBride said again. "Each wondered how to get ahead, how to be the best. Don't you and I wonder that as well? We spend much of our life considering what occupation will help us get more money and greatness. Jesus showed them that being a servant was better than being great. After the meal was finished, He began to wash the feet of the disciples. Imagine Jesus, Who is God, the Creator of everything, girding Himself with a towel and washing the disciples' feet. He explained His actions in John 13:12-15, 'So after he had washed their feet, and had taken his garments, and was set down again, he said unto them, Know ye what I have done to you?

'Ye call me Master and Lord: and ye say well; for so I am.

'If I then, your Lord and Master, have washed your feet; ye also ought to wash one another's feet.

'For I have given you an example, that ye should do as I have done to you.'

"Jesus was showing that service is better than greatness. Twice in the book of Matthew He would say the first would be last, and the last would be first.

"The second thing they were troubled about was grief. Jesus had told them that He would be leaving soon. How that must have broken their hearts. Some of them were probably thinking, 'Why go on if Jesus leaves?' Jesus had a remedy for that as well. To ease their grief, He told them about Heaven. What better way to cheer up the heart of one who is grieving than to tell them about Heaven? Let's read John 14:1-3, 'Let not your heart be troubled: ye believe in God, believe also in me.

'In my Father's house are many mansions: if it were not so, I would have told you. I go to prepare a place for you.

'And if I go and prepare a place for you, I will come again, and receive you unto myself; that where I am, there ye may be also.'

"Lastly," Brother McBride said, "they were troubled over their guilt. Jesus had told them that one of them would betray Him. When the account is told in the books of Matthew and Mark, we find that each one of them asked the Lord, 'Is it I?' They were distressed to know that one of them would betray the Lord that they loved so dearly, but Jesus gave them hope. John 14:6 tells us, 'Jesus saith unto him, I am the way, the truth, and the life: no man cometh unto the Father, but by me.' Jesus was explaining to them that even though they would sin, there was still forgiveness available. If sinners will come to Jesus, He will forgive them, and they can be at peace with God.

"We don't have to be troubled folks," Brother McBride encouraged. "The Lord wants us to have peace. Let's remember these things and use them to comfort our hearts. Let's pray."

It was midnight when Mike crawled out of his bed and made his way to where his father was lying. Since there was not enough room in the wagon for all seven of the Goodtons to sleep, Esther slept in the wagon with the two youngest boys beside her and the twins squeezed in at her feet. Sam and Matthew slept outside under the wagon.

"Daddy, Daddy," Mike whispered, pulling lightly on his father's shirt.

"Mike, what's wrong?" Sam asked, rising to a half-sitting position.

"Dad, I need to ask you something. Brother Mc-Bride said that if we come to Jesus we could have peace with God. What does that mean?"

"Mike, God hates sin and every man is born a sinner. That makes mankind an enemy of God," Sam explained. "Do you know what sin is?"

"You mean like lying, losing your temper, and not obeying?"

"That's right, son. Sin is your worst enemy. The Bible gives many definitions and descriptions of sin. In Numbers twenty-one it's described as slithering serpents, in I Samuel seventeen it's described as a snarling giant, and in Romans 7:24 it is described as a rotting corpse."

"Man, sin sounds awful!" Mike exclaimed.

"It gets worse, Mike. Romans 6:23 says, 'For the wages of sin is death; but the gift of God is eternal life through Jesus Christ our Lord.'"

"You mean, if you sin you'll die?" Mike's eyes widened in fear.

"Yes, but listen to the last part of the verse, '...but the gift of God is eternal life through Jesus Christ our Lord.'"

"Is the gift of God salvation?" the little boy asked.

"Yes. Would you like to accept God's gift of salvation?"

"Oh, yes sir."

Sam remembered the verse his father had used to explain salvation many years ago. He now used it for his son. "The Bible says in John 4:10, 'Jesus answered and said unto her, If thou knewest the gift of God, and who it is that saith to thee, Give me to drink; thou wouldest have asked of him, and he would have given thee living water.'

"Now, that verse gives the whole plan of salvation. First is says, 'If thou knewest the gift of God…' Do you know what you want?"

"Yes sir. I want salvation."

"Okay. Then it says '…and who it is that saith to thee, Give me to drink…' Do you know Who can give you what you need?"

"Only Jesus can, Dad."

"That's right. The next part says '…thou wouldest have asked of him…' Are you willing to admit you are a sinner and ask Jesus to save you?"

"Yes sir."

"Then, lastly it says '…and he' meaning Jesus, 'would have given thee living water.'"

"Doesn't that mean that if I ask, Jesus will give salvation to me?" Mike asked.

"It sure does, Mike. Do you want to ask Him?"

Mike knelt there underneath the wagon and began to pray. "Dear Jesus, I want to be at peace with You. I know I'm a sinner and that You're the Saviour. Would You please save me? Thank You. Amen."

"Well, son, you're now a child of God. Remember that once you're saved, you are always saved. The Bible says in Hebrews 5:9 that Jesus 'became the author of eternal salvation unto all them that obey him' and you just obeyed Him," Sam told Mike, giving his son a hug.

As Mike crawled back into the wagon, Sam heard Matthew whisper, "Thank You Lord."

The next day started out normally, but by midday a horrifying change took place. Mrs. Ghane was fixing lunch and watching her children play. Suddenly, her youngest child fell and began crying for his mother. She rushed to his side, expecting to see only a few scratches, but as she began to soothe him by rubbing his head, she was alarmed that he felt feverish. After sending her oldest child for the doctor, she lifted her son in her arms and hurried back to the wagon.

Greg James, a young doctor right out of medical school, was, like the others, on his way to Miles City. He planned to open up a clinic there, and his wagon was full of medical supplies. Some had teased him, saying that he brought more medicine than he did food. He came quickly to see what was wrong with the child. After a careful examination, he stood up and faced the parents. "I'm afraid your boy has dysentery," he said.

The mother paled. Dysentery was caused by drinking bad water. It would manifest itself in fever, intestinal ailments, dehydration, and often in death.

"Are you sure, Doc?" Mr. Ghane asked.

"Positive," Doc James said, his expression showing his concern.

Ricky Daniels gathered the folks together and told them about the problem. "You all know what dysentery is. Let's concentrate on the three things we can do. First and most important, pray. Second, try to keep the sick ones as comfortable as possible. Third is to find water. We will be slowed down by this sickness, and in a way that could be to our advantage. Every day I want two men to go scouting for water. Some of you already have saddle partners. If you don't, find you one."

They kept to that routine for the next five days. Everybody was put to work. As mothers cared for the sick, it was up to the older children to prepare food. Before long, some of the parents came down with the sickness as well. Doctor Greg spent hours doing all he could, getting little if any sleep. Clint had offered to drive his wagon, so that all the doctor did was help the sick. He would start at the lead wagon and work his way back. After he finished with the last wagon, he would start over again.

All of the women tried their best to care for those that were ill. Carol, who had no children to care for, would fix several pots of soup, and she and Esther would pass it around.

Matthew was a big help, not only to his family but also to those around him. Sam saw him rock babies to sleep while the mothers cared for the ill children. Sometimes Matthew would gather a group of healthy children around him, lead them in prayer, and then tell them Bible stories to help calm them. Sam knew it was the prayers of those children that kept the others going.

# Chapter 27

# THE HAVEN

The twentieth of May found the wagons with only three barrels of water left for the whole train. They were now in Iowa, a little less than halfway through their journey of over 1,670 miles.

"Sam." Esther's voice was filled with fear. "Montana is sick."

Sam's shoulders sagged. Monty was not strong enough to survive the sickness. His premature birth had left him with many problems. The doctor had said he might never fully recover from them. Now, would they lose their little soldier? Sam rushed to his side.

"Daddy," Monty said, his voice barely a whisper. "Daddy, I don't feel good."

"I know, Soldier," Sam said taking the boy's hand. "Listen, Daddy and Uncle Tom are going to try to find some water, and that will make you feel better. You pray for Daddy and Uncle Tom as we go look. Okay?" Sam was trying not to show the boy how frightened he really was.

"Okay, Daddy."

With his other hand, Sam squeezed Esther's. All the words that he wanted to speak but could not were expressed in that moment. Sam bowed his head and prayed for help in their time of trouble.

Sam kissed Montana and crawled out of the wagon. Tom and Matthew already had the horses saddled.

"I'll take care of everything here, Dad," Matt promised, bravely fighting back tears. He knew the danger that Montana was facing. "Please find water," he added.

Sam laid his hand on Matt's shoulder. "We're going to try, son. We are going to try hard."

Sam pulled his boy close. As he did, the twins gathered around him, and Sam hugged all three of them.

Tom and Sam headed west. For a mile they rode in silence, searching for any sign that might point to water. Everything around the two riders looked bare. There had been a drought. The grass was drying up, and leaves were turning brown and dropping from the trees. The sun beat down unmercifully on the parched ground. It was as if they were in the middle of a desert, though at one time the land had been lush and green. The land seemed defeated, and it reflected the feelings of Tom and Sam.

Tom reined in his horse and wiped the sweat from his face. He looked over at his friend. Tom knew that Sam was worried about his son. He also knew that if water was not found soon… He did not even want to finish the thought.

Sam met his friend's gaze. Their situation was desperate. "Come on, Tom. Let's ride."

When they had ridden another mile, their horses became restless. Ears up, they pranced and pulled at the bit, as if wanting to run.

"Sam, do you think they smell water?" Tom asked, trying to keep his horse in check.

"Maybe, let's let them lead us." Hope springing up in them, they let the horses pick their own trail but kept them at an even pace.

Reaching the top of a small rise, they were astonished by the scene below. At first they thought it was a mirage. Nestled between two hills sat a log cabin and a barn. Behind these two structures was a pond fed by an artesian well. The homesteaders had irrigated a small field and planted it to wheat. Next to the house was a bountiful garden that was also watered through irrigation. Though the drought had caused the water level in the pond to decrease, there was enough there for their train. Praying that the homesteaders would lend them a hand, they made their way down.

A man came from behind the house and greeted them in a deep, friendly voice. "Howdy, gents. What brings you way out here?"

"Sir, you're a welcome sight," Tom said with a sigh. "We're from a wagon train traveling to Montana. We're about out of water and dysentery has struck." Tom gave them an overview of the trouble the train was in.

A pretty woman with thick black hair came out of the house. At the word "dysentery," she caught her breath. At first Sam and Tom wondered if she would forbid the train to come. Instead she said, "Hurry, bring them all here."

"Yes," her husband agreed, "we'll do all we can for them. We've got plenty of water to share."

"Thank you, folks," Sam said. Wheeling their horses around, they thundered back to the train.

"Water! Water! We found water!" they cried. They quickly explained to Ricky Daniels, and he gave the order to get the wagons rolling.

When they reached the cabin, they were surprised to see the man and his young son carrying the furniture into the barn.

"What's going on?" Sam asked.

"We needed more room to house the sick ones, so we moved everything out. By the way, my name is Max Pabis. My wife's name is Nan."

Daniels rode up and overheard the two men talking. "Mighty obliged to you folks, Mr. Pabis. I'm Ricky Daniels, wagon master."

"Good to meet you. Bring all the sick ones on into the house."

The Pabis family had spread everything from sheets to blankets and furs on the floor to lay the sick on. All the healthy men lodged in the barn while the ladies tended to those that were ill in the house.

That night a prayer meeting was held. They first thanked the Lord for the haven He had provided them. Then they prayed for rain. Before the prayer meeting was over there was a crash of thunder, and the rain came.

"Isn't the Lord wonderful?" Tom asked, watching the rain come down.

"Just think," Clint began. Since Clint rarely talked unless it was something very important, everyone hushed and listened to him. "God waited until we had good shelter; then He sent the rain. If He'd sent it earlier, more people would have gotten sick and maybe someone might have died." He smiled. "God's always on time."

Day in and day out for two weeks care was given to the sick.

"Here, Esther, drink this coffee," Nan said, as she handed Esther a cupful of the warm liquid. The young mother was tending to her son.

"Thank you, Mrs. Pabis." Esther took a sip as she continued to bathe the boy's fevered head with a wet cloth. "I'm so worried about him," she whispered.

"I know how you feel. When my husband and I first came out here, we nearly lost both our boy and girl. I know praying works, because prayer was all I had to nurse them with." Mrs. Pabis began to tell Esther about all the times God had seen them through their troubles.

Meanwhile, Mr. Pabis was helping the men repair a few broken wagons.

"Where are you folks from, and what brought you way out here?" Daniels asked, after he and a few other men had finished fitting a wheel to one of the wagons.

"We're originally from New Jersey. Two years ago a scout found this artesian well and reported it to the army. The army told the government about it, and the government decided that a settlement should be started here. They began scouting all of New England, looking for people who'd be willing to come out here. I had just surrendered to preach, and the Lord impressed upon my heart the need for my family to come. We prayed about it and decided that we would come as missionaries to this new settlement. So we notified the government and came out here." Mr. Pabis paused to help grease the inside of another wheel.

"What happened to the rest of the people?" Tom asked.

"They were supposed to come out ten months ago," Max told them. "For some reason or another they got delayed. We were beginning to think they weren't coming, but last month a couple of men with two wagonloads of supplies came and told us that the rest of the folks were planning to leave in four weeks. They should get here before winter sets in. That's why we've been cutting down all that lumber." He waved his hand toward a stack of lumber. "My boy and I are going to try to build a building big enough to house all the people during the winter. We should have seven families coming."

Upon hearing that, the men of the wagon train decided to help him build the cabin. After all the wagons were fixed, the men started building.

Two weeks saw the cabin built and all the sickness gone.

"How can we ever thank you all?" Esther said to the Pabis family. Montana, over the sickness, stood at her side. It was the third of June, and the train was ready to head west.

"It was the least we could do," Max said, and Nan nodded. "If you're ever in the area, drop in," he added.

"Mr. Pabis, what would you think about making this future town a station where trains going west could get supplies?" Mr. Daniels asked.

"I think that's a fine idea!" Mr. Pabis said. "Tell you what, when you're finished taking this train to Montana, stop back by here, and maybe you and I'll head back east and talk to the government about that."

"Sounds good. Lord willing, I'll be back. Thanks again for your hospitality." The wagon master saluted and cantered his horse to the front of the train. He turned, and rising slightly in the saddle, he waited until everyone was secure in their wagons.

"Wagons, Ho!" he cried. With creaks and groans the wagons rolled back out onto the trail.

"I'm so glad the Lord led us to that place," Esther said, watching the valley of refuge grow smaller and smaller in the distance.

"Me too. Esther honey, I need to apologize. For a while I began to doubt God. I wondered if I had done the wrong thing, if maybe I'd been mistaken. I wondered if God really cared what happened to us. Then when God directed Tom and I to the Pabis' house, God said to my heart, 'Look, if I could help the Pabis family live out here for close to a year with almost nothing, don't you think I can take care of you, too?' I realized that this was something God wanted us to go through so that we would learn to trust Him more."

Esther laid a hand on his arm. "I felt the same way, Sam. I'm sorry, too."

"From now on, no matter what happens, we'll try to never doubt God again," Sam said.

"Yes," she agreed, and they smiled at each other. Sam turned his attention to the four horses pulling the wagon.

"Dad, Mom, look!" Mike exclaimed. He and Matthew, riding double on Dusty, rode up beside the wagon. Sam and Esther followed their sons' gazes and were speechless for a moment. The two dogs, Rocky and Duke, were running side by side, their tails wagging. During the past two weeks, Ricky and the Goodtons had been too busy to pay a lot of attention to the dogs. Apparently they had sought friendship with each other.

Mr. Daniels rode up. "I wondered where my dog went," he said, after watching the two animals. "Looks like they finally decided to be friends."

# Chapter 28

# INDIANS

The end of June found the train nearing the middle of South Dakota, the land of the Sioux Indians. People began to get nervous, their imaginations leading them to see a wildly painted Indian under every rock and behind every tree. Women who normally let their children run and play at night now kept them close to their side. The men never let their rifles out of arm's reach.

It was early in the morning and the train was just beginning to pack up. Daniels was addressing the men.

"The trail we are taking is through land belonging to a small band of Sioux Indians who want peace. They have promised safe travel to the white men. So if you see an Indian, don't panic and shoot him.

He's probably just curious. Now, we are approaching another forest. Keep on the trail and stay close together. The path is rugged, but at least we'll be shaded. Okay, get your wagons ready."

That day around noon they first saw them. Ten Indians seemed to appear out of nowhere. Ricky brought the train to a halt, and there they stood for a few minutes. The Indians, mounted on rugged ponies, made the first move. Two men began to ride slowly toward the train.

"They want to talk," Mr. Daniels said. "I'm going to ride over to them."

"No don't!" Mr. Trenton cried. "If you get killed, how will we ever make it to our destination? Your job is protecting us, not parleying with Indians."

"Mr. Trenton, if they want to talk, I'll not make the unwise decision of not listening." Daniels fixed the pioneers with a hard gaze. "Don't any of you fire, no matter what you think." He looked at Sam, Tom, Scott McBride, Clint, Raff, and Greg James. These six men were the only ones on the train that he completely trusted to follow orders. "Keep an eye on the others," he told them. Ricky whistled, and Rocky bounded over to him. The wagon master mounted his horse and made his way toward the group of Indians.

"We come in peace," one of the Indians said in broken English. "I am Lone Wolf. I am chief." The young man beside the chief said nothing.

"I, too, come in peace," Ricky said, speaking slowly so the man in front of him could understand him. "I am Ricky Daniels. You honor us by your presence. What can we do for you?"

"We bring news. White Eyes take trail through woods?"

"Yes."

"Must not!" the chief stated emphatically. "Dangerous. Six moons ago, lion come. Kill three horses. Stalk my people. He live in woods. We hunt. Not find. He not fear man. Will hunt White Eyes. White Eyes go round woods. We show way. It not too long different," he added, meaning to say it would not be too much farther out of the way.

Ricky studied the man in front of him. Indians were great bluffers. Could this be a trick to keep them out in the open where they would be an easy prey? Or could there really be a dangerous mountain lion in those woods?

The chief noticed his indecision. He turned his head and spoke a few words in his native tongue. A young boy of about fifteen rode up beside the chief.

"This my son," the chief explained. "Show," he told the boy. With his right arm, the boy pulled back the torn, bloodstained left sleeve of his buckskin shirt. Daniels winced. The young Indian's left arm, from the wrist to the shoulder, was covered with deep gashes, some reaching all the way to the bone. The wagon master wondered how the boy could ride in his condition.

"You know what make wound?" Lone Wolf asked.

"Yes, I do." Ricky had seen two men that had been attacked by a cougar. These marks were identical.

"My son had only knife. He wound lion, anger him. Brother shoot rifle in air, or lion kill him. Believe Lone Wolf now?"

"I do," Daniels answered. Then he said, "This boy needs a doctor, medicine. We have a doctor with us. Let us help the boy. I will bring the doctor to you, if you wish. While he helps your son, I will talk to my people."

The chief was impressed. "Many White Eyes not let us take one of their people. This what we do." He pointed to the young man beside him. "This Little Hawk. He my son, too. Little Hawk go with you. Doctor come to me. You talk to your people. You go different way, my son will stay with you. This way you know we not want to hurt you. I not attack a place where my son is. Little Hawk show you way to go. Go through woods, we not hurt you," he promised. "We want peace with the White Eyes."

Daniels nodded. "I'll go get the doctor." He headed Charlie back to the train.

"Greg, we've got a boy over there that's been mauled by a cougar. Would you do what you can for him?" Ricky asked.

Greg did not hesitate. "Of course." He grabbed his bag out of the wagon and mounted his horse. The two men went back to the Indians. Ricky and Little Hawk left the doctor there and returned to the train.

The injured boy was laid on a blanket and Greg examined the wounds. *How can this boy even stand up?* he thought to himself. He gave the boy medicine to help ease the pain, but Greg knew that treating the injury was still going to hurt terribly. Reaching into his bag, he took out a cloth and soaked it with water. As gently as possible he cleaned the wounds. He took another cloth, soaked it with antiseptic and again cleaned them. Then he covered the gashes with gauze and secured it with bandages. Never once did the boy flinch or show any sign of pain.

After Greg finished knotting the bandages, he stood up. "That is all I can do here, but if you bring him to my wagon I could help him more."

"We wait and see until man you call Ricky Daniels come back." The chief knelt by his son and began speaking softly to him.

For the first time the doctor began to get a little nervous. The seven other Indians did not look mean, but they did not look too friendly either. He hoped that Ricky would hurry up with whatever it was he was doing. To get his mind off the other Indians, he knelt by the boy again and applied a cool compress to the boy's forehead.

"It's preposterous!" Mr. Trenton bellowed. "Why should we believe these Indians? Mark my words, this is a trap. Who knows where these savages will take us. I say stay with the main trail." Several others murmured in agreement.

"Now hold on, folks. What reason do you have for not trusting these people?" their wagon master asked.

"Simple," someone said. "They're Indians. They're nothing but murdering savages!"

"Yeah!" another voice shouted. "Even if there is a dangerous cougar in those woods, why should one animal make us take a different route?"

"If you would have seen that boy's arm, you would think differently," Daniels said. "A cougar with no fear of man is dangerous. He could stalk us for hours and we not know it. Then, when we drop our guard for just a moment, he'll strike so quick you won't know what happened. To top it off, he's been slightly wounded. That'll make him twice as mean."

"How do you know that they haven't already killed this beast and want us to believe he's still loose out there?" Trenton asked.

"I don't know for sure, but I do know this. Chief Lone Wolf took a great chance to come and warn us. He could have just as easily sent someone else, but he came in person. Then he let his son ride into our camp, and if we go this other route, Little Hawk stays with us. The chief won't attack a train that his own son is riding with. Besides, he gave me his word."

"What good is that?" Mr. Trenton snapped.

Daniels saw Little Hawk's hands clench. The young man was standing away from the group. Ricky had thought Little Hawk did not understand English, but apparently he knew what Trenton had said. Though he showed no outward emotion after that, Daniels knew that he was battling to control himself. The word of his father and chief was being insulted. That was enough to make anyone angry.

"I will not have anymore insulting remarks said about the Indians," Ricky ordered. "I say we put it to a vote. I know some of you will want to pray about it first. Go back to your wagons and think about it. Then give me your decision. I'll let you know my vote right now. I believe the Indians." Daniels walked away from the group and stood by Little Hawk. The others dispersed to their wagons.

The Goodtons, Sampsons, and many others began to pray. For an hour nobody said anything. Finally Sam stood up from where he was kneeling.

He and Esther looked at each other and his wife nodded. Sam kissed her, and then went to find Tom. One look at Tom's face told him the decision his best friend had made. Together they went to see Daniels.

"Ricky, the Goodtons and Sampsons vote to do what Chief Lone Wolf said to do," Sam said.

"Clint and I do too," Raff said riding up on his horse. Clint, riding behind him, nodded vigorously.

"We do as well," Mr. McBride said.

"Count us in," Mr. Ghane added. One by one, each family decided to trust the Indians.

Mr. Trenton was the last person to voice his vote. He was so outnumbered that it was almost humorous. "Alright, alright, do whatever you want," he said.

Greg breathed a sigh of relief when Daniels and Little Hawk came back. "I was beginning to think you forgot about me," he whispered to the wagon master.

Daniels grinned, but then became serious. "How's the boy?"

"I need to take him to my wagon where I can sew up those cuts, but the chief wants to see what the folks had to say first." Lone Wolf had explained to the doctor what was going on.

"Chief," Mr. Daniels said, "my people have decided to follow your advice."

The chief grunted. "That quick! Maybe Indian learn from White Eyes. Indian take days to make up mind." Something that looked a bit like a friendly smile flittered across the chief's face.

"Chief," Greg interrupted, "please bring your son to my wagon."

"He go," the chief agreed.

The boy stood up and attempted to mount his horse, but his weakness overcame him. Before he could fall to the ground, both the chief and Little Hawk jumped off the backs of their ponies and steadied him. Little Hawk spoke to his father, and Lone Wolf nodded. The elder son leaped onto the back of his horse, the chief placed the boy in front of him, and the two Indians and the doctor went back to the train.

"Chief Lone Wolf, you would honor me if you would share our fire tonight," Mr. Daniels told him.

"I come." He waved his hand toward his seven men. "They go back to village. Get more and hunt for lion."

Greg led Little Hawk to his wagon. "Here," he said after he had made a pallet for the boy to lie on.

With one hand holding his brother in place, Little Hawk dismounted. He then laid his brother in the wagon. He spoke a few words to the boy, and the injured lad smiled.

"I told him that he must get well quick, or our mother and sisters will be angry that they must do all the work," Little Hawk told the doctor.

"Little Hawk, what is your brother's name, and does he understand English?" Greg asked.

"His name is True Arrow, and he understands what you say. He get well?" Greg noted the anxiety in the older brother's voice.

"I believe so, Little Hawk." At that moment, Carol, Esther, and Cheryl McBride came up.

"Doctor, can we help you?" Carol asked.

"Yes, thank you."

# Chapter 29

# TRAVELING TOGETHER

The day was almost gone, and the train camped for the night.

Greg gave True Arrow medicine to make him sleep. After sterilizing his instruments, he began to work. First, he removed the bandages.

"The Indians must've put an herb of some kind on this to keep it from getting infected. So far it's doing a good job," Greg said. Carol cleaned the wounds and Esther put medication on them. Then with Cheryl handing him the proper instruments and Carol and Esther holding lanterns over the boy, Greg sewed up the gashes. By midnight the wounds had been closed. Cheryl wrapped True Arrow's arm with a bandage.

"There, that should do it," Greg said, cleaning his hands. "How can I thank you ladies for your help?"

"Don't mention it," Esther told him.

"We were glad to lend a hand," Carol said.

"Send for us if you need any more help," Cheryl added, and the three ladies went back to their wagons.

The next morning True Arrow was already feeling better. After he had eaten the soup Carol prepared for him, Greg told him to get some more sleep. He started to protest, but the chief put an end to that.

"You do what man say," he said firmly. True Arrow lay back down, and soon he was sound asleep.

Daniels asked the chief to also ride with them. The chief, surprised that the wagon train would allow three Indians to travel with them, agreed. With the chief and Little Hawk leading the way, the train started on the trail that would lead them around the forest. It was early afternoon when Daniels trotted up beside Little Hawk.

"I'm sorry you heard those things some of my folks said about you and your people."

Little Hawk was silent for a moment. Then he said, "It is hard to see why they can't understand that *my* tribe wants peace with the White Eyes."

Daniels said nothing.

Little Hawk hung his head. "Yes, many of our Sioux brothers have done many things wrong. It makes my heart and the heart of my father sad. He talks to other Sioux tribes but they not listen. Some of our young braves have left the tribe and joined others on the warpath. Those still with us want peace."

"I believe that, and so do a few of my friends."

"Yes, some of the men have been friendly to us. The man with red hair, the one who is always excited, the quiet one, the one who has the face of a fox, the doctor, and the one who sings have tried to become friends."

Daniels grinned at the descriptions of the six men that he trusted. The man with the red hair was Sam Goodton; the one who was always excited was Tom Sampson; the quiet one would be Clint; the doctor was, of course, Greg James; and the one who sings was the preacher, Scott McBride. Daniels liked the description of Ralf Raff best: the one who has the face of a fox. Though Ralf loved a good joke and loved to tease, he could be serious if necessary, and he was dependable.

"Little Hawk, where did you learn to speak English?" Daniels asked.

"I saved the life of an Army scout. In return he taught me to read and write in his language. Then

I taught my father to speak, though he does not read."

"You speak it well."

Sam and Tom invited Ricky Daniels and the two Indians to eat dinner with them that night. The McBrides had been invited also.

Before they ate, Scott McBride prayed for the food. Matthew helped his mother pass around the plates filled with potatoes and meat. As he handed Lone Wolf his plate, the chief asked, "You not afraid of me?"

"No, sir," came the honest reply.

The chief smiled. "I wish others think like you. What are you called?"

"Matthew, sir, but some people call me Matt."

"Matt. I am called Lone Wolf. Do you know why?"

"No, sir."

"I am youngest of five. All above me are sisters. I only brave." Matthew laughed.

"It true," the chief told him. "I am lone wolf, but you have brothers."

"Yes sir, four. All are younger than me." Matt took his plate, sat down by the chief, and began to eat.

Little Hawk asked what it was that they did before they ate. What was this bowing of the head and speaking to someone?

Brother McBride started in Genesis, telling them about creation, the fall of man, the flood, and then led them to the cross of Calvary. He told how the Son of God, the One True God, willingly died to pay for the sins of all men—red, white, black, and yellow. He told them about hell, the place where those that reject the gift of God go, about the never-ending fire, and about the pain that was there. The two Indians listened intently. Sometimes Little Hawk would repeat the words in his native tongue so his father could better understand. The Indians were so interested that they kept asking Brother McBride to tell them more. It was three hours before he was able to finish.

Chief Lone Wolf was silent, pondering what he had heard. He was a big man and brave. He had faced countless enemies, both men and beasts, and had defeated every one of them; yet his heart had never beaten as loudly as it did that night. Never had he feared as he feared that night.

"This new," he said slowly. "I must think." He and his son walked away.

The next day a brave galloped into camp and spoke to the chief. Lone Wolf turned to Daniels. "Again lion attack my people. He hurt a man. His trail is new. Now is time to find him."

"Doc, will you…?" Daniels started to ask.

"Of course I will." Greg picked up his bag and sprang into the saddle.

"He show you how to go," the chief said, pointing to the Indian that had just ridden in. The two men headed for the village.

"Clint, Raff, come with me," Daniels said. The cowboys were already prepared to go.

"Sam, you come, too. With Rocky and Duke along, we might be able to find the cougar." Samuel nodded.

"Little Hawk stay," the chief commanded. "Come," he said, addressing the four white men, "we meet braves."

They rode hard to where they were joined by nine other braves, and the hunt was on. For a half hour the two dogs followed the trail. Then another Indian charged into the small group. His voice was high-pitched and he spoke so fast that the men from the wagon train wondered how anyone could understand him.

At the man's words, the chief's face became more grim. "He has child, girl of four summers. Is gone. Other children see her running into woods when sun come up."

"We've got to find her," Raff cried, "and quick."

The chief looked up at Sam. "Will your Great God help find girl?"

"If we ask Him." Sam prayed aloud, begging God to help them find the child. When they started hunting again, they had ridden only ten minutes when the dogs took off through a clump of dense shrubs. No amount of calling could bring them back.

"What is he doing?" Sam had never seen Duke so deliberately disobey him. Daniels was equally confused.

"Look," one Indian said. He had crawled through the undergrowth and was looking at the ground. There they saw the prints of a child and, on top of them, the prints of the cougar!

"Dogs go where horse cannot. We go round," the chief said, as the others followed him as he tried to find a way around the bushes.

The girl, oblivious to the danger, was sitting in a clearing, playing with some sticks. Crouched on a stone ledge above her was the cougar. Slowly, it made its way down and crept up behind her. Just as it was ready to pounce, Duke and Rocky burst into the clearing.

The child, frightened by their sudden appearance, ran and hid behind a rock. Hissing, the lion turned its attention to the two dogs. Duke and Rocky split up and began to circle the snarling cat, a long-legged, tawny creature that could leap on the back of its prey and break the neck of its victim with one swipe of a powerful paw. The dogs had to be careful. Duke kept the big cat's attention by barking loudly and darting in and out of its reach. Rocky, meanwhile, was making good use of the wolf in him. Keeping low, he positioned himself behind the cougar.

The mountain lion had taken all it could of Duke's pestering. It waited until Duke rushed toward it, and before the dog could retreat, pounced. Duke took a desperate leap to avoid the deadly teeth and claws, but he did not jump far enough. The cat slashed his left hip, making him lose his balance and fall. Before the lion could do any more damage, Rocky landed on its back. Sinking his teethe into the cat's scruff and his claws into its back, he held on. The cougar could not shake him. Finally the cat rolled over, pinning Rocky to the ground. With the weight of the cat crushing him, the dog lost his grip. The mountain lion sprang to its feet, but Duke was ready to take it on again. He bit into the cat's right back leg. The cougar snarled in pain and swung at Duke's side. It missed the first time, but not the second. Duke, not as wise about fighting a wild animal as Rocky was, did not stay far enough behind, and the claws ripped his side. Duke held on to the cat's leg, but he was losing his strength. He finally let go and tried to get out of the way, but the cat swiped at him and cut his other hip badly.

Rocky had been waiting for the right chance. The time had come. The cat had forgotten about him. Rocky lunged and landed once again on the cat's back. When it started to roll over, Rocky leapt off. The movement was so unexpected that the cat lay on its back for a second, stunned. That second was all Rocky needed. He bit into the cat's jugular vain. The cat pushed him away but was losing lots of blood. Though wounded and unsteady, the lion was still very dangerous. Rocky kept him away from the girl and Duke. The latter had managed to get on his feet and place himself in-between the cougar and the girl.

Just then the hunters, drawn by the sounds of the struggle, made their way into the clearing. Rocky saw his master and led the cat to where they could get a clear shot. Eleven arrows and four bullets pierced the cat's tawny fur. The battle was over.

Rocky ran to where the girl was and barked. Her father saw her and rushed to her side and Sam quickly went to Duke. The dog's tail thumped the ground weakly.

"Good job, Duke," Sam said, petting him. "Good boy."

They made a litter for him and headed back to the train. Doc Greg was back and he tended the wounds of both Rocky and Duke.

"They'll be as good as new in a few days," he said, giving both dogs a pat as he tended their wounds.

With the cougar dead, the wagon train could go on without the Indians.

"It was a pleasure to meet you Chief Lone Wolf, Little Hawk, and True Arrow. I pray we will meet again. We want to thank you for all that you have done," Daniels said. The other people nodded in agreement.

"We thank you. You help get enemy of ours. Maybe one day White Eyes and Indian be more friends," the chief said. He turned to face Matthew. "Matt, you young brave, warrior. Want peace, not war. It those like you that make peace or war. You pray to God, do what He say. Be warrior for peace for Him. So you not forget what I say, I have gift for you." He gave Matthew a pair of moccasin boots.

"Thank you, sir!" the boy exclaimed. Somewhat dazed, he took the boots. "I have a gift for you." Matthew gave him his Bible. "In this book are the truths that Brother McBride told you about. Little Hawk can read it to you. Will you let him do that?"

"I do." He took the book and clutched it in his hands. "I believe what you say is true," he said to Brother McBride. "I have Little Hawk read book to me."

The Indians mounted their horses and rode away. Matt knew Lone Wolf would keep his promise. He prayed that, as Little Hawk read the book to him, Lone Wolf and his tribe would accept Jesus as their Saviour.

"These moccasins are kind of big," Matthew said later on that night.

"I think Chief Lone Wolf meant them to be that way," Sam said. "You'll grow into them, and when you're a man, they'll fit. When the time comes, you'll have them to remind you of what the chief said."

Matthew ran his hands over the precious gift. "'Be warrior for peace for Him,'" he repeated softly. From that day on his nickname was "Warrior."

# Chapter 30

# THE LAND OF
# THEIR DREAMS

On the twelfth of August, approximately nineteen weeks since the day they had left Indiana, the wagon train reached the Montana Territory.

"Hurray!" everyone shouted when Ricky told them where they were.

"Folks, here's what we're going to do. The town of Ekalaka is ten miles from here. We'll go there and get supplies. Miles City is about 118 miles northwest of here. It shouldn't take us long to get there. Because of some of the trouble we've had, we're a little behind schedule. Lord willing, you'll get there before winter, but you might not have a lot of time to prepare. So I suggest you get as much as you possibly can now. Purchase those things that will be most needed during the dead of winter."

It took three days for the train to buy the necessary items: coffee, flour, sugar, salt, nails, hammers, saws, and things of that nature. On August the sixteenth they once again began their journey. Three of the wagons had stayed behind, content to settle in the little town of Ekalaka.

"Daddy, where are we going to live in Miles City?" Mike asked that evening as they sat around the campfire.

"Well, we'll find us a place maybe ten or so miles out of town," Sam answered.

"How will we find the right place?" Mac asked.

"We'll look and pray until God gives us peace."

"What'll we do when we get there?" Montana questioned.

Sam grinned as the boys plied him with questions in their excitement. "Tom and I decided that we would build our house first. It'll be big enough for them to stay with us during the first winter if they want."

"Be big, Daddy?" three-year-old Martin wanted to know.

"Oh, Marty, it'll be *really* big. There will be two stories in it, and an attic."

"Could we have our bedrooms upstairs, Dad?" This question came from Matt.

"Matthew, that's a wonderful idea," Esther agreed, "and maybe we could build the house on a hill. Then we can look out our bedroom window and see for miles around."

"Then it's settled," Sam said. He picked up a stick and began to draw plans in the dirt. His wife and sons gathered around him.

"Now," he began, "the bedrooms will be on top. On the bottom we will have a living room, a bedroom for any guests we might have, a big kitchen and dining room, and we'll have a room for storage and for the washtub." The boys groaned at that and Sam pretended not to notice. "In one corner we'll have a study room. In there's where I'll do all my business. Along one wall will be shelves full of books. What do you think of that, Professor?"

Mike had earned the nickname from his love of books. He was only five and could not read a lot by himself, but he loved to be read to.

"I'd like that," came the reply.

"Then in the other corner will be a place for Mom's piano, and on the top floor, Esther honey, I'll build you a sewing room."

"That sounds marvelous."

"We'll have to build a barn, won't we?" Matt asked.

"Yes, son. That will be our second project."

"It sounds like fun!" Mac exclaimed. "Can we help?"

"Of course, Lumberjack. There will be something for everyone to do. Now, it's time for devotions."

The days flew by, and on August 27 they found themselves in Miles City.

"My, I never thought Miles City would be this big," Sam said, gazing at the bustling town.

"It'll get bigger in no time," said Ricky Daniels as he rode up beside their wagon. "The government will be extending the railroad all the way to Miles City soon. I heard that they'll start right after the snow melts. It'll take them awhile, but when it gets done, hold on to your hats, 'cause this place will start busting at the seams. Ranchers will start driving their cattle here to ship them out East. New businesses will spring up. It'll be something to see."

The wagon train camped two miles out of town. Only eight of the thirteen wagons made it to the original destination. The five other wagons had found places along the way to stop and make their homes.

"Hey, Sam."

"Yeah, Tom."

"What say you and I go scouting around tomorrow?" Tom asked.

"Sure. The families will be all right here."

The next day, as they headed for their horses, Sam said, "You know I've been thinking? Maybe we ought to pay for the land instead of filing a homesteaders claim, because suppose we have to homestead on our land, say for five years. Then in comes the railroad or someone else and they decide they want our land. We could have a fight on our hands, but if we go ahead and pay for it now…"

"Then there's no way the land can be taken away from us," Tom finished for him.

"Exactly."

"Sounds good."

They had reached the spot where their horses were picketed. Sam stopped beside Dusty and began petting him. "I'm taking Dusty, Tom."

"Then I'll bring Midnight."

Together the two men rode and searched the area. They went east first and then drifted toward the north. The land was beautiful, but they did not find what they were looking for. The next day they made their way west. It was not quite noon when they topped a hill and their dream became a reality. Their eyes fell upon a rich valley bordered by thick timber. South and west of the center a clear lake sparkled in the noonday sun. A creek wound its way through a meadow and across the valley. In the middle of the valley was a gently sloping hill, the top flat and perfect for a house. Around a clump of trees and up a small incline was another lovely spot to build a house.

"Wow." Tom swallowed and tried to say more, but he could not.

"There must be at least a thousand acres here," Sam said, his voice barely above a whisper. "Look, Tom, two small hills, perfect for building houses on. The land is good for both cattle and crops, and look at all that rich timber. It's perfect."

Tom swallowed again and then said,

> "On a journey we have been
> To find a land so new.
> On a journey we have been
> To see our dreams come true.
>
> And now with joy we see
> The land the Lord saw fit to send.
> And now with joy we say,
> 'Our journey has come to an end.'

"This is it, Sammy. Come on. Let's go to town and check on this land." They urged their ponies into a dead run for the seven-mile ride back to town.

They found out the price of the land and went back to get their wives. Since it was late by the time they got home, they waited until the next morning to show the land to Esther and Carol.

"Esther honey, come on. I want to show you something," Sam said.

"What about the boys?" Esther asked as she finished wiping the dishes.

"I'll take care of them," Mrs. Ghane volunteered.

"Thank you," Sam said, and went out to saddle Esther's horse. After admonishing the boys to be good, the two couples headed out. Before they crested the hill, Tom and Sam had Carol and Esther close their eyes. The two couples separated. Tom, leading Carol's horse, went to the right and found a good vantage point. Sam led Esther to the left and then told her to open her eyes.

"Oh, Sam, it's perfect, just perfect!" Esther exclaimed.

"Tom and I have enough money to buy it. What do you think?"

"Oh, Sam, let's pray first."

After praying, and now sure that it was God's will, they went to town and bought the land.

"Guess what, boys," Sam said, riding back into camp. "Tomorrow we're going to our new land." The five boys cheered.

The next morning, after goodbyes to their friends, they headed for their property.

"Let's pray for this land, just like we did before," Tom said when they reached the border of their property. Kneeling on their newly-purchased soil, the families prayed for God's blessings.

The boys loved the place.

"Dad, there's fish in the creek!" Matt exclaimed.

"We'll have to go fishing soon," Sam assured him.

"Great!" Mac shouted, running around his parents in excitement.

"I love it, Dad," Mike said.

"Yeah, look at all the places to play," Montana said, smiling.

"I like it," little Martin said, jumping up and down.

At supper that night Mike brought up a question. "Dad, what are we going to call our ranch?"

Sam laid down his fork. "You know, I haven't thought about that. What say we let your mom pick out a name?"

"Good idea," they agreed.

"I'll have to think about it," she said. "Give me a couple of days."

After the boys were asleep, Sam and Esther went for a walk. Keeping the wagon in sight, they wandered over their new land, hand in hand.

"We'll build the house there," Sam said pointing to the spot. "Then we'll plant wheat and corn in that field there. When we get settled in good, I'll buy some cattle and start a herd. We'll buy good horses and start breeding them, and maybe we can even harvest some of that good timber. Then, Lord willing, in a few years we'll have a real working ranch."

Esther nodded. "The boys are so thrilled to know they'll be growing up on a ranch." She chuckled. "They already call themselves cowboys."

Sam smiled as he thought about his sons growing up here. "When each of the boys turn ten, I plan to buy them a horse of their own, one they can raise and train by themselves."

His wife smiled and took hold of his arm. "I'm so happy, Sam. This place is everything I dreamed of. Even down to the way it's laid out. I love it."

"Esther honey, do you ever wish we hadn't done this?" Sam stopped walking and looked into her eyes.

"Only once, Sam, when Monty was sick, but not anymore. I *know* this is where God wants us." She leaned against his shoulder.

"The Lord willing, Esther, we'll grow old here together. We'll watch our children grow and get married. This is where our hair will turn gray. Or fall out," he added with a chuckle.

Esther laughed softly.

"I love you, Esther Goodton," Sam told her.

"I love you, Samuel Goodton."

Arm in arm, they watched the sun slip behind the distant mountains. A peace flooded their soul. They were home.

# MY TESTIMONY

Psalms 9:1, "I will praise thee, O LORD, with my whole heart; I will shew forth all thy marvellous works."

Again the Lord has blessed. I thank Him for all that He has done. The completion of this book is only one of the many blessings He has bestowed on me.

I want to thank all those that read the first book the Lord helped me write, Jew Hiders. Your kind words and interest were such an encouragement to me. I know many people prayed for me, and I count that a great blessing.

I have always enjoyed reading and writing. When my family would go to watch a high school basketball game, I would bring books to read. The

Lord must have been preparing me for the time when He would use me to write.

One of the things that really encouraged me to write is the testimony of my Grandma McBride. One day, I asked her to tell me about when she trusted Christ as her Saviour. Grandma told me that when she was young she was reading an Elsie Dinsmore book, and the girl in the book gave her heart to Jesus. Right there, my Grandma asked the Lord to save her because of the testimony in that book. My prayer for these books is that someone will get saved because of reading them. My friend, if you have never seen yourself as a sinner and have never put your trust in Christ alone to save you from your sin, then you are missing out on the greatest blessing you could ever have.

I was saved at the age of six and a half. I don't regret it at all. There's nothing like knowing you are saved and on your way to Heaven. If you're not saved I beg you to accept Christ as your personal Lord and Saviour. The Bible says in Acts 2:21, "And it shall come to pass, that whosoever shall call on the name of the Lord shall be saved."

Whosoever means anyone. There are some that teach that God picks and chooses those whom He will and will not save, but that is a lie. This verse says, "Whosoever".

If you won't get saved, then your life will be a mess. Twice in the book of Isaiah, we are told that there is no peace for the wicked. Isaiah 48:22, "There is no peace, saith the LORD, unto the wicked." Isaiah 57:21, "There is no peace, saith my God, to the wicked."

Then after you die, you will go to a place called hell. In this day and age, people make light of hell. Some people say hell does not exist, but God said there is a hell. The Bible says in Psalms 9:17, "The wicked shall be turned into hell, and all the nations that forget God."

You may say, "Well, that verse says, 'The wicked shall be turned into hell.' I'm really not that bad."

The Bible says in Romans 3:10, "As it is written, There is none righteous, no, not one:"

Everyone is wicked in the sight of God, but if we will put our trust in the shed blood of Jesus Christ, we can be forgiven and made acceptable. Ephesians 1:6 says, "To the praise of the glory of his grace, wherein he hath made us accepted in the beloved."

Won't you please ask Jesus to save you? Then you too can know real peace and joy.

Printed in the United States
73767LV00001B/85-102